A Hangman for Ghosts

Also by Andrei Baltakmens:

The Battleship Regal
The Raven's Seal

A Hangman for Ghosts

Andrei Baltakmens

5

Top Five Books
Oak Park, Illinois | 2018

A TOP FIVE MYSTERY

Published by Top Five Books, LLC
521 Home Avenue, Oak Park, Illinois 60304
www.topfivebooks.com

Library of Congress Cataloging-in-Publication Data

Names: Baltakmens, Andrei, 1968– author.
Title: A hangman for ghosts / Andrei Baltakmens.
Description: Oak Park, Illinois : Top Five Books, 2018.
Identifiers: LCCN 2017059643 | ISBN 9781938938283 (softcover : acid-free paper) | ISBN 9781938938290 (ebook)
Subjects: LCSH: Penal colonies—Australia—History—Fiction. | Murder—Investigation—Fiction. | Conspiracies—Fiction. | GSAFD: Mystery fiction.
Classification: LCC PR9639.4.B395 H36 2018 | DDC 823/.92—dc23
LC record available at https://lccn.loc.gov/2017059643

Cover & book design by Top Five Books

Printed and bound in the United States of America

For when my outward action doth demonstrate
The native act and figure of my heart
In compliment extern, 'tis not long after
But I will wear my heart upon my sleeve
For daws to peck at. I am not what I am.

—Shakespeare, *Othello*

CONTENTS

PART ONE

A PARADISE FOR SERPENTS

CHAPTER I.

Particulars of an Execution

Sydney, New South Wales, 1829

A WOMAN WAS shrieking in the cells when the hangman and the surgeon met inside the gates of old Sydney Gaol.

"Dreadful howling," remarked the gaoler, Wilmot, as he set their names in the gate-book. "Expect you'll find the condemned quieter."

"Then by all means," said the surgeon, grimacing as he wrote his signature, "let us go in."

Gabriel Carver, convict hangman, scratched his version of a cross under the surgeon's name.

All three struck out into the short yard, diving into the merciless sandstone glare. The screams rolled along the pitted yellow walls, blended with the burning of the naked sun. They mounted the high steps and hurried along the terrace. Around the corner, along the row of confinement cells, the gaoler strode to a hobnailed wooden door and threw down the shutter.

The surgeon, Moynihan, glanced at the impassive hangman and stepped forward to peer into the cell.

"Doyle," said the gaoler. "Coughing all night. He's to hang tomorrow. Took with a pleurisy, he says. Malingering most likely. So, is he fit to walk to the scaffold?"

Moynihan looked in. The surgeon was slender, neatly dressed, perspiring in his black coat. He had a long nose and smooth face, but for a small, sharp line of worry or grief centred above the eyes.

The cell was dim and stale, enclosing an iron bed and the hunched spectre of the man on it: a spare, bearded figure, biting on his thumb as he rocked back and forth.

"I shall have to examine him," said Moynihan.

"Here's the surgeon," announced Wilmot, stepping between them and jangling his keys, "to see you're fit to dance tomorrow."

Wilmot hauled the door back. The shade of the cell brought no relief from the clutching heat.

The prisoner peered blearily into the illuminated space beyond. "And what's *he* here for?"—meaning the hangman.

Gabriel Carver was a good head taller than the surgeon. He had broad shoulders—at least, they seemed so by the length of his arms—and wide, dexterous hands, like a fisherman's. He wore no hat, coat, nor waistcoat, only a shirt and a black kerchief knotted around his neck. His features were naturally pale but darkened by the sun: a thick, straight nose, bitter mouth, and deep-set eyes, with the taint of sleeplessness and blood-shot about them. He looked as closely at the prisoner as the surgeon, but did not respond.

Wilmot, squat and unsentimental, with small boots and a tight waistcoat, interposed—"He's to measure you for your ball gown."

The prisoner hacked through a long cough, pushed himself upright with one arm, and was half guided, half dragged out of his cell and onto the terrace. Doyle peered around, turning his haggard face and matted beard, but his dust-crusted eyes, when they settled anywhere, were drawn to the impassive hangman.

"I ain't afraid to do the walk," he croaked.

"No one asked your opinion, you mongrel," chirruped Wilmot.

"I shall take your pulse," said Moynihan softly.

"Don't see as how it matters," said the prisoner, but he allowed his narrow wrist to be taken. The man's right hand was twisted and the fingers curled against the palm. Moynihan lowered his eyes to count and released the hand after a half-minute.

"This malingering dog cracked open an overseer's head with a spade," said the gaoler, conversationally, to the watching hangman.

"I doubt that," said Moynihan quietly, as he slipped his pocket watch away.

"I did, so," croaked Doyle. "He was intolerable severe with me."

The hangman snorted under his breath and looked down at the floor, where the soft, pale stone had been worn to a hollow.

"Killed him, that's plain, ain't it?" wheedled Doyle, plucking at Wilmot's sleeve.

"Now I must listen to your lungs."

Doyle stripped off his coarse yellow and black wool shirt. Even the gaoler looked aside: the man's back was layered with scars and fresh red welts.

"Breath in," said Moynihan. "Out!" He leaned in to follow the exhalation.

Wilmot tucked his thumbs into his waistcoat. "Well? Is he ready for his dose?"

The surgeon tilted his head again. "We shall see. But is there no hope of reprieve otherwise?"

"What do you mean by reprieve?" said Wilmot. "On what grounds?"

In an undertone, Carver said, "Mark you that man's right wrist?"

"What of it?"

Moynihan blinked and glanced at the hangman, as if he were also an unusual case, newly revealed. Then he said, "A fracture, from a fall, I expect, that did not heal cleanly. Look. The bones are not aligned. The fingers only partially open. The hand is weak, and the grasp is feeble."

The hangman shook his head.

"You disagree?" asked the surgeon mildly.

"There was no fall," said Carver. "That is the mark of the flogging frame. If the prisoner is not bound right, he faints or twists in his agony, and breaks the wrist."

Moynihan nodded and straightened, turning to Wilmot. "Can you see a man with a weak hand like this raise up a shovel and strike hard and sure enough to kill?"

"If he could not do it, why confess?" said the gaoler, jangling his keys. "There were informants enough besides, the whole gang."

"That, I admit, I cannot answer," said Moynihan, frowning as he tapped his palm against the man's back.

"I done it for me own peace." Doyle's wheeze came high-pitched, tumbling out of his caved chest. "He wouldn't let off me. Said I made the whole chain slow."

At length, Moynihan looked up. He pressed his lips together for several seconds and said, "There is no corporeal reason why this man could not meet his fate tomorrow. There is some chronic contagion of the lungs. It is not severe. Has the priest been called?"

"Hear that?" said the gaoler. "You'll face it straight then?"

Doyle rested against the wall and resumed biting at the ball of his thumb. In the brief silence, the woman's shrieking intensified, piercing the stones. The surgeon shuddered and pulled at his own wrist. Doyle seemed unconscious of the sound, gazing out over the debtors' yard at the parched sky.

"Detestable racket," muttered Moynihan. Sweat darkened the top of his collar and beaded on the tip of his nose.

"I am putting you under the lock again," announced Wilmot.

"At least let him have some water and clean air," said Moynihan.

"By and by."

"I shall report to the warder." The surgeon stepped to the other side of the terrace to speak to Carver. "Eight stone, I should say," he said softly.

"Five-foot, nine-inch drop," returned the hangman. Only he saw the condemned man wince.

"Rather short," suggested the surgeon.

"Not if you want to keep body and head together when he tumbles," said Carver. "He's thin as a straw."

Wilmot prodded at Doyle and raised his keys. "No more of this sly business. Go in quietly."

The prisoner blinked at the hangman.

Carver had not moved. "What? Out with it."

"You won't let me throttle, will you, mister? I seen me mate Dan Fisher choking on the rope. An awful long time."

"I'm no mister," growled the hangman, "but I won't let you throttle. It will be quick."

Wilmot secured the cell door. All three men kept their thoughts close in the walk around the cell block. The front wall reflected an implacable slab of sunlight and, faint and persistent, the woman's screams from the other side.

"This business of his confession puzzles me, frankly," said Moynihan, at the head of the steps.

Carver, stalking straight-legged a few paces behind, snorted.

"This does not trouble you?" said Moynihan.

"A confession does not surprise me. No folly surprises me."

"He'd not confess if he had no part in it," said Wilmot, with an air of affront.

"Bah—a man here will confess to anything that suits," retorted Carver.

The surgeon tilted his head.

"I don't take your point," said Wilmot.

"He was not brought into the lock and put in a road gang for murder, though, was he?" said Carver.

Wilmot halted on the steps and looked back. "You guess right. He was stealing rum in nips from his master. And on that charge he was waiting for transfer to Van Diemen's Land."

"I don't need to guess. See you his back? You can read the flogger's work there. And then new cuts, like straw laid this way and that. All single lashes from a stick or horse-whip. This fellow lived peaceably enough for many years, long enough for the old marks of punishment to heal. And he was brought back for an infringement and set on a chain gang. And the overseer of this gang lays about him with a whip willy-nilly, and all the prisoners hate him and wish him dead."

"That's the tale. The ward here is too crowded. He would have been sent to Macquarie Harbour, eventually," added Wilmot, lifting his cap a little.

"Aye, Macquarie Harbour. Hell's Gate they call it, for penance and driving cruelty. And in mortal fear of a renewal of his old suffering, flogging, and back-breaking labour, he takes the blame for a murder that the whole gang no doubt contrived, and thereby makes an end to his troubles."

"Takes the blame for the whole gang!" Wilmot shook his head. "Why this specimen?"

Carver shrugged. "He took a cough. He had a weak hand. He slowed them down."

"There is naught in this but guesswork. Mischievous guesswork," said the gaoler, squinting at Carver. "Drunken guesswork, perhaps."

Carver betrayed no sign of present intoxication, but his clothes were permeated with the faint taint of rum. He spoke steadily: "I don't drink before a hanging. Only afterwards. You know that."

"What's to be done?" murmured Moynihan, rubbing one hand at the bridge of his nose.

"There's nothing to be done," said Wilmot, not unkindly.

"That wretch in there chooses his own passage to Hell," said Carver. "So none of this will trouble him after the morrow."

The surgeon took a short, jerking step, shook his head, and looked sharply around the staring walls. "Will that banshee not give over!" he exclaimed. "What is the matter?"

"It has been like that since last night. The woman is confined separate from the others on a murder charge. Screams innocence and will not hear reason."

Moynihan hacked on the word. "Murder?"

"Her master. A free convict by the name of Staines. By all accounts wealthy enough."

Another shriek broke the heavy air of the yard. The surgeon fumbled with his watch chain, but could not catch it with his damp fingers.

"Who does she call for?"

"The chaplain, the magistrate—the hangman in particular, which is beyond reason." Wilmot glanced at Carver, who made no answer, as though recalling his customary reserve.

"The hangman also, you say?" asked Moynihan.

"She is mad, aye, to name the executioner in the same breath as the colonial secretary," said Wilmot. "But she says if the beaks won't hear her, the hangman will."

"She is plainly distressed," said Moynihan.

"Would it please you to look in?" said the gaoler drily.

"Lead on," said Moynihan, with a quick, angry motion of the hand. "Let me see what's the matter."

The surgeon could detect neither concern nor curiosity in Carver, and yet something stirred the hangman, for he followed also.

THE SOLITARY CELLS, separate from the crowded, infested barrack-rooms where most of the prisoners were housed in the main block, stood opposite the old "Females' Room."

Only when the cell door opened did the screaming abate. Moynihan heard a harsh panting as he advanced. The woman within had torn the coarse blanket to shreds, and nothing else was left with her in the cell. He faced a haggard woman squatting on the stones with her hair undone and wild about a pale, greasy face. Her hands were bent and stained with old blood about the broken nails.

"How now," said Moynihan steadily, "what's the matter?"

"Who's this?" she asked the gaoler. Her leg-irons dragged on the stone.

"Assistant surgeon. The gentleman here is confounded by your racket."

She spat on the floor. "I don't want him. I want my particulars taken down properly. I want to be heard before the governor. Better yet, bring me Carver. Then I may relent."

"In time, in time, my lass."

Her voice sank to something rough and cunning. "I ought not to be here. You've no right to hold me here."

"We none of us have a say in that," replied the gaoler.

The woman lunged at Moynihan, and he was startled, rearing and knocking back Wilmot, who had edged in behind him. The surgeon cried out and reached to steady himself, while the prisoner lunged past the guard and bolted to the door. Momentarily, the hangman crossed the opening, fixing his arms to either side of the frame.

The gaoler whirled about. Moynihan caught himself against the wall. But the woman reeled, staring at Carver.

"Who's this?"

"Now, Meg," said Wilmot, "don't you know?"

"Who's this!"

"This is Mr. Carver, the jolly hangman himself, come to pay his respects. Say how-d'ye-do."

The woman swayed and blinked, and lifted her shaking hands as though to caress his face.

"Carrion-crow," she husked. "Turncoat. Traitor. Oh, don't you know me?" And then her heaving breath turned to something low and harsh, like laughter.

Carver stood still and straight; his face was fixed, but the corner of his mouth quirked up after an interval. "So," he said, "Meg Harper. Has it come to this at last?"

Wilmot recovered his balance, and wrapped a thick arm around the woman's neck, hauling her off balance and back into the rear of the cell.

Carver strode forward, and his hand fell heavy on the doctor's shoulder.

"Get out," growled Carver. "You're no use to her here."

The three men returned to the passageway while the cursing gaoler retrieved his cap and shut up the cell.

"It's on you, Gabriel Carver," the woman screamed through the door. "See to it! I know you! Be sure I know you! You'll hang before I do, otherwise!"

Moynihan straightened his coat, and necktie and waistcoat, one by one.

"I take it you know that woman?" he said faintly. A faint burble, like laughter, came from behind the door.

"That woman is my wife," said the hangman. "She'll be quiet enough now."

CHAPTER 2.

The Hangman's Fee

FULL DAYLIGHT SPREAD over Sydney Town. No shadows remained. No relief from the sun in the vastness of this continent rendered prison, a Golgotha of the spirit. In this boundless brilliance, where the sky is blank and impenetrable as a wall, even moral darkness must be utterly concealed, or stand stark as on a bare plain. Inside the sandstone walls of the gaol on George Street, the gallows were made ready, and the executioner tested the ropes, setting knots with an easy turn of his hands.

The spectacle of hanging no longer provided a diversion for the crowds on the street outside the gaol, but beyond the west wall the ground rose, providing a platform for a mob to observe the business within. This patch of ragged stone was called Hangman's Hill, in a familiar way. Onlookers had gathered, feebly excited by the spectacle. Convicts and bedraggled settlers lingered to observe and pass rum with whalers and bow-legged sealers. Aborigines, in tattered scraps of discarded finery, looked on, jaded by all deaths, while ragged children sported with a collection of starveling dogs. Three or four officers had drawn up on exhausted horses and complained of the heat. On the far side of the street, a few fine ladies with parasols lingered and exchanged remarks behind their hands. Flocks of indifferent, raucous birds, brilliant white, tumbled overhead.

The surgeon, Moynihan, idling down the lane from his chambers higher up the street, found the gaoler, Wilmot, off duty, on the edge of the gathering.

"Mr. Carver seems rather particular about his craft," said the surgeon, peering at the crowd and the gallows.

The gaoler was teasing one of the roaming dogs by rattling his keys. "He's a peculiar cove. The convicts hate him for his trade. The officers shun him because he is a convict. Do you not know? No sooner had he stepped off the transport, he won his release from hard labour by taking the assignment as executioner in old Mitchell's place. Answered the call to hang three of his own."

"And what was his crime?"

"We don't speak of old crimes here, but the word was he escaped from the hulks with another prisoner, after some wild scheme to murder a guard fell apart."

"Did he murder that guard?"

"No. That was the other man. His old shipmates would have raised him up as a hero among the prisoners here for that particular exploit, had he not taken up the noose."

"A cypher, therefore. Yet there is something not altogether wild about his conduct," said Moynihan.

"I'll grant you, he's never drunk the day before a hanging," said Wilmot. "And old Mitchell was often dead-drunk, and likely to botch the job."

Moynihan swallowed dryly. "What do you make of his naming that unfortunate woman as his wife?"

Wilmot shrugged. "Convicts make all sorts of queer alliances. There are few enough women. They generally fall in with a likely fellow, or a soldier. But these common marriages don't last. I doubt he'll stand by her, however she may rave and threaten."

The prisoners were brought down for their final walk. Doyle shuffled out last, coughing into a rag.

"His cough is worse," said Moynihan painfully.

"Soon remedy that." The gaoler pushed the dog aside with a thrust of his boot.

"It is a mercy, then, I suppose."

Four, this morning. The youngest, a boy of seventeen, emerged scowling but looked baffled at the raw timbers of the gallows platform. The Reverend Honeychair read from the eighty-eighth psalm, a gloomy favourite among the prisoners, but the crowd roused itself, and a few toasts were proposed and accepted with sour liquor.

> *Let my prayer come before thee: incline thine ear unto my cry;*
> *For my soul is full of troubles: and my life draweth nigh unto the grave.*

The guards cradled their muskets; an Irishman near the foot of the gaol wall began singing.

All four were sent up to take their part under the cross-beam. The hood was offered, and only the wild-looking boy refused, for he had taken the notion that he was a pebble, iron-hard and not to be swayed, even at the end. Doyle dipped his head meekly for the covers. The warder of the gaol looked at his pocket watch. A transport under sail came wallowing up the flawless harbour.

> *I am counted with them that go down into the pit: I am as a man that hath no strength:*
> *Free among the dead, like the slain that lie in the grave, whom thou rememberest no more…*

The hangman placed each noose and turned the knot to the side. His steps alone did not falter on the boards.

There were a few preliminary cheers when the clergyman closed his Bible and began the Lord's Prayer. A scuffle broke out on the edge of the crowd on the hill, compounding the dust.

The warder clasped his hands and nodded to the executioner.

One by one, Carver tipped the condemned from light into darkness. A shudder, a kick; five-foot-nine, well judged. Doyle was suspended, still, a broken stick.

THE HANGMAN AND the guards brought the bodies down, while the soldiers set their caps back on, and resumed their conversation. The assistant surgeon, Moynihan, made a cursory inspection to confirm death. Meanwhile, Carver coiled and stowed the ropes. The crowd outside broke up, a few pausing to make gestures or hurl curses and debris in the direction of walls, the gallows, and its attendants. Carver's face shone with sweat, for he had on a dusty black coat and the heat was immutable, like a weight.

Shortly, Carver left the gallows yard and crossed the open ground of the courtyard to the head warder's office. The old gaol was convict-built, shoddy and unfinished, for the hands that had raised the walls as a last place of confinement in ultimate exile had been weary and unskilled. The office was suspended on raw planks, with enough gaps above and below for the dust or rain to fall through. At this hour of the morning, the room was hot and dim.

Warder Malloch appeared bloated with gases rather than fat, with a square head framed by sparse red whiskers balanced on rounded shoulders. He had been a soldier, had sought preferment and gone into the rum trade, failed at that by drinking into the stock, and somehow come to the gaol on the strength of his old connections. He still visited the barracks every night. He gestured at the bottle on his plain, rickety desk as Carver came in.

"I'm here for my fee," said the hangman.

"Your thirty shekels."

If Carver had an answer to this classical drollery, he gave no sign.

"You'll take a measure, surely?"

"My fee."

Nodding somewhat, the warder rummaged across the top of his desk, found an accounts book, wrote out a line, and then took from another strongbox in his drawer a sum in colonial scrip.

In the interval, Carver poured a long measure of murky brown spirits and settled himself in a chair before the desk. The warder had not unshuttered the windows, and the rum had the same colour as the weak ink with which he wrote in the ledger.

"There is one thing," said Carver abruptly.

"Be prompt, man."

"You have a prisoner," said Carver. "A woman, in confinement. Her name is Meg Harper."

"So I have," said the warder. "You can expect to be introduced on the gallows. Irredeemable creature." He smacked his lips and put down the little tumbler. "A murderess, you know. Monstrous. Cut the throat of her master, old Ned Staines."

"How so?"

"She was assigned to him, under the system. Sent out from the convict barracks as maid and housekeeper. Staines was wealthy, everyone knows. A rare bird. A convict emancipist who served out his term, took to farming, and prospered on his own merits."

"And what reason could they give for her murdering this old man?"

The warder raised his glass again, and peered at Carver across the top of it.

"Should you care? You have been assigned as the executioner these three years and never much shown any other interest."

"Should I not?" Carver scratched his jaw. "I knew her, once. That's all."

"Very well. You keep yourself to yourself. That's canny, in your situation." The warder's flat face folded into a flat, sour smile. "Besides, what is one murderess, more or less, or one murder, where we pile up convicts and crimes like cordwood?"

"Call it my fee," said Carver, raising his head and setting his broad shoulders back. "I take an interest. I have done them some service, and they know it."

The warder shrugged and settled behind his bandy-legged desk. "It is as I said. She was taken by the constables on a bush road. The case is to be heard before Coldrake. He is not inclined to make much of the arguments. The watchword under our new governor is severity. She was found with a sack of silverware from the old man's cupboard. The cause is as clear as daylight."

"What does she say?"

"Her case is hopeless. It is useless to ask."

Malloch drank deeply and poured again. Carver matched him, yet with some caution or watchfulness, for he measured the descending line of spirits in the dusty glass closely. The warder's head nodded, and sometimes he snorted. The heat gathered. The hangman did not stir.

"What date is set for her trial?" Carver said at last.

Malloch started out of a doze. The sound of chains and shuffling feet, the mustering of a working gang, came in from the courtyard. "Still harping on that woman? She's for the gallows. You'll tend her soon enough. No women wanted on Norfolk Island, you know. No reprieve."

"You speak as though it's a settled thing," said Carver. His voice was hard and dry.

"It is a certain thing."

"And yet there is the puzzle," returned Carver, licking his lips. "Why chance certain death for a few ounces of silver?"

The warder set down his glass unsteadily. "It happens so every day. If any felon reckoned up the consequences before he turned to the crime, none of us would be here. You'll get no reason from her, I'll warrant, only brazen denial."

"So that's it," said Carver.

"As you say. Don't linger, then."

Carver stood, and without any outward haste he gathered up the small stack of paper before him on the desk. The warder looked on, sunk in torpor. His trade had made the hangman's face impossible to read, and in the dim room and haze of rum, Carver seemed more a phantom than a breathing man. But the hangman, thought Malloch vaguely, knows the exact worth of any life, since his is the fee for ending it.

"Go, therefore," muttered the warder. "Speak to her if you would. I don't care for her sins, or yours."

Carver slipped his fee into the inmost pocket of his coat and closed the buttons.

OUTSIDE THE WARDER'S office, Carver looked in to the guards' room. He was steady enough, but with a drinker's willed precision, vigilant of error. Two or three guards were there, resting from their rounds in the shadows, but Wilmot was not present.

"What's the matter?" said Abbott, a lazing, pink-scalped bully attached to the day shift.

"I want to see the new prisoner; the woman, Harper."

"You're out of turn. She don't need hanging yet."

"Warder's orders. He wants to see if she's fit to go back to the women's room."

"She's stopped her fussing. Still, won't eat. Won't drink. Twenty lashes will make her amenable again."

"I'm no scourger."

"Then you've no business here but to visit your sweetheart and blacken our door."

"Would you hinder me?" Carver spoke quietly, but he leaned towards Abbott with his hands tightened. The guard leered back, with his thumbs hooked in his belt.

"Now, there'll be no contention on the walk," said another turnkey, a broad, scarred former marine sergeant called Hodge. "Let him be. I'll fetch the keys."

Hodge ambled along the terrace with Carver behind him and unlocked the creaking, uneven door. Carver gestured him aside and went in alone.

Meg Harper looked up warily. Someone had tossed a ragged straw mattress into the cell, and she was seated on that with her head set against the wall. Her eyes narrowed as she scanned the features of the man before her, and then an obscure triumph flickered in her eyes.

"I knew you'd answer," she said. "Soon as I saw you close."

Carver replied, "What is it you'd have of me?"

Meg had a narrow face, a long, sharp-bladed nose, and pointed chin. Her manner had formerly been lively, quick to laugh, question, or harass, and her eyes were wide and warm, hazel flecked with gold. But time had executed its certain changes against her: her tangled brown hair was mixed with white strands. Her eyes were rimmed with red, her lean cheeks hollow, and though she had always been slender, now her wrists showed like knots of bone.

She pushed strands of hair from her brow before replying. "Bring me out. Steer me past the gallows at least. You have the warder's ear, I don't doubt. I'll own to taking the old man's silver, but I swear I did not kill him. I'll not hang for that."

Carver sighed and rubbed his jaw. "Why should I help you?"

A pinched, sure smile tugged up her lips. "For I know you, I do. Gabriel Carver! And I could tell a pretty tale about you. A very pretty tale. And then what would your office mean? You might find yourself on the wrong end of the noose again."

"Turn king's evidence against me? Who would believe you?"

Meg tsked. "Have you no tender feelings? Man and wife, that's what we were, or don't you recall? You know it. I ain't seen my husband since he were took off first to the hulks. But I've heard his name in a hundred curses since I came here. Gabriel Carver. The hangman. Holds himself cold and hard and proud and separate from us all. But I did not kill that old man, and *my* fine man, my

Gabriel Carver will not let that go. So I called for the hangman, and here you appear."

The cell was no more than a few paces across. Slowly, Carver took off his coat and lowered himself to the ground, and his outstretched leg and boot almost touched the other wall. "Why did they catch you on the road with the old man's plate silver?"

"Wages owed," she said, leaning forward. "I worked for that withered tyrant for three years, no better than a whore, and the assignment system my bawd, and so I took what I was squarely owed."

"Did you trouble yourself to ascertain if the old man was dead first or not?" said Carver.

Meg shuddered and rearranged her ragged dress. "I found him, so I did, cold in his own chair, and raised the alarm. The rest of the scum bolted directly, and I knew that there would be nothing but accusations and hard suspicion, whatever I did." She shrugged. "So I don't know where he kept his money—he was closer than close about that—but I could lay hold of his table-wares."

"Did you not think you'd be caught?" said Carver.

She shook her head. "We're all caught out here. I just wanted to see how far I could go."

"Who did for the old man? Had he many servants?"

"It was one of the black devils," she said swiftly, "from out in the bush."

"Pah!"

"They're mighty sly. Why, the constables should be out with the dogs right now."

He laid his hand flat on the pressed dirt floor of the cell, and shook his head. "I need facts, not wild guesses, if I am to get you out of this. The scene of the crime is material. Tell me everything: how it passed, how you came upon him, who was there, anything else."

"The old man never slept much. When he weren't out in the kitchen in the morning I went into the house. He wasn't in his bed so I found him in the parlour, stretched out in the dark in his best chair, with his throat cut and the blood gone thick."

"You didn't sleep in the house?"

Meg scratched her lean left arm. "Cookhouse. I can bar the door. There are plenty of convict hands on the property who could get ideas otherwise about the larder—or me—and Staines locked the larder cupboards overnight. To be doubly sure, I suppose."

"Old Staines passed the night alone in the house? No wife?"

"Had one, once. There was a tale you could never hear the end of. Irish lass. Ran off with a soldier, he said. Officer of the corps. Took a small fortune with her. That made him close and crafty, I reckon. Wouldn't trust another woman ever again. He was a grasping, bitter old fish. Always marking the content of his cupboards and the level of his bottles."

"I don't care about gossip," said Carver. "What did you do then? Why not raise the hue and cry, get the constabulary out, if you thought it was the black man at work?"

"This talk makes me thirst ache something. Can I get some water?"

"Do you not have some here?"

Meg's voice dropped. "I threw it at them."

Wordlessly, Carver clambered to his feet and went to the cell door where he could call for water. A battered tin cup duly came, filled with lukewarm water from a stale barrel. Meg drank it quickly, but when she returned the cup she touched Carver's hand and he did not withdraw.

"I had a wish to walk the roads and go far and free. The old hands say that there is a way to buy your passage home, if you have enough tin. I thought to sell the plate in Port Middlebay or thereabouts."

"As well try and walk to China," snorted Carver.

"Well, the old man was dead, and I have no wish to go back to the Female Factory."

"There's the matter in fine," rumbled Carver. "He trusted you enough to sleep in the kitchen, why would you cast that aside for a mean sum in plate and the noose?"

"Now there's a plain, canny man!"

Carver waved this aside. "What of the knife, the razor, whatever made the cut?"

"I didn't see it."

"Was Staines given to entertaining? Did he have many guests?"

"He had callers all the time, but never the Currency, the high-and-mighty free settlers who have him bounded on all sides. No, mostly free convicts like himself. He was deep in the emancipists' cause. And the old man was hard as an old stump."

"Throat-slitting, that's a sure way to kill a man, but it takes strength, or speed, and a steady hand."

"In London, we knew enough cutthroats and pads who could finish the task."

"We're not in London. There's no call to speak of it."

"I'm a farmer's daughter: I'll stick a pig, not an old man."

For the first time, Carver allowed himself a half-smile. "I'm inclined to take your word for it, but that's not enough."

"You can make them hear."

"Hold. I still have no part in this."

Meg scowled. "You are their man, their hangman. You can turn the warder, the magistrate, or the police constable. There is that soft-voiced surgeon, the new fellow, at least."

"These men hate my office, for they make it necessary."

"And what of your office, if they knew you as I do?"

Carver heaved forward, his face dark. "Hush your voice. I won't be threatened," he hissed. "I should not have answered when they said you called me."

"But you did. You were afraid of what I might know. The hold I have on you: it's stronger than rope or chains."

"So you might say."

"Then take my part, and follow your conscience."

"My conscience is withered; it's no use to a man here."

"Stubborn," hissed Meg, "and proud. But I know what I know. I won't dance on the fatal tree alone."

"If I take this up for you, I must see the place itself," Carver half muttered. "There is a chance that the constables missed something. But I can no more leave the town than you can. I am no ticket-of-leave man to go where I will, but assigned to the warder."

"I'll wager they don't follow you too closely, at least when the condemned cells are empty. Would anyone come looking if they thought you dead drunk for a day?"

Carver rose, leaned down, and picked up his coat, which was crumpled and covered with dun prison dust. "I commit to nothing," he said, "but I will set my mind to it."

"There was a man on the property," said Meg eagerly tugging at the seam of his trousers. "Overseer. Ralph Devers. He and the old man were close together in some plotting and planning. But they had words between them. Fierce words in my hearing."

"Why did you not speak of this before, put your evidence against him?"

"You find him, my pretty man, and I will. He ran off before the rest of them."

"Ran off? Did you see him after you found the old man dead?"

Meg blinked, and a faint, cruel smile touched her lips. "Why, I did not. He will know what happened, I'm sure. But he won't be keen to say."

"And how am I meant to find him, if the constables can't?"

"He used to ride out on one of the old man's horses. Down many times to Sydney Town, he would boast."

"Where in the town? On what business?"

Meg scowled. "He said, once, that he was looking for Staines' runaway wife. I reckon he drew out the tale to keep our master interested and find as many reasons to ride out as possible. He's found a crack to hide in there, I'll hazard."

Carver stepped into the blistering heat of the yard. Prisoners, overflowing from the crowded dormitory, had spilled into the yard also, and were shuffling up and down in a line, shackles jangling, under the eyes of the guards. All their progress was but to reach one wall, turn, and return. Carver halted and panted like a wounded man under the beat of the sun, struck by weariness and thirst. A prisoner, limping by, turned a black look towards him. Carver returned the look with a steady glare, and went on to the gatehouse to set his mark in the warder's book.

CHAPTER 3.

Curious Guests

A FEW MILES INLAND, a gang of convicts hauled a cart loaded with broken rocks. Heat and red dust made them insubstantial, unreal as the peeling, grey-barked trees scattered in ragged stands across the unbroken plain. Where the dust settled, Gabriel Carver followed. His feet dragged on the pitted road. From time to time he drank, without pausing, from an earthenware jug in his hand, but the small beer did not refresh him. Intermittently, a squatter, settler, or constable would pass on a horse, but he was not troubled to show his papers—a fortunate turn, for he had none that would suit.

The sun had advanced, the jug been discarded, and a dry, hot wind began to move across the Cumberland Plains from the haze of hills to the unseen ocean, when Carver stopped at a fence of broken spars on the side of the road. He rested, panting, but something of the wary hunch of the gaol had been left behind with the thin beer, and his gaze was steady. In the distance he saw a spreading ironwood tree, alone among the sparse fields, with thin yellow grass clustered about its roots. Flies buzzed and gyred before him. He followed the track towards the house.

The homestead at Three Mile Creek stood desolate at the end of the late October day. Carver surveyed the main house, the walled kitchen block and the distant cluster of open barns and ramshackle wooden huts. He advanced to the shade of the deep verandas and stood for a while in the cool margin. Crows hopped and croaked on the roof. Then he plunged in at the door.

The servants and hands had abandoned the place, lawfully or not. Only the memory of the murdered man remained: the texture of his character in the plain dining room and the stiff, hard furniture, the simple bedroom, the narrow fireplace. The hangman had not a grain of superstition, nor any latent aversion to the signs of death, and looked on all this unmoved.

In the front room, which must have served Staines as office and parlour, the buzzing and rising of myriads of hard flies showed him the tacky bloodstain that had run down to the seat of one of the two heavy armchairs by the hearthstone. Carver raised his head fractionally, as though to test the air, and then searched the room without haste. He went to the desk, glanced at the scattered papers and open drawers, and scowled at the sideboard and the mantelpiece, where a clay pipe lay with the tobacco ash cold within it. Carver looked down again, to the same bloodied armchair nearest the fireplace. A glass had fallen by the side of the chair and rolled through a few degrees. Carver knelt on one knee and scooped up the glass, glaring at a chip in the side. There was a pale, dry residue against the curved side of the vessel. With an odd relish, Carver sniffed at the rim. Then, ignoring the swarming, irate flies, he crawled a little across the floor where the lesser spatters of blood showed. He looked up also, at the black specks whirring about the ceiling.

Rising, he peered into the one cabinet with its door ajar, grimaced, and touched the lock. Glasses to match the one on the floor, and a set of rough clay tumblers, were disturbed; but the fleeing workers had abstracted all bottles of spirits. Quickly, Carver rummaged through everything that remained, and briefly held one glass up to the light before leaving it standing again. Then, he turned out of the room and went a few steps into the old man's bedroom, which he surveyed impatiently.

By now, his thirst was almost painful, and so he crossed out of the house to the kitchen block. At the small cistern, almost hungrily, Carver pumped out enough water to guzzle with his hands and wet his dusty face and the kerchief knotted around his neck. Still dripping, he left the main house, and ambled towards the largest cottage, which he took for the overseer's quarters.

Flocks of bright green birds dove screaming through the air, and white clouds above the brown fields were tainted at their tops with pink and apricot shades. In this inverted world, even the summer night drew on swiftly. Chattering, quarrelsome black bats stirred in the trees.

The plank door was unbolted. The stem of a broken pipe lay in the red dust outside. Carver peered into the cottage room. The bed and rough table were disordered and slovenly. Carver blinked at the bottle stoppers that were strewn across the floor, and his sight fell on a pair of dice dropped and forgotten near the hearth. There was a prisoner's sea-chest at the foot of the bed, but it revealed no sign of boots, belt, or knife, only a smattering of clothes.

Carver returned to the farmhouse and stepped into Meg Harper's kitchen. For some time Carver sat in thoughtful silence at the crooked and beaten kitchen table, until he heard the sound of a horse approaching from the road.

Carver walked out to the front of the house. As he stepped clear of the shadow of the veranda, a voice called, too sharply, "Hold, or I'll shoot!"

"Shoot who, you popinjay?" returned Carver, in more even tones.

"Step up, then, and say your business here." The rider was dressed in a grey uniform, with a few threads of gold ribbon around the cuffs, and a stiff round cap. He had a musket laid across his knees, which wavered uncertainly as the horse shifted. A thin beard was starting on the chin, but he had a rather delicate and bony face, awkwardly long and straight. The policeman was little more than twenty.

"I am Gabriel Carver, hangman at the Sydney Gaol. My business is with the scene of the crime."

"The hangman be damned. You are some bushranger or thief, come to pick over the dead man's property. Hold still, by God, or I'll shoot."

"Here," said Carver, "you may read my papers."

"Lay them on the ground there."

Carver set a folded slip of paper on the packed earth beyond the veranda, and at a gesture from the mounted man, he stepped aside. The man slid off the horse and then went to examine the papers. He glanced at the signature, read the description, and then squinted at Carver, whose face was half in shadow in the low light.

"It says you are the hangman, but you have no leave to be anywhere beyond Sydney Cove."

"And who are you? And by whose authority do you intervene in my business?"

"I am constable Ellington, of the district police. I am here to keep convicts and trespassers off the property—not that it's your business to ask," he added, after a delay.

"Wait till you know my business better. Come in and have a drink. Riding the bounds of this property must be a thirsty occupation," offered Carver.

Ellington stuffed the papers into his belt. "You have no lawful business here. You have escaped, for all I know."

Carver grinned at the policeman. "No lawful business, but a righteous purpose."

To Ellington's consternation, Carver began to walk away along the path to the house. He crossed the grass, making towards the distant, black branches of the lone tree that marked the edge of the property from the road.

"I shall shoot you if you flee," offered Ellington.

"Arrest me, when I am done. Take me to your sergeant. Or better yet, the nearest magistrate. I fancy I have something to report."

Carver passed through the grass, in the long light of the faltering day, and the policeman followed him, flicking the reins over his horse's neck.

BEYOND THE TOWN, the gum forests had been broken and hacked apart by the growth of the colony, pierced and sectioned by bullock tracks, homesteads, and ramshackle grog-shops. The native people had been driven out from their settled terrain, though their spears still terrorized stockmen and settlers on the margins. The kangaroo, likewise, had submitted to slaughter to make way for parched cattle-runs and herds of scrawny mutton. But scattered over the plains there remained great stands of trees with richly variegated brown bark: cathedrals of rising dust, the air dense with the pine-scent of eucalyptus, the forest floor dry and red and dark, haunted by stealthy animals.

Carver walked along the track in the stifling shadows. Ellington followed on horseback, hunched over his musket.

Somewhere, there was a crack, like a branch breaking, and a hushed rustle. Ellington reined in; his horse padded the ground.

"Why do you stop?" said Carver, who had not broken his slow, easy stride.

"Bushrangers," muttered Ellington. "Escaped convicts, native hunters."

"What do we have to steal?" asked Carver.

"You're not wearing a policeman's uniform."

"Fair point," Carver conceded. He turned on his heels. "Do you know how many labourers Staines had?"

"A dozen or so."

"Are none of them to be found?"

"They will be arrested. There is nowhere for them to run. Then the magistrates will examine them, and one will spit out the truth."

"Not if your man thinks he has already found it. And there was an overseer for the convicts."

"Convict overseer. He's missing as well."

"Ahh. And don't you think he's worth having a word with?"

"You think this man quarrelled with his master and murdered him," said Ellington, stirring his horse to a walk.

"I am sure only that the full truth hasn't come out, and that don't sit straight with me."

All sound seemed to draw away from the two men, and the long, bladed leaves of the trees hung heavy. Far away, there came a snap, like gunshot. Ellington looked up.

"I am tasked to find Staines' overseer, if I can," said the constable.

"Then ride on," said Carver, and he resumed his even, slow striding walk along the brown trail.

MRS. ANTONIA FITCHETT, Miss Fairbairn before her marriage to a stuffy Calvinist lawyer twenty years her senior, was in conversation with William Fordham but so alert by temperament that she heard, above the whining saw of night insects and the improbable bellowing of little frogs in the distant creek, the approach of a rider and then her maid answering the door. When she saw Kathleen hovering at the entrance to the dining room, unsure of the disposition of the gentlemen, she excused herself from the party and slipped out to see who was there. As she stifled a yawn in the hallway, she told herself brightly that her motive was hospitality and not escape from the *ennui*.

The night was not fully dark, with a bewildering array of stars and a steady half moon. She recognized one of her husband's constables on his lean roan horse, but then a second man appeared like a wraith at the horse's flanks: not tall, but wide at the shoulders and upright in his bearing.

"Who is it?" bellowed her husband from the dining room, before she had a moment to phrase her own greeting.

"One of your men, dear," she returned. "And...someone else."

This man stepped forward into the frail light of the oil-lamps disrupted by the whirling, idiotic moths, "I am Gabriel Carver, ma'am, executioner to the warder of Sydney Gaol."

"You don't look like an executioner," she blurted.

"Should I be grinning and capering under the fatal tree?" he replied evenly.

"No. I mean: I don't understand why you are here."

The mounted policeman rattled off, "I caught him trespassing on Staines' run, without a clear account of himself. He is a convict, and has no pass."

"Consequently, I am brought here to your husband," concluded Carver.

"We have guests." Antonia gestured at the windows.

"Well, I cannot wait in lockup while the constable sends to find out the truth of my purpose."

The man before her was watchful, calm, expectant. "Very well," she said. "You had best come in."

"Bring the fellow in here!" a voice shouted from the window. "It had better be damned important—begging the lady's pardon."

"Is it important?" said Antonia, as though she were trying to guess the answer to a parlour-riddle.

"A life and a death rest upon it," said the executioner.

"He says he knows who killed old Staines," announced Ellington.

"I know who did not," said Carver, before passing within.

The dining room was filled with stale smoke and the scent of hot rum. Fitchett, the police magistrate, sat at the head of the table. He had set his knife and fork side by side on his clean plate, but it was not he who had called for the stranger to be brought in. Mr. Fordham, land-owner and one of the so-called Currency, the true coinage of empire, was returning from the window. The deacon of the parish, Mr. Hoare, and the chief recorder of the district had pushed their chairs back and were lounging in conversation. Only Fitchett seemed like a man out of place at his own table.

"I hope, my dear, that our evening is not interrupted on some slight pretence," he said. Fitchett was tall, with a small head and a long neck that merged smoothly with his chin.

"Begging your lady's pardon," said Carver, "but I am here to tell you straight that the lass you have in the Sydney lockup is not the one who did for Staines."

"Then since I examined and arraigned her myself," said Fitchett, "you are here to tell me I am wrong, decidedly like every other felon that passes before my bench."

"You are wrong," said Carver.

Fordham soothed himself with a cough.

"Impudence," remarked Mr. Hoare. "And pride."

"This is not an approach calculated to your advantage," said Fitchett, pressing his front teeth together.

"At least hear him out," said Antonia. "He has come out of his way by his own account."

"Lock him up, have another glass, and charge him tomorrow," said Fordham cheerfully.

"Do you know who Staines' guest was on the night he died?" said Carver.

"He had no callers," said Fitchett. "I have established that."

"Then have you established to your satisfaction why someone went to the trouble of leaping out of the bush to tidy one of the dead man's good glasses back into his cabinet?" said Carver.

"The fellow is trying to fox you now," said Hoare.

"The cabinet was unlocked, and though the labourers had made off with the rum, I counted five glasses, and a ring in the dust for one more, and there was a stain on the boards and a chipped glass rolled away at the side of his chair. Now that would mean only that the old fellow had a dram beside the fire that was lit to keep his old bones warm and the biting swarms away, except that the glass stood up in the front in the cabinet was touched with blood. A smear from the finger and thumb, I would say." Carver edged from the door towards the dining table as he spoke.

"Oh, I see!" said Antonia Fitchett.

"If you see, my dear," said the police magistrate wearily, "then you can surely enlighten the rest of us."

"The glass was picked up by someone after Staines was dead," she said. "This shows that Mr. Staines had a guest that night. For they took a glass together. And then one glass was dropped, by Staines or his guest, and the other glass was returned, and hastily cleaned."

"Nonsense. Staines was by himself. His glass was disturbed in the struggle, that is all."

"What struggle was that?" asked Carver. "For excepting the pilfering, the room was not overmuch disturbed, save for a pool of blood on the chair itself. I have seen how blood flows in strife and agony, and but for the first jet, there was little of it sprayed around, and that, I would judge by the crawling flies, struck the ceiling above the chair."

"If you would, sir," said Fordham, "a lady is present."

"I would not know how much blood to expect," said Antonia softly.

"Who would have thought the old man had so much blood in him?" said Carver, under his breath. "All the same, the desk was turned over. That room is all order and disorder compounded. It don't fit."

Fitchett gestured irritably at the dry plate before him. "The serving woman fled the scene first, and the rest followed, after pilfering from their dead master. Perhaps she disturbed the glass you speak of with her own blood-stained hands. And made a futile effort to find money in his writing desk. She is implicated by her own acts."

"She took what she thought was owed her, and more, but that is her nature," said Carver. "But the old man locked the cupboards at night and left her to sleep on the hearth: do you think he would therefore trust her so far as to share a friendly glass that night, or any other?"

Fitchett hissed between his teeth.

Antonia Fitchett glanced at Fordham near the window. "Your place is close by Staines'. Do you know who visited him?"

Fordham crooked his head. "You could as well say I visited him in secret, for I admit I have designs on his property. He had a fine parcel of land close to town, and access to the creek water."

"Then it's as well for you that he is dead," remarked Carver.

"Mr. Staines had no next-of-kin. The colonial secretary will determine what happens to his property," interposed Fitchett.

"And then someone in the governor's office will profit handsomely by inducements. Which is to say," continued Fordham, "that I could not speak properly of anyone visiting Staines. The old man was a party to the emancipists' cause, and convicts and squatters came by at all hours and hatched their plots to sway the colonial office in their favour, I'm sure."

"There is no solid proof this imaginary visitor was ever there," snapped Fitchett.

Ellington coughed behind Carver, but the hangman said, "The floor reeked of fine brandy, hardly an old hand's drink. There was good tobacco smoked there that night also, in Staines' pipe and perhaps another's. You could still smell it."

"Tobacco smoke?" Fitchett snorted. "Humbug!"

Ellington pitched a little towards the magistrate and said, "Begging your pardon, sir, but there *was* a horse tethered under the big tree by the road, not long before Mr. Staines was done in."

"You see," said Mrs. Fitchett, "hoof-marks, no doubt, left in the dust to show someone hitched a horse and approached the house on foot."

"Not so much hoof-marks as other leavings," said constable Ellington, looking down.

Hoare smirked at his wine-glass, and Fordham hooked his thumbs in his waistcoat. Fitchett stood up suddenly.

"Is this the limit of my authority, in my own house, to be corrected by my constable, a flogger, and my wife?"

The others lapsed into silence. Carver folded his arms. "Respecting your authority, sir, you have the say of life and death in this case, else I would not stand here. At the very least, this visitor is a material witness and clearly none know who he is."

Fitchett held out his right hand. "Show me this fellow's papers."

As he read, Fitchett said, "It is not usual for the hangman to scruple at the guilt of the condemned. Why chance a flogging to come out here?"

"This woman is known to me," said Carver, "from before we were stowed on the hulks. You might say I owe her something. She is a thief, but no murderess. I thought it right to see the stage of the crime myself, and judge what she told me."

"You have some reason to favour her," Fitchett observed, "with this account of flies and blood-stained glasses. Is that all?"

"Surely it is his role to serve the law in his sphere as you do in yours, my dear," said Antonia Fitchett softly.

"The crime is not hers," said Carver doggedly. "And besides, if she cut the fellow's throat, where is the razor or knife that served? Was she taken with it? A woman would use the first blade to hand, out of the kitchen drawer. A man would bring his own knife—and take it with him."

"These convict women," said Hoare, "can show remarkable strength and a very masculine ruthlessness. No doubt she threw it away."

"You are here to muddy this business and protect your doxy," said Fitchett.

"I come here in good faith," retorted Carver. "I have no connection with this woman now. If you don't believe me, then write to my governor. Better yet, ask Moynihan, the assistant surgeon at the gaol."

"I shall do that," said Fitchett, "assuredly, I shall. And you will wait for the reply."

Carver laid one hand flat on the back of an empty chair. "Does it not occur to Your Honours that if this woman is innocent, a murderer is abroad in your district while you sit at dinner?"

"I will not be browbeaten at my own table by a damned functionary!" roared Fitchett.

"Angus—"

"Nor yet by my wife."

"Let her speak sense to you, if none can be brought in by other means."

"Ellington, cuff this man and bring him to the lockup."

Carver turned swiftly on the constable. "I will walk myself into any cell you have."

"Take him out of my sight," said the magistrate. "The evening has been spoiled enough."

"Nonsense," said Fordham. "Pay him no mind. Pour another glass."

The policeman had retreated to the hallway. Mrs. Fitchett came out after Carver, drawing her long skirts through the dining room door.

She glanced at the hangman. His eyes were reddened by dust and his mouth grim and set in contempt.

"My husband is not convinced by your findings," she told him.

Carver blinked and seemed to appraise her in a long glance. The convict's hard wariness faltered. "But you think better of them, I hazard."

"You offer only a glass, an unusual bloodstain, a trace of tobacco—and the leavings of a horse—instead of common sense."

"The problem with common sense is that every man's common sense conforms to his prejudices," said Carver.

Mrs. Fitchett allowed herself a small, quick smile.

"I shall speak to him again, if you are sure this woman is innocent."

"Did you know this man Staines?"

"He owned a great deal of land in this district. He was a moneylender I believe, to all sorts. He argued with everyone, and frequently called on my husband to intervene in his disputes. He was stone hard, and suspicious. He did not like women."

Now the hangman grinned crookedly. "Then you judge in your husband's place how a serving-woman got the upper hand of him. Goodnight, ma'am—I thank you."

The policeman had taken his arm, and the pair of them were moving away. Mrs. Fitchett heard her husband's voice, low and querulous, in the room behind her. She smoothed her skirts and lowered her head to fix her face into a form of demure calm. Moths blundered and beat themselves against the covers of the porch lantern, as the policeman and his prisoner went out.

THE LOCKUP, on the long rise behind the main mass of Sydney Town—for Fitchett's house stood a good, staid distance from the chaotic port, the barracks, and the rows of convict cottages—was a rough wooden shed, with posts whose bark was still peeling away, and crooked planks that sprouted long splinters like quills. The packed-earth floor, with its covering of straw, suggested the movement of rats, in addition to the human vermin huddled along the walls in fetters.

Ellington looked down as he undid the padlock on the door.

Carver did not flinch at the darkness or the shapes half-revealed within. Ellington glanced back at the police station-house. His shoulders slumped. "There will be better news in the morning."

"In the morning, a killer will be another day away. Drinking and carousing in The Rocks."

"You must go in."

Carver tilted his head towards the constable and said, in a low voice, "I shall set myself beside the door. If any man within should recognize me and propose to make mischief, I shall start up a racket that would rouse the devil himself."

In answer, Ellington pushed him forward, and Carver scuffed the threshold with his boots, raising the dust and various pleas and curses from the men inside. The constable clicked and rattled the lock for good measure and returned to the barracks to sleep.

• • •

"ANGUS, DEAR," called Mrs. Fitchett, while her maid Kathleen was combing her hair, "did you write to the warder and the surgeon yet?"

His voice came from the other room. "I shall, in my own time. The insolent fellow just left. Called me a fool to my face, and in front of guests."

"Do you not think the case is worth a second look?"

"On the basis of some fiddle-faddle? You are too trusting. These convicts will spin any lie they please to get around you. You must show them a stern face and never waver. The convict woman is guilty of something, sure enough."

"But is that something murder?"

"That will be determined at the hearing."

"But does this man not have an interest?"

"He has no more interest in right and wrong than the horsewhip in my hand. He is an instrument, and fit for it, no doubt, by his looks."

Antonia Fitchett looked at her own face, pale and oval, in the mirror she had carried twelve thousand miles from Dundee. *Could I have ever seemed such an old maid?* she wondered. *I should have married earlier, or not at all.* But she said, without raising her voice again, "But he is your instrument, dear, and you represent justice."

She heard her husband sigh and say, as though from a great distance, "We are all judged under Heaven, my dear, and found wanting. I represent the law, public order, and His Majesty." Then he wished her good-night, and she listened closely for the click of the latch as he shut the door between them.

CHAPTER 4.

Taking Refuge

IN THE TORPOR of midday, Ellington opened the lockup and found Carver still with his back against the post beside the door, seated at his ease, but dishevelled and wild, like a half-famished goshawk retrieved from the mews.

"Did your governor write to mine?" said Carver, with a dry-throated cough.

"He did so, this morning, and the answer came from the warder."

"What answer?"

Ellington coughed in his hand. "'Carver is a damn fool, but he is mine own damn fool. He is to return immediately. There is work for him on the morrow.'"

"I see," said Carver, pausing to stretch. "The gallows don't sleep."

Mrs. Fitchett was waiting in the front room of the station when Carver and Ellington passed through. The police constable paused.

"Ma'am?"

"Mr. Carver," she said, "I heard that you would be released. I would that it were sooner."

"There ain't many who would hold that view," he replied.

"You risk your position, as it were, to help this woman. There is more to you than is apparent."

"I came up here to judge for myself by the scene whether she was lying or no, for on past acquaintance alone the answer could be one or t'other."

"And what did you find?"

"She is not telling the whole truth, but she did not cut that old man's throat."

"You think it was this unknown visitor, because of this marked glass, the horse tethered outside the yard, the stain on the floor, an odour of tobacco."

Carver shook his shaggy head. "There was no fine tobacco smoked that was different from the usual, though the old man's pipe was out. I told your husband that to impress on him the particulars of the scene. Such things bear heavily with men like that."

Mrs. Fitchett looked down at her light little parasol. "I see."

"What of the case? Will your husband not reconsider?"

"The woman will be tried in Sydney in five days. There must be some proof, some palpable fact that can be laid out before that. I will speak to my husband. I will keep the matter before him."

"I have had time to think on that. This man Devers, Staines' overseer, has not been seen since, and he is sure to know something. By his quarters, there's a man with a taste for gambling and drink. So I have an inkling as to where he might be found."

"That is our business, not yours," said Ellington sharply.

"Then go about your business," snapped Carver, "and I will take to mine."

"I am to take you back to Sydney Cove," returned Ellington. "You're not wanted here."

But Carver stood a moment longer, and inclined a subtle fraction towards Antonia Fitchett. "I am grateful, ma'am. I cannot show it, but I am grateful."

He was gone before she thought to even offer him her hand. She waited many minutes more in the shadows of the station house, before raising her parasol and going back out to the waiting pony-trap.

TWO BLOCKS FROM the old gaol, on a narrow, steep lane surrounded by timber-yards, a saddlery, grain stores, public houses, and huddled cottages, was the low shack that Carver retired to sometimes to sleep, to drink alone in the bleak cage of his thoughts, and where he stored the lengths of rope with which he conducted his duties. Inside it was as hot as only bare walls and a tin roof can be, but it was dark and out of sight. Carver stumbled to the hearth, uncorked a jug on the mantelpiece and poured the contents into an earthenware cup. He drank, poured, drank again.

The bells of the old fort on the island in the centre of the harbour tolled one o'clock. Carver scratched speculatively at the stubble on his jaw. Then he went to the back wall and reached up into the space between the rafters that held the roof and the top of the clay-brick wall. His fingers found a folded leather satchel, which he brought down. He undid the straps and drew out no money but a book. The pages were yellowed and thickened, as with a passage over water. The front cover had been lost, leaving only the fly-leaf, spotted with stains. Slowly, the back cover was coming apart.

Carver returned to the chair and half-table beside the chimney piece, poured again, drained the cup, and sat with the book open before him. He opened the thick volume and read intently, as though from a prayer-book. Sometimes, his heavy head fell forward and his eyes half closed. Sometimes, his eyes left the pages altogether, and his lips moved to tell out the words.

AN ILLUSTRATOR or government surveyor, looking out from a ship as it went wallowing up the harbour, still dazzled by the green sea and the high golden cliffs of the heads, would make out at first the ships at Sydney Cove, the frigates, prison-transports, fishing smacks, whalers and sealers, round merchantmen, and the tangle of masts and spars and ropes, like a great net set at the end of the journey. To compose a soothing view of the colony, the artist would turn, on the left hand, to the stone columns of the governor's mansion, the customs house, the barracks, the colonial offices, set out in pale sandstone among the high palms and tropical trees. On the other side of the water, the draughtsman's eye would fall on a cluster of shacks, taverns, and rickety terraces, as bleak as the rookeries of St. Giles, clutching in bedraggled and haphazard chaos to the high ridges: The Rocks, a heap of driftwood and jetsam cast above the high-tide line, where the stray souls, free convicts, sailors, poor settlers, whores, and rum-sellers had washed up and pursued their several diversions.

As evening came on, Carver descended George Street towards the distant plash of water and the call of sea-birds. As he neared the first rum-shop, his gait altered, taking on a sort of side-stepping unevenness. Oil-lamps were starting up along the steep, filthy lanes of The Rocks, and the hubbub of voices rose. Men were smoking and drinking on the steps. Carver pushed his way roughly up to the threshold of the public-house, peered for a moment into the open door, and then pitched in like a thirsty drunk.

Dice rattled on the floor, a fiddle shrilled at the other end of the room. A few smoking lamps could hardly break the darkness. Carver prowled among the benches and stools with a wary eye on the clustered faces. If anyone recognized him, they gave no sign.

"Take a drink or get out," said a rough voice. "We'll have no skulkers nor skivers in here."

Carver turned about. "I'm looking for a man," he said hesitantly. "Name of Devers. Swore he'd stand me a drink here."

"Don't know him. Not here." The speaker had on a leather apron, a squat, sun-burnt plug of a man.

"Where would he be then?" moaned Carver, with every sign of drunken bafflement.

"Up the hill. Flat in the gutter. Don't know. Get out," returned the other.

Carver shook his head and passed by the man. Only when he was out on the street again did he straighten and look up. The approaching night fastened its hold upon the harbour and the fresh wind from the sea faltered. Slowly, Carver walked on.

Harlots called to soldiers and whalers as Carver pressed up the hill. The air was laden with the stench of human refuse, boiled beef, and seaweed. Carver dodged a pair of caterwauling drunks, who were being followed by three hungry youths. He saw the prison guard, Abbott, standing at a door supping a tankard of ale, and sharply turned another way. He pushed into the heat and din of a rum-house on the next corner, and this time set down a few pence for a measure. Seated, he drew a square of paper and a pencil out of his pocket and spent ten minutes or more laboriously writing on these, making marks and crossing out lines. He tore off one corner, and for good measure sprinkled a little rum on the sheet. A florid woman approached him as he made his way outside and he shook his head. He went on among the crooked lanes, shoulders hunched and head down, though his eyes moved always.

At the next public place he stopped the serving-man and produced his scrap of paper. "Devers," he rasped. "Sly cove. Has a taste for grog and the dice. Owes me the debt on this note. Won't be found, unless you know him."

The man was stooped, sweating: shook his head.

Carver went out again. He flourished his note and told his story at the door to a brothel. A patron of the house, red-eyed and with a bloated nose, stumbled against him, tapped the side of his nose significantly, and gestured at the darkened lane. "Ask the rats. They sniff out everything."

Carver snarled and was about to turn when one of the women said, "Try the bawdy houses up the hill. The trollops know everything that passes hereabouts."

Carver nodded and went on.

At the edge of Fort Street, a man stepped out of the dark as Carver passed, squinted, and hissed, "Hangman, hangman. Lackey. Traitor."

Carver's fingers clutched about the knife in his pocket, but he shied away into the shadows of another wall.

But then, after another round of drinking and swearing oaths and waving his note, Carver heard an old man, say, "Nancy. Nancy Baird. Call on Whistling Nan, and she'll direct yer."

The wind from the sea had choked and there remained nothing to cool the byways of The Rocks. Men, women, roaming gangs of soldiers with their red tunics unbuttoned drank rum and bellowed defiant ballads as they reeled along: stupefying drink to parch the throat and heat the heart, promise merriment, and then render confusion and finally numb forgetting, for cast-offs at the end of the world.

A WOMAN WAS resting in the dust with a bottle in the laps of her skirts, next to a boisterous grog-shop. Carver leaned down over her and spoke a name. She shook her head and mewed a string of incoherence.

"Whistling Nan," said Carver harshly.

The woman pointed towards a doorway.

Carver approached with a loose gait. There was just enough light by the grog-shop to show the slight form of a woman or girl in the recess. "Evenin', darlin'," she said. "Looking for company?"

"Perhaps. If you're the one called Nan," said Carver.

"I am that." She stepped out with a little flick of her skirts.

The top of her head came but midway to Carver's chest. A girl, he judged, of sixteen at most. She was dishevelled, with a pointed face that had the mark of hungry days and the scattered scars of smallpox across her forehead and cheeks, but her mouth was tilted in a grin and her chin was round and pretty. He could not guess at her crime, or the long journey of her short life that led to the magistrate's bench and transportation.

"What's your name?" she asked.

"I'm called Gabriel."

"A fine name," she said with a nod. "Scriptural and so on."

When she spoke, he saw the missing tooth in the front of her mouth that added a faint whistle to her words.

"It don't come of a Bible verse, not in my case," he replied.

She seemed to consider this, pulling a little air in through the gap in her teeth. "A tug for tuppence."

Carver shrugged. "What if I should want more?"

"What more?"

"I'm homesick, and I miss my English lass."

"Come round the corner then," she said, with a turn of her head. "I have a place; come there with me."

"Is it far? My man might get worried. He's an awful worrier."

"Let's go see him, then. I have rum, tobacco, tin in my pocket, and, to speak plain, I'm taken with you, Nan."

She folded her arms across her waist and gave him a reading look, measuring him against all harm and profit.

"We'll talk to him, see," she said, "and make an arrangement."

She turned around the side of the building, down steps so dark and constricted he would not have guessed they were there. Carver followed her, with one hand on the stone wall to guide himself. At the narrowest point, the girl slipped on a loose fragment of stone and Carver, without pausing for thought, shifted to stop her fall. Her frame was light as a child's in his hands. She did not shake him off, but carefully found her balance. Then she moved again.

Her voice came back to him, wistful. "Do I remind you of her?"

"Who's that?" he said, surprised.

"Your English lass?"

Carver stiffened. "That was a long time ago, and beside—"

"Perhaps she did you ill, but it don't matter to me if she did. Here."

Here was a low, straw-brick hovel hacked in at the side of the hill and roofed with scraps of wood and bark. Carver stepped in, lowering his head. There was a faint glow near the hearth, where a man was sitting on a bare chair. The man drew on a clay pipe, but there was something sickly about the tobacco.

"Who's this?" said the man.

"Devers, ain't it?" said Carver.

The girl lingered at the threshold. "Here's Gabriel, to make a spot o' business."

Devers drew on his pipe, and his features floated in the glow. Devers was long-limbed, and lean with it, and at first his face, with its prominent jaw and teeth and high brow, was even-tempered, pleasant even. But as he puffed and blinked, something cold and blithely self-interested peered through his lowered eyes.

"What's your pleasure?" asked Devers, pointing the stem of his pipe towards a rickety stool on which stood a hunk of salt meat and a portion of bread.

"You are Ralph Devers, overseer to Matthew Staines before he was done for in his own parlour."

"Are you here for me or the girl?" returned Devers, putting his pipe down.

"All in good time," said Carver evenly. "You see, I happen to know Meg Harper, who is under the lock a mile from here right now."

"What's this?" said Nan. "Who's Meg Harper?"

"Are you still nattering?" growled Devers. "Step out and ply your trade."

"I don't understand," said the girl sulkily. "Will he go with me or not?"

"Do you know who this is?" said Devers.

"No."

"This is the hangman of Sydney Gaol. Would you want his hands all over you?"

The girl's voice rose. "Don't be angry with me. He has sad eyes."

"Out, you trollop! Leave us in peace."

"Your master's death leaves you pretty free and easy," remarked Carver, once he had heard Nan's steps retreating in the lane.

Devers stretched out one leg and glanced at the sparse room, the scavenged furniture and heap of bedding in one corner. "It suits well enough, for now. And how is darling Meg? A fine figure of a woman, though I daresay you knew her in better days."

"She's screaming and tearing her hair in confinement, and mortally afraid of the noose."

"Poor woman. I wish her well."

"You damned hypocrite," said Carver heavily.

"What do you say?"

"That you sit here, at your ease, living off the earnings of that girl. And you know as well as I do that it would have been you up in the gaol, afeared to your soul of the gallows, had the constables but caught you fleeing your master's property. But you discovered your master dead first, didn't you? And rather than raise the alarm, you searched for whatever cash and notes of hand he held, and took yourself off down here."

"So says the hangman," scoffed Devers. "You get your fee by dead men."

"And you were an overseer, and you would have worked ten, fifteen men at any time, and been free with the bloody cat, no doubt."

"What do you want here, Mr. Carver?" said Devers, tapping his pipe against a boot.

"I want a quiet life, beyond the reach of all you damned fools."

"I find that hard to credit."

"Then I want to know why you are here, and who laid a knife to Staines' throat."

"You think I killed the old man?"

"Did you not have words between you?"

"Did Meg tell you that?"

"There's truth to that, then, or you would simply say, 'Nay.'"

"The old tyrant was a convict like you and me, a machine-breaker before that. He could turn his hand to cropping and milking better than others. There were precious few of his sort back when they were parcelling out land on the plain. He was lucky to find water and good earth on his hands. He had little plots here and there, when he decided to settle close to town. I was the one to set on his gangs every harvest, and he refused me a ration of rum or a share in the gain. What sons or kin did he have to take the lot after he died? Assigned man or not, there were words between us. But it was a steady position, and I had no cause to end it."

"You must have had a mighty shock when you came upon the old man dead—when was that? Early in the morning?" said Carver.

Devers grinned, showing the long yellow teeth of his lower jaw. "Let us understand each other. Meg told me a thing or two about you, as well. You squirmed your way out from under a sentence for murder."

"You seem pretty close to Meg," said Carver.

"I wouldn't say so." Devers scowled. "Your glowering there at my door puts me out of sorts."

Carver shifted his weight but did not approach the hearth. "Tell me who was in the habit of calling on the old man unknown, after dark, and I'll skip up the lane most merrily."

Devers shifted and rested his hands between his knees. "I don't know. He was deep in with the free-convicts, the emancipists. They had their endless petitions and complaints, but the new governor won't hear them. And then the Currency, his oh-so genteel neighbours, were dead keen on acquiring his land."

"Who else would wish him ill? What about his wife?"

Devers looked up, cocked his head. "You heard of her, then. Well, she ran away with a soldier-man and took a good portion of his hard-earned tin with her, so he said to anyone who would lend an ear to his bile. But she is gone, sure, and won't come back."

"What do you mean by that?" said Carver sharply.

A drunk passed outside; they heard laughter and a woman muttering in anger.

"I mean that she's a ghost, and chasing her won't turn up nothing. Your murderer is riding free in the bush, a hundred mile or more away. Or it's them black devils."

"And if you are certain of that, why are you hiding in a whore's squat in the back of The Rocks?" said Carver. "What's your business here?"

Devers half closed his eyes, and Carver traced the smirk behind the pipe. "That lass is my passage home. As soon as we raise enough money between us, we are sailing free."

"Unless he has outlived his sentence, no convict can step on his majesty's ships without an Absolute Pardon," said Carver. His neck was beginning to ache with stooping under the grimy roof and low beams of the hut.

"The rats know," said Devers dreamily. "Do you see? They dig deep in the dirt under the floorboards. Their little tunnels and nest are all about. They have a mighty clever way of going here and there."

There was movement at the door. Carver pivoted immediately. The girl had returned, alone. Nan was whistling between her teeth and singing a fragment of an old song. Devers seemed surprised, as if he had forgotten her business. He rose, displacing the stool. He was a tall man, with some inches over Carver.

"What?" he said. "Back again."

"I'm lonely out there," the girl protested.

"Then go find some company," retorted Devers.

"Ain't you decided yet?" she asked, glancing at Carver, puzzled.

Devers glared at Carver. "Move on. You won't hear aught else from me."

"You're not done, my friend. The constables are looking for you."

"And so?"

"You set Meg Harper in the clear. You tell them you saw a rider that night walk in boldly to the house, tell them you heard a scream, that you found the man dead yourself, that night, none the wiser. You were afraid. You ran. And when you had enough of drink and whoring, you came back."

"Quite the tale you've brewed for me. And if that's not true?"

"I don't care one whit for the truth."

Devers paused, licked his lips.

"And if I choose not to go back, big man?"

"Then your easy life is over, and I'll tell the constables you helped yourself to the old man's secret cash-box, and slunk away before anyone else knew."

Devers seemed to curl in on himself, as though at the touch of the lash, but his lips drew up and his long, plain face twisted, as he forgot his torpor of tobacco and rum. "I see now. You and Meg are of the same mind. You mean to set the whole of the murder on me."

"Oh, darlin'," said the girl. "We know you didn't do it."

Devers glared at Carver. "He don't. But he guesses more than he should. And acts less friendly than he poses."

"Turn in your evidence, or every informer from here to Port Jackson will sing your name. No more gammon and grog for you," growled Carver.

With a roar, Devers hurled himself at Carver, and Carver, caught off balance, tottered back across the low threshold, spinning about Nan. Carver stumbled in the filth of the narrow lane and fell, catching his hand among the stones and fragments of brick. The air stank of stale spirits and worse. Devers followed, but he did not hurl himself down on Carver like a tavern brawler; he began to circle, looking for a place to kick. Carver scrambled to rise. As he gained his feet, Devers aimed a swinging punch at his head. In the darkness, he missed the cheek and pummelled the side of Carver's head. A sound and sensation like the rushing of a vast wave struck Carver.

He thought, coolly, as though he were a spectator to his own rage, of the knife folded in his pocket. The girl was screeching in distress. Devers loomed before him. Perhaps he expected submission, but Carver punched hard at the soft notch between the ribs and the belly, and Devers folded like a broken spar and went down on his knees.

Men and women were turning out all along the lane to review this entertainment.

The girl plucked at Devers's shoulder, but he batted her hand away. "You brought him," he snarled. "You let the devil in."

Carver cupped his bruised hand. His head pounded and burned. There were too many eyes now in the lane, glimmers of light from smoking lanterns, querulous voices. "Just remember what to say," he growled. "A horseman, that night." He backed away, while Devers slumped in the dust and the girl, Whistling Nan, wept over her fallen champion.

CARVER WALKED SLOWLY, hunched and deliberate, out of The Rocks. The side of his head ached like a lost love recalled. Ship's bells tolled in the harbour. The hangman winced. There was no breeze, and to his jaded senses the night seemed tainted, and the memory of the girl, her missing tooth, and forlorn ditties worked like a goad on him, raising memories he had long thought set aside, or drowned in rum and the Southern Oceans. Shortly, he found a tavern crowded enough for him to feel unseen, and he took a measure of harsh spirits, cleared his throat, and drank again. The pain in his head tightened like a clockwork screw to something throbbing and contained, but the drink did not dilute the bitterness in his mouth. After the last hour of the day had passed, in defiance of the curfew, he resumed his walk to the gaol precincts. The moon sank low in the sky, coloured like grey sand. All those who passed him were rendered insubstantial, delivered to a desolate landing.

• • •

"CLEVER MAN," said Meg Harper.

Carver pinched at the bridge of his nose and said, "It's not resolved yet, but Devers makes himself suspicious by his actions, and the police magistrate will find him and examine him soon enough, for I have informed them of his whereabouts. I'm damned if I know why he chooses to hide himself. Or why he is so smug about it."

They had moved Meg to the women's infirmary at Moynihan's word. The linens were patched and tattered, but the room was bright and quiet.

"Where did you find him?" said Meg.

"In The Rocks. Where else? There's a man who won't stray far from his pleasures. Pimping for a doxy that goes by the name of Whistling Nan."

The lines about Meg's mouth deepened and hardened at once.

"He means to live off this girl until he saves enough to take ship out of New South Wales—did he ever speak of that?"

"Speak of what?"

"This plan. Not the girl—that surprised you—but his taking ship, while a convict still."

Meg looked down at her hands, flat against the blanket. "How should I know that?"

"You told me where he would be."

"That's where he went, often enough."

"And you yourself on foot, walking swift in the other direction. Well, I expect he had already taken the old man's horse."

"There nothing you can make of that," said Meg, her voice dull and low, as if she spoke to a guard or chaplain.

"No," said Carver carefully. "But Devers was awful familiar with you. Insufferably so. I wonder why you did not follow after."

"Are you jealous?" said Meg, wrinkling her nose.

"Not I. But these things trouble me like the flies."

"I ran because I was afraid." Meg had grown sullen again.

"So you were. You didn't expect to find the old man in that way. That's the truth. You panicked. Fled with whatever you could lay your hands on. But did you think...?" A low half-chuckle of sudden discovery escaped Carver. "You did! You thought Devers had killed the old man."

Meg recoiled. "Why should I think that?"

"Because you had talked of it, hadn't you? At least, the two of you had shared the notion of stealing Staines' money."

Carver was answered with a glare. "We talked of many things around the kitchen table. Wild ideas. Aye, theft and escape, sometimes. Staines was a convict like the rest of us, but he treated us like dirt all the same."

Carver grinned coldly. "But finding him dead and murdered, that was a dreadful surprise for you. That's why you were on your way to Port Middlebay, alone, with a sack of stolen sterling—plates, forks, and knives! Since you guessed Devers would go to Sydney, you thought it politic to walk the other way, rather than be taken as an accomplice. Well, Devers made good his escape, and now he's lurking in The Rocks, drinking and smoking and living off a whore's wages."

"He's a dog," said Meg bleakly, "and a fool."

"What? Did you think to make another husband of him?"

"What of that? You shouldn't care."

"Enough. I don't care if you had set your cap at him. What did the two of you talk about?"

"We speculated the old man had some money set aside. Devers spoke of some debt between them. That's true. There was no call for talk of murder, though. We just never found out where he hid it. When I walked in that morning, I thought Devers had done it, got drunk, tortured the old man to make him talk. I tried to get as far away from him as I could." Meg's eyes did not stir from the dark, rough-cut beam in the ceiling above her.

"But then you were caught on the road, with the evidence of a crime about you, and you were desperate for someone to find Devers. You had heard my name often enough, so you called for me. So, why all this wild talk of bushrangers and the Black Man?"

Meg blinked, slowly. "That's no wild talk. My hands were clean: that was all. You won't get a man like Devers to confess a thing. Who else, then?"

Carver made a careless gesture, as though to throw this off. "It could be bushrangers still. I half-doubt Devers did kill Staines. But he has some other purpose in mind. You and he thought to flee the system, and you will both pay in your way."

Meg Harper closed her eyes and laughed. "I would not expect you to be that particular about who was guilty of what."

Carver looked around. The surgeon, Moynihan, was coming, straight-backed and neat, between the rows of cots.

"Devers has something to hide," he said, "but for whom, and why, I cannot divine." He shook his head slowly. "I can make nothing of this folly of sailing out of the colony. It is death for a convict to go back before his sentence is done. Lifers can never return without a full pardon. Stowaways are always caught."

"That was a notion of Devers'. Something he picked up about the gangs on The Rocks, when he went looking for Mrs. Staines," said Meg. She shrugged. "Perhaps it was him after all."

"He says not. And if he couldn't persuade Staines to tell him where his money was, why would he give up a place as an overseer to skulk on The Rocks?"

"Most likely there was no money," said Meg wearily. "Staines' wife stole it when she went away."

"Where is this wife now?" he asked.

"Devers said he knew," returned Meg. "But he was close with it. She was Irish, you know. Probably ran away with the rebels."

Moynihan stopped at the end of the low bed. "It doesn't matter," said Carver, glancing at the surgeon. "When Devers is examined he will say whatever he needs to and spin any tale to give them pause. I have settled your case. You'll be charged with the theft, but not the killing."

"He will lie to save his own skin," said Meg, but her voice was charged with satisfaction.

"He'll lie, all right, but if he makes the right lie, both of you will dance free. I've done my part," said Carver. "Now Fitchett has another bone to gnaw."

He turned and nodded to the surgeon, and then scratched his head and looked back to Meg. "When you came upon the body, did you mark the wound?"

"He was dead and set about with blood. What do you mean by wound?" said Meg.

"I mean, was it broad, like a gash—" Carver traced a line across his throat with his thumb—"or otherwise?"

Meg wrinkled her nose. "As best I could see, it was the other sort, deep and short. Neat, here." She touched her fingertips to her neck. "But you're a strange one, you are. What's that to you when all is said and done?"

"Nothing," said Carver, unsteadily, as though this were the first thing to puzzle him. "A wise prisoner sees more than he says, aye? Well, it was a black scene, where the old man died. I have not seen its like…for some time passing. But if it wasn't you nor Ralph Devers who did the deed, then I fear this is something that won't square off, no matter what the magistrates decide. That troubles me. But we are quit, you and I. Naught remains between us."

"When I walk free," said Meg, "you're free of me. All forgot. You'll be my Gabriel no more."

"I never was," he said. "And you should not mention this business between us before the magistrates, for if they think I am any more than partial to you, they will throw out everything I find."

"Is that so?" said Meg. "Or do you have another reason to keep that between ourselves?"

"This trouble of yours leaves a sour taste. I need a drink of something stronger to wash it clear."

But Meg Harper no longer looked at him. She drew up her knees on the thin mattress and looked out across the ward, diminished and forlorn.

Carver nodded, and made his way out between the rows of orderly beds, a broad, dark figure eclipsing the bands of sunlight from the high, thin vents in the walls. Meg Harper turned over, and Moynihan, with a sigh, patted his pockets smooth and moved on.

IN THE LAST WATCH of the night, Bennett gave thought to his berth on the sealer *Moira Day*. But he was fuddled with rum and sickened at heart by the sound and stench of the fur-seal slaughter, and so he staggered away from the shoreline towards the rows of buildings along the point called The Rocks. He could not remember in which of the several raucous dens along the road he had left his shipmates. He had gone up to Sydney Town with French and English coin in his pocket, and now it was mostly gone on furtive women, cards, and drink, and he was alone, and reluctant to sleep yet. The footing in the alleyway was uneven, filled with broken stones, and he was not used to steady land under his feet, for he kept swerving this way and that. It was dark, here, as well, and the motley of walls, fences, and gates hoarded deep shadows. He heard footsteps behind him and pulled up with a sharp intake of breath, and then he was ashamed because it was only a street-walker, alone, a woman slighter than most, though she seemed to know her way in this place.

As she passed him, he heard the woman singing under her breath, and a faint whistle as she breathed the words. She turned a corner, and Bennett drew a deep gulp of air and watched the bright antipodean stars wheeling overhead.

Then he heard the shrieking, dreadful to his ears, worse than the scream of a gale on the Southern Ocean, and as near. He ran to the next corner, and there was the same small woman, screaming, braced in a crooked doorway, and too bright, fatally bright, for her skirts were on fire, a river of flame in the dark.

CHAPTER 5.

A Rope to Hang By

SOUTHWARK UNDER the rain. Boatmen calling from the river. Spars and ropes, dark-wet, descending and dripping. Coal-smoke and fog at the back of the nose. Carts rattling and skidding along the muddy streets. The rain touched his cheek and cooled his face, and he smiled, recalling a fine, white hand on the handle of a parasol. But a cart was coming closer, rumbling over the cobblestones, and the smoke made him cough and choke, and someone called a name—"Carver! Damn you! Carver"—and the whole alleyway was filled with the din and shake of wheels: rain, river, and white hand retreating.

He woke. Corporal Ellington was kicking the side of his bed with his hobnailed boots. A resolved pain flared behind his eyes, and his throat ached, raw and foul. "Enough," Carver croaked.

"A drunken executioner," Ellington exclaimed. "A swine in muck!"

Carver wrenched himself upright and set his feet on the ground. "What's the matter?"

"Ralph Devers is dead," said Ellington. "We found him, we did."

Carver would have spat on the ground, but he was too dry.

"Hanged he was, and left all in shambles."

Carver bowed his head. When he could stand to, he looked up.

"And the girl?" he croaked.

"What girl?"

"Nan, she's called. Was she there?"

"Set fire to herself, poor fool. Knocked over an oil lamp trying to bring him down. Burned bad; like to die."

Carver heaved upwards and pushed past Ellington to the table. There he poured from a jug and drank the tepid water in long, harsh gulps.

"And why are you here?"

"Did you not hear me? Devers was hanged. The noose was around his neck. And where are all your lengths of rope?"

Carver put the cup down. "You've looked already."

"You keep the tool of your craft in good order. One's missing."

"We'll see about that. Who sent you?"

"My governor. He has a question or two for you and is in no melting mood."

Carver glared at the policeman, who straightened his cap and his cuffs. "Then I will answer," he said, standing and clenching his fist to stop the tremors in his arms. "I swear I will come quietly, if you allow one thing first."

THE HOSPITAL MORGUE, chipped out of red stone by convict hands, was cool and damp enough to give Carver some relief. Devers had been laid out on a stone bench, naked and rigid. The tall man seemed frail and spindly in the half-dark of the cellar.

"I don't think this is proper," said Ellington, in a hushed voice from the door.

"How was he hanging?" said Carver.

"I don't know. I haven't seen him till now."

"Then what did the men who found him say?" grated Carver.

"They say he was strung up from the long beam."

"Strung up, you mean dangling clear of the floor? Out with it."

"No. Hoisted to his knees. The hut was an almighty mess. The lass couldn't get the noose over his head before she blundered into the lamp." Ellington paused, cleared his throat. "The noose had thirteen turns to it."

Carver grimaced. "Did it now?"

He pulled the dead man's head back and peered at the neck. Ellington looked away.

Carver straightened. "I'm ready to see your governor."

THE POLICE MAGISTRATE, Fitchett, was seated, straight in back and solemn, at a small desk in a bare room at the police house. He had laid out before him an inkwell, blotter, quills, and some sheets of paper, in a severe grid. He schooled his face into stillness when Carver came in, but his lips were set in a narrow, flat line. The midday sun flashed on the distant harbour, and the room was close and hot.

"Is this a deposition or an arraignment?" said Carver.

"A fine distinction in law, but then, I expect you are well versed in procedure."

Carver crossed to a sort of bench or box below the windows and, without asking, sat down. "Then why am I here?"

"Stand before the magistrate," shrilled Ellington.

"I'll stand when he can constitute a good reason why I am here."

"A hangman goes forth to find a man, and lo! that man is found—hanged, to boot. Is that reason enough?" said Fitchett, with dreary mildness.

"You suspect me of this thing?"

"Can you prove otherwise?"

"Thirteen turns of the knot," said Carver, clicking his tongue behind his teeth.

"What?" snapped Fitchett.

"Thirteen turns. A hangman's noose to most minds. But nine suffice. That's what I use."

"And knowing that, you might have added four, for good measure," returned Fitchett.

"You think this is played like a parlour game?" growled Carver, pressing his palms against his skull.

"Stand up when you address His Honour!" roared Ellington.

"I shall lash you for insolence," said Fitchett, "if you do not answer me straight."

Carver pitched forward and bent over the magistrate's neat little desk. "Ask your question. I've yet to hear one."

"What account can you give of yourself for the early hours of this morning?"

"Dead drunk," interjected Ellington. "That's how I found him."

"I dropped two souls yesterday morning," said Carver.

"Perhaps three," said Fitchett, making a mark on the paper.

"I did tell you he was lurking on The Rocks myself!" exclaimed Carver.

"And perhaps you thought better of that after a few drinks. Perhaps he was not so tractable to whatever plan you concocted."

"Can you not see it, man?" said Carver, rubbing his forehead.

"What is there to see?"

"There are ten thousand proven felons within a mile of where we stand, and any one of them would do bloody murder to further their ends. But this is different. This is evil considered. Your murderer coaxed old Staines into quiet and cut his throat, and now with Devers, he strangled the man first with a thin cord. You can see the marks of it under the dents of the knot. And then hung him up. Well, he couldn't get him high enough, whatever he thought to do. Not many of us could. You would need two men or a pulley or be mighty heavy to do that. So he left him half-suspended, and set a lantern out just so, to show what he had done, which that poor slip of a girl must have knocked over in her haste to get the rope from off her man's neck. He used the hangman's knot! Knowing I had been by. This is cold, purposeful work."

Fitchett bent and twisted the quill in his hand as he spoke. "I know only that a prominent man, a respected former convict is dead, and that another man sought in connection with that death is also murdered before he can be brought before me and examined, and it speaks to disorder and malice, and I *will not have it.*"

"At least you cannot lay this at Meg Harper's door," said Carver.

"Perhaps that is what was intended by this foul deed. At any rate, the case is hopelessly muddled. But that does not mean she is free from guilt, only that perhaps she had an accomplice. It may be as well to keep her under lock and key a little longer."

A green gecko scuttled along the wall behind Fitchett's head, and Carver watched it pass. He drew a long breath. "Devers spoke of taking ship from New South Wales, of returning to England even."

Fitchett's frown deepened. "Did he so?"

"A convict, his master dead and murdered, making ready to escape the colony. And chances are he was not alone."

"Impossible—it is death."

"But a mighty strong inducement to mischief. That's a reason to murder two men. I fancy the governor himself would take an interest in such matters."

"I see." Fitchett made another mark on the paper before him. "We cannot have that." The magistrate looked up. "My wife is a romantic. She believes you have a talent for uncomfortable truths."

Carver stepped back from the police magistrate and glanced at Ellington, who was still stationed just inside the room. Fitchett remained impassive but flushed, as with the heat, and studied the tip of his pen. Carver's headache was reduced to a point of gouging pain behind the eyes, but his thirst had multiplied.

"I will draw this rumour out," said Carver heavily. "If you permit."

Fitchett nodded, as if he had just read out a neat judgment of his own devising. "I will make your insolence serviceable yet, Master Carver. Prove that you are not part of these crimes, and your sentence may be improved. But you will not breathe a hint of this, or approach any witness without Corporal Ellington."

"If I am to gather information, I must have leave to pass beyond the gaol. Staines and Devers were asking questions about Staines' missing wife. I must find out more about that."

"I shall make out an order," said Fitchett. "My clerk will amend your papers. Return in an hour."

"Then I take it I may go."

Fitchett smiled, and for a moment Carver saw the straight set of his features moderated by a flash of cool intelligence, and the magistrate nodded to Ellington, who shifted minutely aside.

Carver walked slowly down the steps of the station. The multiplying light dazzled him. He shook his head, like a dull beast harried by dogs and flies. *Cornered,* he thought. *Befuddled. And put out to assignment by that magistrate. Hangman and informer. I set out my head and the noose passed smoothly over, and now we must see whose hand is on the lever.*

CHAPTER 6.

The Rats' Line

FULL MORNING, and the tide was rising. The warm southern waters, holding and sifting endless reflections and charges of light, lapped at the stone edges of the port. Gabriel Carver stood near the water, listening to the ships' bells and the cries of a multitude of sea birds. There was little material change in his stance, but his eyes were clear and he had shaved with the same old razor but a steadier hand. He scanned the ships at anchor. Soldiers, red-faced, cursing, and tainted with the slime of the bilges, were coming down the gangway of the barque *Prosepine*. Sulphurous yellow smoke emerged in puffs from the scuppers of the ship, rousing flights of white gulls. When the last soldier had made his way off, the gangways were drawn up and sailors scuttled across the deck. The *Prosepine* was bound for Calcutta and London, but the searching soldiers and noxious smoke had scoured her holds and bilges of any prospective stowaways.

Carver observed this business from a low stone wall. His attitude was one of calm indifference, unnoticed by the seamen, dockhands, chandlers, and shipping clerks at work in the relative cool of the morning. But he appraised the scouring of the ships very closely. As the barque raised its sails to the faint breath of air, his mouth quirked and he shook his dark head and began to walk in the direction of Elizabeth Street. Only a long lizard sunning on a pile of rocks not far behind him marked his departure.

PETER MOYNIHAN, surgeon, kept chambers on a shady stretch of Elizabeth Street, in a leaning brick pile already half smothered in vines that bore a profusion of heavy red flowers at all times of the year. When it rained, water flowed from the kitchen to the front door without interruption. The front room was cool, with high, shuttered windows, and here he sat, glancing through some old letters, when he was roused by unexpected knocking at the door. He looked out at the window before answering and saw the hangman. He folded the letters and retied the ribbon around them, and then went to his door.

"Mr. Carver."

"Mr. Moynihan."

"I am pleased to see you, but own to being a little surprised."

"Given that you are mostly concerned with keeping bodies and souls connected, and my task is otherwise?"

"No, no. Only that I gather that your business with Meg Harper is over."

"The case against her falters, but we are yet subject to the tyranny of petty men, and must therefore make common cause," said Carver cheerfully.

Moynihan shook his head. "I don't follow."

"Find your boots," said Carver. "I have checked at the gaol and you are not called for. I will explain as we walk."

Moynihan looked uneasily at the sun, but nodded, and closed the door briefly before returning in brown boots with a wide-brimmed hat on.

The two men walked. Moynihan leaned forward into his stride and went quickly, forcing even Carver to increase his pace. They followed a route among the serried ranks of houses of merchants and settlers, all closed, shuttered, and hostile to the sunlight.

"What is the matter?" said Moynihan, when Carver had held his silence long enough.

"I am not famed for making requests or begging favours," said Carver.

"I cannot aid you on that account," returned Moynihan.

"There is a girl, a slip of a thing, in the women's infirmary. She is afflicted with burns, bad burns. I do not know if she will live or die."

"I do not attend at the infirmary," said Moynihan.

"I must speak with this girl," said Carver. His jaw clenched. "I must know what she knows. But she has good reason to mistrust me, and someone must gentle her."

"And you select me, therefore."

"You are a surgeon. You have been across on the transports. The convicts trust the surgeons and are grateful to them. This girl will trust you."

"I still don't understand. What is your business with her?"

"You know of this case with Meg Harper and the emancipist, Staines. Well, Ralph Devers was Staines' overseer, and he got murdered himself. She is—was—Devers' doxy. A whore, but with a plain soul. Devers, in his cups, with his belly full of gammon, boasted to me of a plan, a passage to England, before he died. I must know what the girl knows about this."

Moynihan stopped and raised his hat, fanning his face with the brim. "It is plain folly," he said sharply. "Phantasy. Convicts used to believe they could walk to China inland from Sydney Cove. Those that tried starved or were speared for their ignorance."

Carver laid his broad hand heavily on the slight surgeon's shoulder. "I must know. Names, rumours, boasts, dreams. Whatever it is. Whistling Nan, they call her. All that she knows or guesses or was told."

Moynihan set the hat back on his head, adjusting the brim to bring his face into shadow. "On whose authority?"

"The police magistrate, Fitchett's. He has given me this task, for I am snared in it, and he must have information. He's high-handed and dreadful afraid of what the convicts may do if this is true. And if the colonial secretary should find out, it will make the magistrates look like fools, or rogues. Besides, the girl may not live long."

"How was she burnt?" said Moynihan softly.

"She knocked over a lamp when she went to get her man down," said Carver. "This murderer, he needed to light his task, for it is no simple thing to hoist a dead man up and down."

"As well you know," said Moynihan mildly. "But you say 'he' as if it were a certain thing."

"It took a man's strength and some craftiness, with rope and a beam handy. But a man and a woman together may have prevailed, I suppose. The girl may know something on this count as well. It took great effort to string Devers up."

"Perhaps he was being punished," mused Moynihan. "That is what the idea suggests, by association, as it were."

"That is what you must ask the girl," said Carver. "Will you go or no?"

"I do not like the sound of this. You are the executioner, and I am a surgeon. It is not our place to name the guilty—would you be judge as well as hangman, sower and reaper?"

"The system don't care who men are or what they would do, only that our hands are set to the task, and some order is ground out of this chaos. I must show why Devers had to die, or the blame will revert to me."

"I see. But you cannot show why this girl had to burn," said Moynihan.

Carver lowered his chin, and looked down into the brown dust of the road. His voice was troubled. "'Poor fool,' the constable called her. 'Poor fool.' Take pity, at least. Someone must, for she is all alone in this place. Hear what she has to say; she will not speak to me, or any magistrate's man."

Moynihan shook his head, and seemed about to turn back down the street. The sun had touched the edge of the surrounding roofs, and all the windows were shuttered and secretive. The surgeon raised his hat again. "Your craft has made you cruel," he told Carver. "But I will do as you ask. Call at my rooms tonight."

"I shall. And my thanks upon it."

"And what do you do now?"

"Staines had a runaway wife. And Devers was looking for her. It is little enough, but it is another place to look for the cause of all this."

The surgeon blinked and said, "I doubt you will find much, but there is a chance, I suppose. If you come by news of her, I should be interested." But the hangman had already turned away.

"GOD, WE KNOW, for the scriptures tell us so, is just," said the Reverend Honeychair, in a wavering voice, pausing long enough to smile, as though taken by the novelty of his insight. "And assuredly, God is also stern, yet as a loving father, guiding upon one hand and correcting upon the other."

The parson frowned, as though puzzled by this last exception. A dry wind sighed about the chapel, which was raised out of pale timbers, the chinks filled up with a daub of red earth and straw, and starkly whitewashed within. A dog, left on the patch of scorched ground outside the doors, yapped to itself.

Honeychair seemed to regain his thread of thought. "We are promised that God loves all us sinners equally, but assuredly, there is not one iota of sin within us that He does not see and excoriate. As we are all equal in His love, we must be all equal in His justice and deserving of the correction He doles. Our state is surely the work of Providence."

Some ten or twenty convicts sat in the back pews, chained at the ankles and nodding in the chapel, while scratching at a multitude of insect bites. One or two looked up at this last premise, but the rest kept their heads down and shifted in the uneven, rough-cut pews.

"We are not given to equal estates," continued the parson. "But we are equal in this. Some of us set forth our hands to minister and correct..." Honeychair's voice faltered a mere fraction as Gabriel Carver stepped out of the shadows about the doors and levered himself without urgency into one of the pews.

"Yea—even unto the ends of the Earth. And blessed are they who stand meek before justice."

The Reverend Honeychair looked down, satisfied at the aptness of the last turn of phrase. The congregation rose with a rustle of hymn-books; all except Carver, who stood without urgency and looked around at the gathering. In the front pews, Fordham, following the parson's glare, craned his neck slowly and nodded pleasantly at Carver. Antonia Fitchett was singing, with her head raised, on his right. A few of her fair hairs glowed bright in the light from the apse.

Presently, the service was concluded and the prisoners were shepherded out. Carver rose, but lingered. Fordham passed him with a quizzical nod, but Mrs. Fitchett stopped before Carver and offered her hand. She was taller than he had noted at first. Her face was angular, with nothing conventionally pretty about it, and yet it concealed a growing towards grace, and a fine, quick mind.

"Your husband is not here?" said Carver.

"My husband is a free-thinker, and adheres to a stricter doctrine than the Reverend Honeychair preaches."

"I am not sure. The reverend has the manner of a meek parson, but his conclusion is sharp enough."

Antonia glanced at the empty pulpit and then down at her hand, which rested in Carver's easily. "I have sometimes thought that myself," she murmured. "Like you, he is not all he seems."

Carver drew his arm back.

"I do recall that there is some matter in the scripture that does not wholly concern judgment or punishment," said Antonia.

"You will not find it applied here," said Carver.

"You are a cynic."

"I don't give false hope." He gestured, and edged a little out of the pulpit.

"So, indeed, you are not here," said Mrs. Fitchett, "for the sermons of the Reverend Honeychair."

"I must know more about Staines, and his man Devers. This was their parish."

Antonia frowned. "This is my husband's work you do."

"Aye, because he cannot be seen to do it himself. He must have a convict to ask questions in dark places."

The chapel had almost emptied. Several had turned to see the magistrate's wife talking with the man in the rough black waistcoat.

"We must go out," she said. "Come."

In the shadow of a gum tree, with the thick, oily scent of the leaves about him, Honeychair was shaking hands with one or two of his flock, and sometimes in conversation with Fordham, who toyed with his riding crop and frowned as Mrs. Fitchett and the hangman emerged. But Fordham recovered his good humour enough to remark, as Carver strode up: "The insolent fellow, with the odd trick of noting things. What spoor are you trailing now?"

"Staines," said Carver. "Who in the parish knew him best? He had associates, old servants, farmhands, business partners at least?"

"I don't know if this is really proper," began Honeychair.

"My husband compels it," said Antonia.

"Don't look at me," said Fordham. "It would be improper. The convict strain and all that: we don't mix."

"He sat in there every Sunday, got married there in front of a respectable churchman, no doubt," said Carver. "What was his wife's maiden name? I hear of her at every turn, and no one can name this shadow."

"I don't know." Honeychair was perspiring under his heavy clerical robe. "There is the register, I suppose."

"Then bring me to it," said Carver.

"Surely—" Honeychair began, with a watery grimace, glancing at Mrs. Fitchett.

"Mr. Honeychair scruples," said Antonia, picking her way between the words, "because he is not sure what you will make of the register."

Carver took a half step backwards, but his grin was fierce. "I can tell out the words of the old hymnals well enough. I think I can make out a name at need."

"Perhaps we may make an exception, in the circumstances. Nothing should stand before the magistrate's investigation, no?" said Fordham, with an airy gesture.

"Then you must show Master Carver what he needs," said Mrs. Fitchett brightly.

"Very well," said the parson. "But you must stand aside now."

Carver glanced at Fordham from the minister, frowned, but stepped back into the shadows of the tree. The parson turned to Fordham. They shook hands. Mrs. Fitchett seemed to have some idea of speaking again, but her maid was close by and gesturing. Carts and carriages were moving along the track, raising dust. She took the parasol from Kathleen. Carver watched her go, slim and straight-backed.

THE DAY HAD thickened and brought black clouds to lurk above the harbour. Carver, walking down towards the cove, had thought at first that the regiment was firing cannons on the green at Hyde Park, but six or seven flashing threads of light in the glowering sky corrected him. It began to rain heavily when he hammered on the surgeon's door, the imperious rain of the sub-tropics in dense, oily droplets.

Moynihan opened his own door with a lamp in hand, nodded in recognition, and glanced up at the black sky. The gargantuan hiss and roar of the rain drove out all possibility of speech until Carver and Moynihan were settled in the cramped parlour. Then

Moynihan closed and latched the outside windows after drawing in the shutters, and sat himself in the chair before the empty hearth.

"What's the good of facts?" he said abruptly. "The facts are our betrayers." The surgeon's face was pinched and worried.

"You have seen the girl, then." There was no challenge in Carver's voice, only an enquiry that sounded like the stirring of sympathy.

"I saw her, dammit. And she was pitiably anxious to please. She remembers the surgeon on her transport. A good man. I did not mention you."

Carver nodded, with his chin low on his chest.

"Is she likely to recover?"

"I cannot think so. Her burns are grievous. In these tropical conditions, a fever is sure to find her."

Carver passed his hand over his face, and then leaned forward. "What did she say?"

Moynihan had an open bottle at his elbow, and he poured from it again. "I had not the heart to quash her illusions. She dreams of walking on the Suffolk Downs. I doubt if she has ever seen them: some description that Devers conjured for her. She was a street-walker from an abominably early age. Then she found herself transported in the Female Factory—awful place, all labour and lashes. She escaped as soon as she could and took up her old profession. Expecting no better, that man played on her sympathies and dreams of a passage home."

"But how?" said Carver urgently. "There are but two ways a convict can return to England. Serve out the sentence, or get an absolute pardon from the governor himself. Any other escape to an English or Irish port is but a passage to the gallows."

Sly lightning licked about the edge of the shutters, but the report was distant.

Moynihan raised the bottle slightly and tipped it at Carver, but the hangman declined with a sharp shake of the head, which was almost a shudder.

"She knew but little of the details. 'The Rats' Line,' she called it. For rats sail where and when they will, from one end of the Earth to the other. A convict's dream. That was Devers' business with her. I wonder if it was just an incentive to make her work harder. I had the impression that she, through Devers, was connected with the chief or the head of one of the criminal gangs on the rocks, which style themselves fellowships and circles. I tried to press her, but our talk made her weak. She had more a mind to talk of fields she had never seen. The wandering of her thoughts was pitiable, intolerable."

"How, and where, would they meet this chief?"

"She did not say, precisely. But when Devers went himself, he often spent her earnings in a grog-shop on Potter's Point. And once or twice she found him in close conversation with an Irishman, she says."

"Is that all?"

"I dosed her with morphine for her pain. That, at least, was one material good I could leave her."

"Precious little then," growled Carver.

"Aye, precious little."

As suddenly as it had started, the downpour stopped, as if guzzled up by Leviathan. A false sense of a gentler rain followed, composed only of drips and drops from leaves and the eaves of the terrace. Water ran hurriedly down the little street.

"I lack subtlety, I suppose," resumed Moynihan, after the pause, "because I cannot hazard why a few missing convicts should be of such great import, nor how the murder of Staines and his man Devers are connected."

Carver had slumped in his chair, stretching his legs before him. "We are transported. We are consigned to the ends of the Earth. And we are therefore as good as dead to the realm and its judges. There can be no hope of reprieve, only suffering and toil to terrify the wretched classes who remain behind. How can a system such as this tolerate one iota of reprieve? How can convicts grow wealthy enough in this penal colony to contemplate their own release? They can, I suppose, but no convict can return to haunt English shores without the system's leave."

"There is enough suffering and toil in England to make me wonder why anyone would want to go back there, if they had felt the contempt of English law," replied Moynihan.

"Why did you come here, and stay?" said Carver mildly.

Moynihan drank again before he answered. "My family bears an ancient name, but that is no certain means of preferment. I had always lived a sort of marginal life, sailing in and out of debt. There were other circumstances I choose not to recall. I have brothers and cousins all making their fortunes here and there, in the army or the law. A surgeon's place on a transport is an excellent opportunity, or so I was told."

"And why do you linger?" pressed Carver.

"One must have money to establish a practice. The office of hangman, I imagine, is easier to acquire."

"I had only to raise my hand," said Carver gravely, "but it was no simple thing. The convicts in the colony have an expression, a form of praise. They call a prisoner a pebble, a stone, when they are hardened to all punishments, to all injuries and insults. So it is with a man in my position. I have my faults, surely. But as a boy I was a quick study, and I have taken to this lesson well. The only way to see the inside of a stone is to break it. But I am not needlessly cruel, and I did not step on to the gallows to satisfy my nature."

The surgeon studied the man in the other chair, but the brandy he had consumed confounded him, and so he murmured, "Perhaps you feel more than you say, therefore. We may both pity that poor girl, in our own fashion."

"She should not have been there," said Carver tautly.

"And to survive here, and prosper, I begin to see, you must perforce still the whispers of the past in your head. We should all need a sort of slaughterman for memories, a hangman for ghosts."

Moynihan grinned crooked and sad at the dark shape the other man made, farthest from the closed windows. The night insects resumed their business, and the damp, warm air hummed.

"You are right," said Carver. "It does not pay to remember too much. I cannot repay you for this service."

"I apologize," said the surgeon. "I have pressed too far. In truth, I have drunk too much."

The chair creaked as Carver rose. "Leave the light," he said. "I'll find my way out."

"You didn't answer my other question," said Moynihan, not stirring.

Carver nodded. "Whoever killed those two, Staines and Devers, whatever they intended, it was on account of something valuable, something worth a terrible risk and cold preparation. That is the connection. It is the same hand and the same will, surely. But I cannot see the rest."

"What will you do with this information?"

Carver was on his feet. "A grog-shop. Potter's Point. An Irishman. Smugglers, perhaps. I do not know yet. But there is a prisoner in solitary, a pebble, a rock, who will know."

CARVER STEPPED OUT into the blackened street, which had been sluiced by the onslaught of the rain. The warm stone was steaming, and threads of mist rose towards the storm-wracked sky. To the north, flickers of lightning, rapid as the shuttles of a loom, gave an eerie, intermittent green-blue illumination to the bastions of cloud. Carver drew up his collar and walked. The memory of Antonia Fitchett, bright and quizzical in the summer sun, fluttered about the border of his thoughts. He brooded also on the burnt girl and fragmentary names, coils of rope, broken glass, and dark ships in the harbour. A man roused from a stupor might feel such incidental things pressing very hard on his attention, as his dull senses reach for clarity, and so each incident and memory pricked and goaded Carver. He was not accustomed to curiosity after so long suppressing all questions of his own past, but he was curious now. He was not accustomed to kindness or pity, and the surgeon had invoked both. Even regret he had smothered deep, and that haunted his steps down the hill. A palm frond cracked and toppled from a tree in front of him. Once or twice, his imagination reported movement and stealthy steps in the lanes that he passed. But the hangman's scant comfort remains, that of all the killers abroad at the given hour, he remains the most prodigious.

CHAPTER 7.

Jolly Boats and Grog-shops

THE PRISONER SAT square on a low stool, leaning forward with his wrists crossed and his elbows on his knees. The floor below him was laced with trickles of blood and water. The man was massive—weighty in bone and sinew. His skin was darkened and toughened by the sun, but his back showed a mass of whitened scars, even under the scattering of bloodied, weeping streaks that revealed the tracks of the recent lashing. His scalp was razored and beaded with particles of sweat. Still he sat on the stool in the prison dormitory, breathing steadily and perceptibly. His name was Croyden.

"Sounds like—a grog-shop round the point from Snail Cove," he said eventually. "You wouldn't be the first to ask. But you don't strike me, Carver, as the type to go calling there."

"Indulge me," said Carver.

"Bah. It's a meeting place for Irish scum, rebels, worse dogs than the Blacks."

Croyden was a hard man, obdurate in his defiance of the lash: a pebble. Not to be broken by any means, his reputation and his prejudices were immovable.

"What are they about there?"

"Mutiny and bloody mayhem. Recollecting Castle Hill. They'll have nothing to say to a proper English hangman, if you take my warning."

Carver nodded, and Croyden continued his slow, shuddering taking of breath.

"Someone said a cove might find out something about a venture called the Rats' Line there."

Croyden grimaced and seemed about to spit, but either his mouth was too dry or the gesture too painful to finish. "Who told you about that little sailing club?"

"Drunken cully on The Rocks," said Carver.

"It's a joke for gulls, canting speech. Blather and talk."

Carver leaned back from the lashed man. Flies dodged and buzzed in the darkened air of the long cell. Other prisoners watched Croyden and Carver with sullen eyes, but none dared interrupt.

"Nonetheless, where is this grog-shop?"

"Fellow I know, Maggsy, said it was on a point in a bend of the Parramatta, half-mile or so past Cockatoo Island."

"Maggsy?"

"Convict. Sound. Went straight. Made a bit of coin herding sheep in the back country. But don't be thinking you'll walk into that den of Fennian rebels and Sodomites and find a warm welcome."

"I'll take the measure of that myself," replied Carver.

"You've been warned."

With vast and terrible deliberation, the pebble reached down to a shallow bowl where a fragment of sponge was steeped in water and weak vinegar. He raised the sponge, and let a trickle fall across his back. Angry flies rose and whined. Croyden let a long breath hiss from his crooked mouth.

Carver nodded, and Croyden watched him retreat. "I won't yield to any damned lasher," said Croyden. "Nor bow and scrape before any of them. They can beat a righteous man to tatters and never harm him."

"Nothing is good or ill," returned the hangman, "but that thinking makes it so."

"You're a damned heathen," said Croyden.

THE NIGHT WAS clear, and a yellow moon, half-eaten, sat close to the edge of the cliffs and bluffs of the harbour. A jolly boat, with Carver at the oars, skimmed over the glassy water in the lee of Cockatoo Island. Hungry things slithered and splashed in the waters lining the edge of the tangled stands of mangrove. Presently, the skiff slowed and worked against a slow current, turning into the pockets and bays of the tributaries. Carver looked up and took his mark on the wavering point of light on the horizon. Steady at the oars, he turned the boat to the land.

He lodged the boat in the palisade of roots in the shallows. Then he waded until he came to a rough jetty of bound wood. A narrow track, cut through the tangle of mangroves and tall grasses, led up the hill. Carver, dressed as a ticket-of-leave man—rough coat, cap, and slipshod boots—looked up to the top of the ridge above him, at smoke curling under the stars, and heard voices and the whinny of a fiddle and beat of a little drum.

At the top of the path squatted a long house, built of mud bricks on a cleared patch of land, with great trees looming above it: substantial for one of the countless grog-shops the free convicts had established at all points of the colony. Men lounged among the posts of the long veranda, with bottles and tankards between them. Smoke and light and noise issued from the open doors and long windows. Coming out from the brush, Carver pulled his coat closer and lowered his head. His firm steps became a weary, crimped shuffle.

A few heads turned in his direction as he approached, but they betrayed no interest. He passed in at the door and stood on the threshold as if perplexed by the lamplight and oily smoke of the eucalyptus logs. A man in a leather apron was attending one of the four or five long wooden tables that filled the room. He looked up at the newcomer and barked a few words in Gaelic. Carver smiled as though embarrassed and beckoned the aproned man closer.

The serving-man grimaced and came near, stooping to hear him as the musicians hastened their tempo.

"I want to speak to a man," said the newcomer, almost inaudibly. "About getting on a boat."

The serving-man hissed an insult and looked away. "You're a mighty fool. Get out."

But the convict grasped his sleeve and drew him nearer. "I have money," he hissed. "Maggsy sent me."

"Drink, and don't speak," said the other, pulling his shirt free and stamping away.

Carver sidled about the room, watchful and nervous, until he came by an abandoned stool. He had barely dared to crouch on it when the serving-man returned and pulled him to his feet. They crossed between the crowded settles. Carver winced at the glances cast his way.

One door led out to the kitchens. These proved as hot as a smithy, with spits and kettles in the fireplace and a brick bread oven. Carver peered into the steam and smoke. By the fireplace, but facing the room with her eyes on the three maids and the sweating cook, sat an ancient woman on a low, round-backed chair of polished native cedar. Her hair was stark white and closely drawn up; her face was wide, puckered around a toothless mouth, seamed, and sun-blackened. The eyes, buried in folds and creases, were sharp and sure as a raven's, a cool green.

The serving-man said, in Gaelic, *"This is the English-speaking stranger, mother."*

"I don't like his look," replied the crone. Her voice wheezed and grated. *"His boots are muddy but his hands are too clean."*

"What does she say?" asked Carver.

"She says a bad tide cast you up."

"Who is she?"

"This is Mother O'Doul."

"And who are you, while we're about it?"

"Callum O'Doul."

"Tell your Mam that I have money." Carver leaned forward as though petitioning a magistrate. "Pounds, shillings, and pence."

"I can hear you right enough if you don't mumble," said Mother O'Doul. "Where did you come by this money?"

"I have it off a station-man out at Three Mile Rock."

"Did you kill this man?" she asked, eyes gleaming.

Carver twisted the toe of his boot on the stone floor. "I don't know if I care to say."

The old woman had a coarse shawl heaped about her shoulders but seemed impervious to the heat. "What would you here? Seek grog and whores in the town, if you want them."

"I'd rather an English lass—in an English bed, if you follow me."

The old woman tilted her head back and opened her mouth like a hungry bird and let loose a yelp of derision.

"Well," said Carver in hurt tones, "they told me that someone here knows the way to get on a ship, if you can pay."

The mouth snapped shut. "The man who sent you here is a liar." Mother O'Doul barked a command at a dithering maid hovering over one of the kettles.

"Oh, but your Irish rebels, your agitators and mutineers, you can't tell me they wouldn't give everything they could for passage back to Dublin, to defy the English again, lawful or no."

O'Doul settled under her shawl and her eyes fixed on the man. "You speak like you know us."

"I've come across a few of your kind in the gaol-yard."

"Sixty year ago I was shipped here like so much baggage by the cruel English. A girl of sixteen. Over the years, I've seen men and women set off, north and west, by boat and by foot, to find a way home. And only that one lass made it. The rest left their bones in the bush for the chain-gangs to find, or came back, whipped and tied like animals, at the hands of the Blacks."

"You've no need to scold," said Carver sullenly. "I'll find a whaler to take me to America. Maybe you know one of them."

"Show us what money you have," said Callum, eagerly, who had little moved from his station at the hearth.

"I didn't bring it all. I know your sort."

"If you knew us," said the old woman, "you wouldn't be here."

She barked a few more words in Gaelic. The kitchen racket of knives and spoons did not change. Carver straightened suddenly and stepped back.

"Where are you going?" said O'Doul.

"Whom did you call?"

"Did I call someone?"

"You mean to rob me!"

A boy, coming in from the common-room with a handful of tankards, opened the door at the same moment Callum reached for Carver's collar. Carver knocked his hand away and pulled the boy off balance into the path of the man and the old woman. He dodged into the next room and lunged for the farthest door, but he was tripped, tangled in legs and stools, and fell between two of the long tables.

They were on him then. Carver was kicked and shaken, and several hands reached down to clutch at his arms and shirt and hair. Then he was hauled upright and slammed backwards onto the thick table, still thrashing and growling. A plate was lodged in the small of his back; a fork dug into his shoulder-blade.

And then they fell silent. The door to the kitchen opened and Mother O'Doul appeared. One hand clutching at her son's shoulder and one hand on her stick, she advanced in a grim processional. Every man in the crowded room attended her.

"You damned hag," said Carver, in a low voice, "you mean to murder me."

"No more than you murdered the old convict-farmer on Cleveland Plain," she replied.

"Who is this man?" said her son.

O'Doul smacked her lips and said in English, "That there is Master Gabriel Carver, executioner to the Sydney Gaol."

As though the very touch and presence of the man was dreadful, the hands on him loosened and one or two drew back. Carver levered himself up with a gasp.

"Pfaugh!" spat the old woman. "Did you think a little white ash in your hair and oakum in your cheeks would deceive these old eyes? Your hand took off three of my grandsons, seven of my kin."

"Aye, and Patrick but a month ago," said another.

"And Liam."

"And Davy. I saw him set the knot."

Carver looked up, and every face in the room contained a dreary accusation. Bare knives were laid on the tables.

"I'm not here to answer to you all," he said.

"Why are you here?" returned O'Doul, quizzical.

"Look," said a man next to him, suddenly. A hand thrust into his pocket and before Carver could catch at it, it was withdrawn, clutching the curved handle of a small-bore pistol.

"You mean some mischief after all," crowed Callum, taking the pistol.

"Tell us the who sent you hither—no quibbling, mind—and you may walk free. Otherwise, I'll leave you to the company, and they will do as they will."

"A hanging," said one man.

"Break his hands," another proposed.

O'Doul silenced them all with a wave of her stick. Carver plucked wads of cotton from inside his cheeks.

"This isn't my business. This is police work. They task me with it. But cross me and you cross the police," said Carver.

"You're not one of the police, to be sure," said O'Doul.

Carver shook his head. "No. But I'm fit for low places."

O'Doul glanced sharply around. "Low work in low places, indeed. But what do they suspect?"

"They want a murderer, the one that killed Staines on his farm and throttled Ralph Devers in Sydney Town."

A sly smile twisted the old woman's toothless mouth. "We see your hand in that second killing."

"Why should I kill a man who was of use to me?"

"A police informant, you mean."

"A witness to the other crime."

The old woman hobbled closer, and the hands on Carver tightened. He could smell the stale rum on the breath of the man clasping his shoulder.

O'Doul peered at him with her raptor's eyes. "What did this man Devers tell you?"

"He boasted about his plans to leave the colony. He told me he found a way onto a ship from here. A prison rat's passage, under the noses of the administrators."

"So why did he tell you to come here?"

"Didn't he come here himself, once or twice? Or is there another grog-shop on this point?"

"Did he say that himself?"

"He said the Irish knew the best ways in and out of the colony."

O'Doul's head flicked up. "You're a fool. The man was lying, so."

Carver grinned dangerously. "And you're so pickled in falsehood and plots you hardly stop to think on them. You quiz me for fear of what I might know."

"You can pull my words apart like a lawyer, you won't find what you need here."

"Then it's time for us to part."

"Who sent you?" hissed O'Doul.

"The magistrate, Fitchett."

"Fitchett's a prig and a fool. Say again, and if you lie, Danny here will start taking off your fingers and you'll tie no more knots."

Carver glanced over his shoulder. "There are too many eyes and ears here, don't you think?"

O'Doul shrugged. "All good Irish patriots, who know when to speak and when to hold their tongues."

"And not an informant among them?" Carver glanced at Callum. "Don't threaten me. I know enough flayers and torturers to know you don't have the lead in you."

Callum hefted the pistol he had taken, and his thumb brushed the hammer.

"He's right," said O'Doul with a sniff. "We've trespassed with family business on this good company. Besides, this mob has stopped drinking. Take him out."

At a nod from Callum, two men hauled Carver off the table and shoved him back towards the kitchen. Kicked and jostled, he was propelled to the next door, which opened without ceremony on the back of the grog-shop: copper-kettles, washing lines, a dusty yard, scratched over by chickens by day. The red clay was dark under the half moon. Broad-backed cockroaches scuttled out of the light from the opening door. There was a haphazard woodpile to feed the kitchen fires, and a pair of hatchets stuck in the worn stump of an old tree. A lantern, suspended from a hook by the door, attracted flittering moths. A green snake coiled about the rafters of the overhanging roof.

Carver was released. O'Doul edged out over the stone step, and one of the maids scurried behind her with a stool. Finally, the old woman was seated like a duchess at the theatre.

"Now," said O'Doul, "I want the whole of your business: who sent you, who told you, what do they know?"

Carver drew in air between clenched teeth. A breeze stirred along the river, bringing the muddy smell of the mangroves at low tide. "If you give me the name of the cully that hanged that man Devers and tried to put it on me," he returned, "I'll tell you all the police know, sum and substance, of your gang of rum-runners and malcontents."

"I'll send you to Hell, and you can make inquiries on your own, if you don't speak respectful."

Carver shrugged. "Our speech is at an end."

He turned away from the noise and reek of the kitchen, the circle of men, the old woman, and began to walk with easy steps towards the edge of the yard and the kitchen garden. Beyond that stood a stretch of long grass and then the ghostly, bare trunks of the trees.

"I will shoot you down if you take one more step," shrilled Callum O'Doul.

"Then shoot," said Carver, without breaking his stride, "if you have the nerve for it."

There was a sound like the quick tearing of a page, and then a thunderous crack, and the whole clearing was illuminated in a stark flash.

"Damnable fool!" screeched O'Doul.

Carver ran, with the shot ringing in his ears, leaping the low fence of the yard and crossing the open grass towards the line of gums and ashes at the edge of the clearing. The trees and the open sky admitted him. A thin, shrill whistle came from the tree-line, as if in answer to the shot, and then a man shouted and horses' hooves were beating against the dry earth. Carver filled his lungs with the night air and laughed. From between the trunks a dark horse and rider emerged, bearing towards Carver. He stopped, and the shadows of swift horses, whinnying and snorting, the men on their backs leaning forward, passed him on both sides. Carver turned as the ranks of mounted police drew up before the inn. A shotgun was discharged upwards in the sky: a fountain of sparks erupting. Six or seven men ran in disarray, some towards the edge of the headland. A shout went up as the door he had passed not long ago was battered open, and he saw uniformed men swarming against the light.

• • •

LATER, WHEN ALL the tumult was stilled, Carver stalked along the front of the inn, where the policemen had gathered up and shackled a handful of men who sat, slumped, mostly on the ground or along the low porch. Constable Ellington was leafing through a handful of papers. His cap was missing. His face had a bright sheen, flushed and eager.

Before Carver spoke, Ellington said, "Fencing stolen goods. Harbouring escaped servants. There are two wanted bushrangers here. Not a bad night's work, acting on information."

"I would rather have found the man who stole my own rope than a dozen poxy bushrangers," returned Carver.

"Suit yourself," said Ellington, scanning another pass. "Perhaps we should have ridden in more slowly."

Carver clenched his jaw. "I would say I was tumbled. Someone here knew I was coming, and they laid a trap for me. They knew my name, and they were ready. There's another puzzle."

"Well, the guv'nor expects you to call on him tomorrow, so you can make your excuses then," said Ellington.

By the door, Callum O'Doul stood handcuffed, glowering at an armed policeman. A few feet from him sat Mother O'Doul on a bench, with a young woman tenderly patting her shoulder. O'Doul mugged at every policeman that passed like an aged beldame gone witless. Only when Carver passed into the edge of the lamplight did she spare him a glance, a flicker of fury and calculation mingled, and then she looked up again and smiled, softly.

"You should be dead," charged Callum, aggrieved.

"You did me a service," said Carver lightly. "There was no shot in the pistol—it was meant for a signal."

Callum glared at his mother, who betrayed no interest in her son. She blinked as if in puzzlement at Carver and flashed a hectic smile at Ellington. The hangman opened his mouth, drew breath, and then clamped his lips shut. He nodded and grinned at the old woman, and then strolled away from the gathered policemen and prisoners, whistling fragments of an old tune.

CHAPTER 8.

Death and the Lady

ARCHIBALD FITCHETT was not fond of tea, but the delicate white bone-china cups he possessed served as emblems of the rank and responsibility of the colonial magistrate, and he therefore took tea in his study every morning, usually while he listened to his constables reporting.

As he contemplated the teacup, his expression did not alter when he said, "A clutch of Irish smugglers harbouring a few runaway servants and the subjects of two or three warrants. It is tolerable work for an informant, but we are no nearer the murderer of Matthew Staines or Ralph Devers, or any unauthorized departures from the colony."

"They are connected to it somehow," said Carver. "They quizzed me closely, with all manner of threats. They wanted to know how much I knew. If I were but an informer, they would have beaten me and sent me along, none the wiser. They are hiding something; that's material."

"And what do you propose, therefore, to do next?" said Fitchett, without emphasis. "I have not yet retired my suspicions of you."

"I have a notion that Devers' molly, the girl who was with him, may know something material."

"Then bring her out, and let us question her directly."

"No," said Carver sharply. "She is injured; she may be dying." He shook his head. "But the whores talk to each other. They share many things."

"I shall grant you three days' grace. Make the best of it you may. Bring me some material proof of the rumour." He set the teacup down with a grimace.

EJECTED FROM THE magistrate's chamber, Carver almost tripped over the maid, who was dithering within earshot of the panel doors.

"What is it?" he snapped.

"If you please, would you take a drink of water before going back down to the town?"

"I don't have time for water."

"The *mistress* said it was *awful* hot today, and you should take a *cold drink* of water, in the *kitchen*—if you please, mister," said Kathleen with much screwing up of her face.

Carver stopped and opened his mouth. "The mistress, you say."

"Yes. She said so especially."

"Then I will go."

The kitchen, set a little aside from the house in the shelter of the walled garden, was already warm with bread baking in the brick ovens, but the doors were open to the yard, where the herbs and vegetables flourished. Antonia Fitchett hovered near the table, where a cup of water stood. Her eyes were glittering, and she began as Carver entered: "Mr. Carver, what have you discovered?"

"A great deal of trouble."

"But do you draw closer to the answer to the two murders, for they are very much the talk of our colony?"

"I have stepped in the hornets' nest and roused them up. But I have no one to charge, nor certain proofs of anything. And your husband is not inclined to patience."

"Oh." Antonia became flustered. She smoothed her skirts and looked down. "I had thought, given your coming here….At any rate, what did you learn when you examined the records at the church?"

"I learned that the marriage of Ruth Tremaine and Matthew Staines was witnessed by a Colonel MacNeish, which strikes me as notable."

"MacNeish! I know him, we must call on him at once."

"We? Call on him?" Carver grimaced. "I am not one of the Currency, nor your husband's office clerk, but a convict. And you are a married woman."

"You need not trouble yourself to remind me of that! But I am no colonist's wife, afflicted by nerves and fatigue. And your case holds that rare quality for me: interest."

"In truth, you may be able to assist," said Carver mildly.

"We must contrive something. We must sound out the colonel. Surely when you went to the Reverend Honeychair you had some thought of discovering a clue to this business."

Carver rested one hand on the plain kitchen table. "The reason why Devers had to die, perhaps it is connected to the missing wife. It is the one matter between him and Staines that there is no account for."

Antonia smiled, a quiet illumination that only Carver saw. "Then we will introduce ourselves to the colonel, as if by chance."

"You cannot do it alone. If there is any danger, I must be near."

"Of course. But you and no other. Archie cannot know about this."

"Now I must go," said Carver. "Send your maid to find me, when you are ready." Abruptly, with a crooked grin, he swept up the cup of water and swallowed half. Then he said aloud, "Thank you for the water, ma'am. It is bound to be hot again."

• • •

COLONEL ARTHUR MACNEISH, formerly of the sixth dragoons, had since the Rum Rebellion consigned himself to a fixed routine. He breakfasted before the parade bell and never stirred beyond his veranda during the hours from eleven to three, but once a day, in the enervated late afternoon, he walked past Hyde Park and along the road that Macquarie, with his palpable mania for public works, had commissioned beyond the Government House towards the headlands. As his flesh had shrunk about his bones, the colonel had come to feel any breath of cool air most particularly, and so the heat of the westering sun held no fear for him. He walked with a heavy hawthorn stick, but the Domain was closed to common strollers and convicts, which was no small part of his satisfaction in strolling there.

Nevertheless, he was surprised, though not displeased, to see, somewhat in the distance and looking out from the land, the shape of a woman. She had, he thought, a pretty figure, somewhat long about the limbs but pleasing in the waist (the colonel had suffered setbacks and left his hopes for a wife far away), though her dress had something of the severity of the wife of a colonial official about it, and was no doubt years or more out of date.

He made no haste in approaching her, and watched instead her curving back and the wind fluttering the edge of her parasol. She turned when he came near. She had a pale, angular face, clear eyes, a row of light freckles across the high bridge of her nose, a clever mouth.

He stopped to raise his hat.

"Colonel MacNeish," she said, with but a trace of hesitation.

MacNeish let his hand drop. "I'm afraid, madam, that I have not had the pleasure."

"I am Antonia Fitchett. You know my husband, of course, the magistrate..."

"A fellow Scot I perceive."

Mrs. Fitchett glanced to one side, and MacNeish noticed, then, the man sitting a little further down from her on the dry grass.

A heavy, square-shouldered fellow in a coarse black coat with a broad-brimmed hat.

"I do believe I must offer my condolences," said Mrs. Fitchett.

"Must you?" said MacNeish lightly. "And for what, pray?"

"For I understand you were a friend of Matthew Staines, the man who was—well, in such dreadful circumstances as my husband will not describe in my hearing."

Perhaps MacNeish paled: there was something ashen in his countenance that decades under the Imperial flag could not burn out. "Dreadful indeed," he said.

"But more so to his friends."

"Quite." The colonel lowered his stick.

"That is, I believe you were a friend of the family, since you witnessed Mr. Staines' marriage in the parish registry."

"It was more in the matter of business: I was supply-master to the regiment, and Staines had a gift for teasing crops out of this damnable thin soil, when most convicts were city scoundrels."

"But perhaps you could help us find that poor man's wife, his only kin in New South Wales."

Mrs. Fitchett smiled, and MacNeish raised his hand as though dazzled by glimmers of the sun on the waters.

"I can pass on only gossip. Regiments are rotten with gossips, worse than flies on—beg your pardon—horses."

"We believe any information could be material."

"Forgive me, madam, but you say 'we' as though this were not an entirely private matter."

Mrs. Fitchett looked to her left, and the man sitting behind her rose, brushing the dust from his clothes. He thrust his head forward, like a ragged crow at the woman's side.

"This is Mr. Carver. He acts for my husband."

"He is no constable, I hazard."

Carver spoke: "My office is of another sort."

"Forgive us," said Mrs. Fitchett. "A matter such as this requires extraordinary presumption, I am learning."

"What I may communicate," said the colonel, "is too tedious for this pleasant portion of the day. I dine every night at Kember's Hotel. Perhaps you—and Mr. Carver, if he is free—will join me there."

"Tonight," said Carver.

"Then I wish you good afternoon, Mrs. Fitchett, Mr. Carver."

The colonel tipped his hat again, and walked on. Sunlight glimmered on the brass buttons of his coat.

Carver nimbly stepped up to the side of the path.

"I have done as you ask," said Antonia. "You have been introduced. The colonel will speak to us. I cannot guess what you think he will tell us."

"He is hiding something," said Carver. "He avoided your questions twice."

"Are all your speculations so dark, Mr. Carver?" she asked.

"Only the ones that prove true."

"You are glib!"

"No. But I have seen enough dark deeds to know which way this one runs."

The shadows had begun to grow long under the clustered pines and acacias, and along the banks of hibiscus and thorny bougainvillea of the Domain. Only the air above the cove remained bright and sharp. Sea birds rose and wheeled over the orange rocks. Antonia Fitchett turned to the smokes of the town, a dirty smear against the wavering horizon.

"Then you think me an innocent," she said.

"I think you the magistrate's wife."

"I have a convict maid, a convict cook, convicts to water my garden. I have heard the children playing at games of lashing and shackling. I have known babes that threaten their convict nursemaids with execution. I am as familiar with transportation and assignment, the whole grand and awful design, as you. I am a magistrate's wife, and I am as close confined by that as any felon."

Carver raised his chin and looked at her face, the two high points of anger there. "I make no presumptions, I hope."

Antonia shook her head and began to move away along the path. "No. But you forget we are both bound to our duties."

Carver pushed a hand through his hair and then he followed, watchful as a hound.

Constable Ellington was waiting at the gate with the magistrate's fiacre. Nearby, the colonel's heavier carriage was also drawn up, while his driver sheltered in the sketchy shade of a palm tree. Carver stepped forward to offer his hand, but Antonia went lightly into the carriage and only then turned to him.

"I will call on the colonel tonight."

"We shall both call: he is expecting me," she replied.

"Is that proper?" he asked.

She laughed, to his astonishment. "A magistrate's wife, meddle in a crime before her husband? It is not proper in the least. But since when did you concern yourself with what my husband thought proper?"

Carver was about to step forward and put his foot to the carriage step, but the horses pranced forward, the wheels ground the dust and gravel, and the carriage pulled away as Carver hopped aside. Antonia, upright with her hand on the door, did not look back.

KEMBER'S HOTEL, on the tapering corner of Adelaide Street in the best part of town, had a long, deep, second-floor balcony to provide shade by day and capture the few wafts of lukewarm air by night. The balcony was scented lightly with jasmine. Carriages, fiacres, and traps rolled towards Government House, the barracks, and the park, and up again with a tripping, delicate air—with the aim of being seen, for the ladies could gain a clear view of each other, their broad hats, and feathers. The indifferent bats whirred in the immeasurable darkness overhead, and sometimes an ibis loosed one of its hideous strangling cries from beneath the sprawling fig trees in the park.

Carver waited on the dark side of the street to join Antonia for her appointment with MacNeish. Before he could move, he saw Fordham, on an excellent riding horse with a light, high step, stop and tie up outside the hotel. The gentleman seemed to expect a meeting, for he twitched his riding crop and glanced along the street. Briefly, his gaze passed over Carver. The hangman drew back under the fig trees.

Soon, another man, also riding but leading a second dusty horse, arrived, dismounted, and was greeted by Fordham. Fordham went to the unsaddled horse to inspect it. His movements were deft and quick as he shifted from the teeth to the flanks to the fetlocks and the hooves. He held out his hand abruptly and spoke to the other man, who hesitated and then passed Fordham a kerchief of his own, which Fordham used to brush the pasty dust off the horse's forelegs. Fordham stood and shook his head.

Carver, who had no eye for horse-flesh of any quality, made to cross the road unseen while Fordham and the other man began to argue. He had put one foot on the steps to the hotel when he was hailed from behind: "Carver! There's a fellow, I suppose, who knows how the unjust prosper."

Carver turned. "Mr. Fordham."

"This man here," chirped Fordham, "is bent on selling me a horse he has kept on dry pasture this month or more. Not a bad nag, you know, but not quite worth what I'm paying."

"I wouldn't know, sir," said Carver stonily.

"But you, I'm sure, care for cheats no more than I do," said Fordham, and for a moment he appraised Carver as closely and surely as any stock or property.

"As I say, that's not my business."

"Hmm, quite. You have business at Kember's of your own. Not your usual drinking place, I suppose."

"Can't say. Magistrate's business."

"Confidential. I understand you perfectly." Fordham turned back to the man in the long coat who was shifting from side to side behind him. "Let us knock the price down to something sensible, and let Mr. Carver get on with his business."

The man growled something that seemed to indicate assent. As swiftly as he could, Carver slipped away through the doors of the hotel.

COLONEL MACNEISH had set about his third measure of grog when Mrs. Fitchett and a "gentleman" were announced to him in dire tones by the steward. Colonel MacNeish set down his tumbler and sighed.

"Forgive me, I had expected, perhaps, Mrs. Fitchett only."

Following the respectably sombre magistrate's wife, Carver had put on his executioner's coat, and in the fluttering light of the paraffin lanterns he resembled a grave and thrifty parson making a county visit.

"I should also hope to further your acquaintance," said Carver flatly.

"Quite so," returned the colonel serenely. He pointed to an empty wicker chair. Antonia settled herself there, her skirts rustling, while the colonel busied himself with a pipe and matchbox. Carver leaned against the balcony, with the rattle of carriages and the beat of horse hooves behind him.

"It is an unhappy story," said the colonel, "here where so much comes to an unhappy end, and I must own to my part of it."

"You mean what happened to Mrs. Staines?" said Antonia.

"No, I mean my part in bringing together all of the players in this sorry business."

"You knew Staines," said Carver, from the edge of the light.

"I knew Matthew Staines as a convict in the hungry years, when our ill-formed colony barely knew how to feed itself, and all that vast acreage beyond this pretty harbour proved an illusion, nothing but meagre soils and bitter scrub. Out of a thousand convicts from the rookeries of London or the slums of Dublin, there were but a handful of country men who knew how to hitch a bullock or turn the soil. Well, Staines was one of those. He was an agitator, a machine-breaker in Hertfordshire, enamoured of the nonsense that lost us our American colonies and turned France into a bloodbath, but he could read the land and raise a crop. He was granted a small plot of land at Parramatta, and there was water on his little parcel of land. He prospered, took to horse-trading and money-lending, and took more land, including a section at Three Mile Rock. I was a supply officer at the time and had plenty of dealings with him."

"You were friends, then," said Antonia.

"I should not say 'friends' exactly, my dear." The colonel had a long clay pipe at his side and he leaned over with a twist of paper to pass the end through the lantern flame. "It would not do for an officer of the garrison to be on friendly terms with a convict, but we had a deal of business to do together and were on good terms, in the main." The colonel turned the lighted twist to the bowl of his pipe, puffed, and drew smoke, while the tobacco glowed like an ember in the darkened balcony walk.

"You knew his wife also," said Carver.

"She was assigned to him, at first. By then he had any number of convicts working his properties. He had acquired his ticket-of-leave earlier, and then Macquarie himself, a sound Scotsman otherwise, but given to coddling the convicts and their aspirations, signed his conditional pardon."

MacNeish leaned back and puffed a little more on his pipe. Antonia heard the whine of mosquitoes along the rail, and was grateful for the smoke.

"The colony has always been bedevilled by a lack of women, you know. Leads to dreadful business—lady present—not to be mentioned, and so on."

"What was her name? Where did she come from?" snapped Carver.

"Ruth...Tremaine, I believe, was her maiden name. Irish lassie, filled with fire for the cause. Futile, ye ken, for there is no profit in it. Not in Dublin no more than Castle Hill. She was unusual, I should say, among the usual run of female convicts, mostly felons and petty whores—if the lady will forgive an old soldier's plain speech—in being an educated woman, though a firebrand, a pamphlet writer for the Society, and a modern-day leveller. An unhappy young woman, rather squat and dark to my taste, but with a certain sharp and passionate manner that was not unappealing."

"So how did she come to marry Staines?" said Carver.

"A young woman in need of protection married a dry old man—there's no mystery there, I hope," said MacNeish.

Antonia Fitchett did not look at either man but turned her face momentarily from the light. Her long hands were clasped in her lap, right over left. "It is not so curious, I think."

"And then she ran away with a soldier," said Carver.

"You are too hasty, sir," MacNeish admonished. "Captain Pryor was a gentleman. He was foolhardy, but his intentions, I am persuaded, were always good."

Carver did not respond, but settled against the outer balcony, and so MacNeish turned to Antonia, after drawing a few long streams of smoke.

"I am no longer a young man, but I recall the first years of the colony: hunger, tedium, and discipline. But Captain Pryor, I will say, had a young man's enthusiasms and a young man's illusions. When he arrived, our officers scrambled for land and convicts to work the land, and they traded, principally in rum. Those were our diversions. Well, that high-minded jackanapes Bligh was a considerable navigator, but he had a positive talent for cultivating insubordination. When things came to a head between the governor and the regiment over the trade in rum—I assign no particular malice to either side, mind—Pryor's hopes of a profitable post were dashed, and by the time Macquarie was set above us to bring some sound Scots sense to the whole business, he chafed at the bounds of his commission and his duty. I daresay, like many young officers, he thought often on the campaign against the upstart Napoleon and feared all his hopes of daring and command were spoiling in the Antipodean sun.

"I mention this to set the scene. Old soldiers grow garrulous, my dear, in the long tropical nights. I took an interest in Pryor. He took an interest in turning some stretch of land into an estate. We rode out to Three Mile Rock often. Staines was proud of his acquired respectability, his wife, and board, and Macquarie encouraged his sort of ambition. Mrs. Staines served us. She had adjusted her manner to the new condition, but I do not think her reformed in any fashion."

MacNeish laid his pipe aside. His voice sank, and somewhere a frog began to chirrup while carriages rolled beneath the balcony. "I will but allude to the circumstances of a young woman elevated from penal servitude, a young man resentful of the impositions of his duty and ambitious to prove his abilities. These matters are all part of the texture of garrison life. We are also constrained by distance and discipline, and the temptations of the Serpent are manifest in this second Eden. There were opportunities to exchange notes, long rides along the boundaries of the town, glances in church."

"You mean he seduced her," Carver interjected.

"You are a plain man, I see. I mean no such thing. Begging the lady's pardon, but I should say that Ruth Staines was a reluctant young wife with a distracted husband in a foreign land and was moved to make trial of her own escape."

The colonel's pipe had smothered while it was set aside. The colonel reached for it and frowned. With a smooth, sudden motion, Carver leaned in and took one of the spills from the side-table and held it to the lantern flame. He offered the smouldering paper to the colonel, who used it to relight his pipe. Antonia looked out into the dark, her face composed as though for a portrait, her eyes cool and unreadable. The hangman straightened and returned to his place on the edge of the light.

"But they planned to—what should I call it?—run away together," she said, with the same distance in her words.

"They were romantics," said the colonel. "That's their damnable fault. Condemn them for that."

"How did they contrive it?" said Carver eagerly. "How did Pryor mean to get his convict mistress back to England?"

The colonel shook his head with a low chuckle. "My dear fellow, whatever put that idea into your head?"

"Where then?"

The colonel drew on his pipe, and the embers flared. "There were rumours of fine grazing lands in the ranges, of hidden convict settlements, but I believe they fled to the islands of New Zealand. There are always whalers and sealers going between the colonies. All it would require would be a small ship and a willing captain, and the means to keep the crew quiet. Why half the sealers in the Southern Ocean are absconding convicts." The colonel smiled indulgently at Carver.

"She stole from her husband to pay for the passage for herself and her lover, and he abandoned his regiment for her," said Carver flatly.

"Could she have worked it all to that end?" murmured Antonia.

"I always believed there was something calculating about that woman, a wee hard stone in her heart."

"You put it all on her," said Antonia.

"Pryor was ambitious, quick-tempered, foolish, as bold men are foolish when confined. I do not excuse him."

"What did Staines do then?" asked Carver.

"He was a plain, honest, thrifty chappie, for all his rough edges. He raged at his loss. He cut himself off from all civil society, my own included, I'm sorry to say. He took an interest in emancipist matters. Pestered the governor about land and title."

"And did he not try and find his runaway wife?"

The colonel knocked his pipe against the edge of the table, and embers tumbled and flared. "I cannot say. I believe he called once for a native tracker, and the woman, being a convict, was sought by the police. After it was clear she was gone, he prospered again under the late governor, and his fortunes were somewhat restored. Then, I believe, he began to make new inquiries through his overseer."

"Why's that?" said Carver.

"Perhaps he had a thought to marry again."

"And you have had no news of Captain Pryor since?" said Carver.

"Should I have?" returned MacNeish, with a keen glance.

"You were on friendly terms, did you not say? You seem to know his mind on several matters."

"I have not heard from the man, nor should I expect to. He dishonoured his commission and his regiment, and misused an introduction I made for him. As a matter of honour, I would refuse further confidences."

"Mr. Staines and Ruth Tremaine had no children?" said Antonia.

"No. None."

"But if Ruth Tremaine appeared now, she would inherit, as next of kin?"

The colonel shrugged. "As these things go, I expect so. It is curious that he never moved to excise his wife from his will."

"Perhaps," said Carver slowly, "he had no fear of her ever returning."

MacNeish fell silent, laying down his pipe and returning to his grog.

Antonia said, in a low voice, "We are very grateful, Colonel MacNeish. We do not mean to revive memories of a painful incident."

"Do not think of it, my dear," said MacNeish. "I only regret that my recollections cannot bring you any closer to the murderer of that upright man, a true original."

Carver leaned forward abruptly. "Did Staines know or suspect what passed between Pryor and his wife?"

The old colonel paused before answering. "I cannot speak to his knowledge one way or another. He was careful in his dealings and canny with his friends, even before marriage. I will say that scandal and gossip fly exceedingly fast in our little colony, and we have nothing to occupy ourselves with but our sins. But you should know that convicts hold their thoughts close and their secrets even closer."

The hangman bowed his head as if in thought. Then he stepped in and took Antonia's hand as she stood.

"A little air, perhaps," she said, with a fainter voice. "Good night, colonel."

Carver followed her to the far end of the long balcony. The tentative breezes of evening had faltered, and the night was still and cloying. In the distance, a woman's laugh rose and terminated in a grating shriek. Antonia leaned out across the railing and breathed deeply.

"That wretched tobacco! Archibald has no vices to cultivate, but I am still glad smoking is not one of them. What do you make of the colonel's story? I cannot see how it helps us."

"Chances are the old hypocrite is lying, or at least he passes the truth off with shoddy goods," said Carver, through closed teeth. "There is something wrong with all of this, something that buzzes in my head like a fly in a jug. What is it we're seeking here? It is almost as if Fordham wanted us to know about them, when I went to the church."

Antonia leaned back. "Do you think Ruth Tremaine was the vixen he makes her out to be?"

"I do not believe that Captain Pryor was the gallant gent we have heard him made out to be. Why preserve his reputation over hers? Why should they not stand equal in robbing the old man?"

"She at least had the courage to let her passion serve her, and would not submit to exile and confinement."

"You admire her," said Carver.

Antonia raised her head. "Why did you consent to become the hangman?" she said.

Carver's face was dark, composed of faint planes and the black pits of his eyes. "I was sentenced for life also. But the hangman is removed from hard labour, and there is the chance, by and by, of a conditional pardon. Why did you marry Fitchett and follow him to the world's end?"

"I had four sisters, and my father was a dull Calvinist minister in a poor parish."

"Then we both do as we must."

"You are a better liar than MacNeish. You are well practiced in it, I think."

Carver took care to stand away from the rail, where he could not be viewed from the street or the parading carriages. "We both of us see more than we ought to. You test me, and I should rather be your friend, and have you think me a little more honest than most do. But I must bear a double life, for what I have done—and failed to do. I took the hangman's place because even on the scaffold no one looks straight at the hangman. I had good reason to keep myself out of sight, and whatever I have become, I am no fool. You alone may claim the privilege of looking at me as I am."

"And yet," she murmured, "you remain a mystery."

Carver turned back. "He smokes English tobacco, the colonel. Mark that. He has connections and trades still. New Zealand! As well to say they sailed away to China across the inland sea. I should like to know more about his business."

Antonia laid a pale hand on the rough wooden rail. "I shall enquire, if you like. If Ruth Tremaine and Captain Pryor feared discovery, that would be a reason to silence the emancipist."

"That is a desperate turn," said Carver.

The colonel, meanwhile, had refilled his pipe and took another paper twist to relight it. He looked back along the balcony. On the edge of the lamplight, the tall woman in the wide skirt was a pale sketch, faintly reflective, her head slightly turned as she leaned towards the man, who had become a mere absence, a black interruption in the night, poised at her shoulder. *Death and the Lady,* thought the colonel, closing his teeth on the end of his pipe. *There is our subject this evening, assuredly: death and the lady.*

CHAPTER 9.

A Token, Given in Affection

THE FEMALE FACTORY, established for the provision of useful work by female prisoners, was dedicated to grinding virtue out of these women as much as manufacturing convict weeds—and convict shrouds at need. A totem of the logic of the system, it was hated and avoided. Many of those who passed its gates found whoring and petty crime preferable to labour and correction on its stifling, dusty floor, picking at threads in the heat and vermin. But it had a small infirmary where women were taken for the lying in, or for injuries and diseases. Here the officers had carried Nan Tucker.

Early in the morning, before birdcalls racked the sky, the hangman appeared at the gate. He blustered past the guard and roused the night warder, who was dozing in a chair by the guttering lamp. He had a fixed, feral grin and a hard, quick way of talking. He would not go until he had spoken with Nan Tucker. The warder examined his ticket-of-leave and other papers, and lighted the way across the yard to the infirmary. There they descended to the cool cellar where Whistling Nan waited for her last journey. She had died in the night and been washed and laid out in a pauper's shroud: they had but to stitch her in it.

The warder was indifferent to such changes, and therefore did not mark the moment the hangman faltered and lowered his head. Then Carver approached Whistling Nan without fear. Gently, though there was no call for it, he examined her necks and arms, avoiding the livid burns along her legs and sides, and held up her hands, with the smooth, sunburned fingers. All this he did in silence. Only when he had laid down her right hand did he turn, as quick and composed as before.

"Where are her things?" said Carver, in the same rallying tone.

"They were collected when she passed," said the warder sleepily.

"Then bring them here, woman. And who took them?"

"Purvis was here last night."

"Then fetch Purvis."

The woman hesitated. "The dress was burned. We didn't keep it."

"Go! Fetch her things," growled Carver.

Presently, the warder brought down a scrap of knotted linen and Purvis, the nurse. Grey light tinted the cellar. Carver could hear women groaning as fires were lit and water brought in. Purvis was squat, dough-faced, with small-pox scars running along her face and forearms.

Carver unknotted the cloth. "Ribbons," he said, "lockets, keepsakes." He paused. "Are these all her rings?"

"All that she brought with her," said Purvis, swallowing a yawn.

"All? Then where are the rings she wore? For there are pale bands about her fingers and thumbs."

"What bands?"

"I will speak to the surgeon that called on her. If he says she had anything else, I will come here with the constables and we'll turn over every miserable inch of your room," said Carver.

"She did ask me to look after this for her," said Purvis dully. "Before she was took. I forgot, so I did."

Purvis pulled something off her own finger and dropped it onto the cloth. Carver snatched at it. It was a ring, larger than most, like a signet, with an oval, green stone carved into letters. The band was sterling silver. It was too big for the girl. Carver guessed she had worn it on her thumb. Briefly, he held it up to the bar of light from the slot that let air into the cellar. He squinted at the rim of the setting.

Carver put it down again, among the gauds and ribbons Nan had collected. The hangman stilled himself, and all his bluster and fierce energy he set aside. The women behind him fell into a dreary squabble that he heard no part of. He had retrieved enough sentimental tokens from the hands of the dead to feel no repugnance or shame, but here was one more thing, surely a strand in a long rope, winding and winding, that had caught the dead girl and would lead to another knot and a fatal fall. Winding and winding: and he thought of the girl, Nan, tripping merrily down the cracked steps before him, and here, in the quiet of the mortuary, he took up the strands again.

CONVICT LORE maintained that the first man to hang in Sydney Cove had been taken to a tree where the gaol now festered. Convict lore also held that a beam of that ironbark had been split and adzed for the first convict gallows, but then the same rumour related that the Devil himself had shown Captain Phillips the tree, which not even the soundest empiricist could refute. At noon, two more souls mounted that scaffold and tumbled to their doom. One, Gifford by name, kicked and choked and wheezed before he was stilled. The crowd on the hill hissed and jeered in disgust. The hangman, scowling, trapped the man's flailing legs and quieted him with a hard, sure tug and all his weight. Standing in the shadow of the scaffold, he looked out above the walls and saw two men lounging away from the main mass of onlookers. They had both broad-brimmed hats that hid their faces, coarse breeches, convict boots, and they alone seemed uninterested in the business of the gallows.

When his job was concluded, Carver passed by the warder's office as Abbott and Wilmot came out. Abbott was in a gleeful mood, and he laughed and clapped the hangman on the shoulder, and called him a good fellow for bringing in those Irish rats. Carver, hot and more haggard than usual, stared at him and did not speak until Abbott had passed down the corridor.

"What business does that damn fool have to put my name to it? It was a police raid." He looked at Wilmot, who shrugged.

"Don't mind him. He seeks to improve his office and impress the head warder. Hangings make the prisoners restive, and he will go out and find a few to beat, and pick one for the lash, for their suffering proves his resolve."

"It don't signify to me," said Carver. He moved off, paused, and looked around. "But here, I want to find the owner of a ring."

"What sort of ring?"

"A man's ring. Took off a whore. But she wore it on her thumb, so I'd say it's a gift from a fancy-man."

"Judge Foyle, could it be?" returned Wilmot, with a half-laugh.

"Who's Foyle?" said Carver sharply.

"Oremus Foyle? Why, he's father to half the bastards born in the town," said Wilmot with a leer. "At least, that's who the whores name in the register, for they mock him so. Frog Foyle: a madcap who drinks while he hears cases from the bench. The other half name the Reverend Marsden—for his hypocrisy."

"It has the look of a clerk's ring. There is dried ink around the setting," said Carver dubiously.

"For gauds and such, try a fence if it has been stolen, or a Shylock for pawning," said Wilmot, straightening his caps and settling his keys.

WHEN CARVER STEPPED out of the gaol, the heat had grown: close as the executioner's hood and vast as empire. The sky was shaded like slate near the horizon. Two men who had been lounging on Hangman's Hill with a view of the prison roused themselves. They made a fuss of fanning their faces with their hats, but they watched closely enough, as Carver ambled towards the foreshore.

Carver had thought first of the moneylenders who were drawn to the stray pickings of the shore. Soon he came within sight of the shipping yards, counting houses, chandlers' stores, the Customs House, quays, and piers of the crowded port.

On the waterfront, in the close heat, two men in low, wide hats appeared as from the shimmer of air. They walked without haste towards where Carver stood. The hangman faced the sky, as though waiting in vain for some cooler flourish of the breeze. Then, as the men came within fifty paces or so, they were revealed clearly. Carver stepped sharply away towards the sea wall. One of the men tapped the other roughly on the shoulder, and they broke into a run.

Carver dashed down the piled stones that made a rough flight of steps to the narrow shelf of rock and sand below the sea-wall. The ground was littered with a debris of broken sticks and oyster shells, green kelp, fractured barrel planks, and hanks of rope. Carver heard scuffling steps behind him. The hangman went with quick, sure steps. He twisted past little ketches and bumble-boats, moored on the strand, crossing a slipway slick with slime and ducking under the piers of a long jetty. At his back he made out pebbles and shells grinding, heavy breathing and curses, and he grinned.

But the heat stopped up the mouth and made his head spin. He got down in among the shadows of fishing boats pulled up close, piled with stinking nets, and waded out among the lapping waves. Still, the two men behind him came nearer. Carver crouched and pushed against the hull of a cutter. The footsteps faltered and then turned uncertainly, this way and that.

"What would you?" he called, his voice dispersed by the low water and the clustered boats.

"You're the hangman," came a voice.

"Since you saw me hang a man, I suppose I can't say no."

"The O'Doul wants something of you."

"You can tell the old hag that I can no more get her Callum out of the gaol than I got him in there."

There was another long pause, as though the speaker were catching his breath, but when the answer came the voice was nearer and softer. "That's not what she wants."

Carver pressed closer to the hull of the boat. Wavelets stirred sluggish about his ankles. "Then what the devil is this about?"

The voice came softly from the shore. "You know, you thieving mongrel."

"You're mad," said Carver, under his breath. "But to what purpose?"

The hangman hunched down and gathered in another breath of salt and rotting fish and wet wood. There were no more footsteps, only the one voice from the shore. Then Carver glanced up to the gunnels, even as he sensed a flicker above him, a variation in the immense sunlight. Carver reached up and grabbed at the man who loomed above him on the edge of the boat. His hand caught at a shirt and arm, and he hauled down. Carver twisted and the man plummeted into the shallow waters. Staggering backwards, catching the hull of the boat to steady himself, Carver kicked out, not knowing if he connected with seawater or flesh. Then he surged towards the shore.

Some eight or nine yards away, the other man who had occupied him while his companion crept from boat to boat kept watch on the strand. Carver noted the low hand covering the blade of a knife. Behind him, the man who had fallen sputtered and bellowed in rage.

Carver ran again, but this time with no thought to evasion or hiding, only speed, for he had guessed their business at last. The hot sun seemed like a hand on his chest, pushing him back.

He careened up a slipway and back onto the dusty track of the foreshore. Then he broke into a run again along the waterfront.

The midday glare had driven most souls inside. He glanced back to see the two men again, struggling to the top of the sea-wall. Carver turned uphill into the twist of lanes and little alleys. He pushed on, angling back towards George Street and the precincts of the gaol. Still he heard ragged breathing and cursing, echoing along the close walls of the warehouses around him.

Rising above the shoreline, alternately running and pausing in the meagre shadows to look behind, Carver made his way to his shack, jogging up the lane and past the timber yard. He had lost his hat, and his coat sat heavy with cloying sweat on his back.

The door was ajar. He pushed in. Mother O'Doul sat neatly at the head of his table, calm as a dowager aunt calling on relations. In front of her, under one crooked finger, was a tattered book. A thick-jointed man lurked by the hearth.

"You," said Carver, the breath burning in his throat.

The old woman tutted, "What time of day is this to be out?"

"That's not what you're looking for," husked Carver.

O'Doul sniffed and the edges of her mouth turned down. She flicked the pages of the coverless book. "No. Some theatrical dainty is this. It was well hid. But this is not the treasure of the man I take you for."

"Then you take me wrong," said Carver. "And not for the first time."

"Who said I was looking for such a thing?"

"You sent two fools to watch over me and distract me, while you conducted your burglary. They let the thing slip. You're looking for a thief."

"Hmm." The set of her mouth did not change, but the old woman's black, bird-like gaze still flicked about the room. "Have you any tea, Mr. Carver?"

"No."

"Men never think about the tea," O'Doul grumbled. "For ten years I went without a drop."

"No tea," Carver repeated. "Nor the other stuff."

The old woman looked up at Carver. "Do you mean to live like a blessed saint?"

"I mean to keep a clear head."

"That's not the hangman of old. Seamus!" barked the old woman. The big man with the broken nose sidled over to the board and turned back with three chipped cups.

"I'll thank you to keep your damned hands out of my cupboards," growled Carver.

"We won't stand on ceremony, will we?" said O'Doul. The cups were filled from a bottle in Seamus's care.

Carver suddenly felt his head aching, his knees tightened with the effort of his uphill run. He slumped at his own table. O'Doul nodded in satisfaction and beamed at him. Carver tipped the hot liquor to the back of his parched throat. "I swear I have nothing of yours," he said.

"You come like a spy into my homely house. You get my son arrested. You ask questions about murders and the Rats' Line, and claim to be in the service of the police magistrates—a hangman, a secret, prying fellow if ever I saw one. Saints forgive me, but I don't take your oath that easy."

"You've searched my house. Search me if you like—here." Carver stripped off his sopping coat and hurled it at Seamus, who was sipping delicately from his mug.

O'Doul raised a calming hand. "No. I don't expect you have it by."

"What do you want?" said Carver.

"You know well enough."

"Let's not talk as if we were both fools. It's too hot."

The old woman blinked slowly. "I wonder, that night when you brought the constables to my door, why you did not name me also."

Carver laughed. "Dare the wrath of a hundred Irishmen who already take me for an informer as well as hangman for turning their Mam in? I did you a turn. I expected a turn in return."

"What sort of turn?"

"What sort of thing are you missing?"

"Book. Not like this. Notes. Accounts. Ledger book." O'Doul pursed her mouth. "Or *leather* book, he called it, which makes no sense."

"So it's not your book. When was it taken?"

"Night ere last. But they want it back, and soon, something fierce, my boy."

"I'm not your boy. But perhaps we two can be of service to each other. What's in this book?"

The old woman gestured across the table. "There. Drink up again. I don't trust a man who won't take a friendly glass. Rum deadens the mind, but *ouskie* makes it burn clear."

The glass was filled, and Carver drank again with a single motion. O'Doul seemed distracted, meandering in her thoughts. "What's the point of it, I say. The English kept us in their rotting hulks for five years past the fens. And then they sent us here, to break the land or let it break us. Floods I saw, like God's own. Driftwood fifteen yards high in the trees. But we went back and turned the mud over and built our houses again. Ran horses. Brewed beer. Sometimes the governors give out land, and sometimes they take it back. We wept for the blessed martyrs and buried our babies and raised sons and daughters, and went on. Who dreams of the bare green hills and hunger, and English bayonets on the roads while we are here? What we have, it's too much to our profit to threaten for the want of a book or dead men's tales."

Carver's thoughts were running too rapidly. "Tea," he said. "And sweet English tobacco. And whiskey, and peppercorns and cloves, and white china, cotton, lace, you trade in it and smuggle it in. But there is this other trade, too. The Rats' Line, you called it—I heard you—my ears are sharp. Trade coming to you, every now and again, for those who can make the price, bodies going back to the Old Country. But now the one has put the other in danger, and you are mortal afraid for your little concern." He paused, while questions and guesses whirled in his head. He was too dry and sun-struck to think clearly.

O'Doul nodded, slowly.

"I'll put a stop to the questions," said Carver, "if you leave me be."

"Drink," said O'Doul. "When we have drunk three times in company, we are good as kin."

Seamus poured. Carver grasped the glass and swallowed. "But a little less than kind."

O'Doul did not correct him.

Carver slapped the glass down, and the old woman nodded once. "Agreed, then. You return that little book to me, and all the trouble between us will be forgotten."

"Tell me one thing," said Carver, turning the glass as though to screw it into the wood. "Did you do away with Staines because he asked questions about his headstrong Irish wife long gone with an English officer?"

O'Doul plucked up her shawl and made ready to stand. Seamus shifted to her shoulder. "No. He had a mind to ask some questions, and sent his man, Devers, in his stead. But Devers was no fool and knew where he shouldn't meddle. Unlike some I call to mind."

The old woman hobbled out of the shack. Carver said no farewell, but rose, and took up the book she had left behind, and then laid himself out on his hard bed. He heard O'Doul's voice raised in admonishment outside, but he closed his eyes and lay still, breathing very deeply, until the room seemed still again.

CHAPTER 10.

The Assignment System

A LINE OF CONVICTS, new from the transport and so lean and hobbling, uncertain of the ground that no longer heaved like the ocean, was herded up to the barracks at Hyde Park by soldiers and bayonets. A few stared in wonder at the white parrots and the hook-beaked ibises that strutted in the dirt before the barracks gate. It was late in the day, and many free convicts were sauntering in the street in the shadow of the building.

For the night they would be shackled again in some dim hall. And in the morning the inkwells would be uncapped, the blotters straightened, the registers opened, and the sheaves of forms set out, and three hundred men and women would be entered into the assignment system—name, place of birth, profession, charge, date of arrival, and sentence noted and inscribed with steel nibs, a binding stronger than forged steel.

Until then, the clerks were clambering down from their high stools and desks, buttoning their coats, knocking the dust off their cuffs, and coming out of the barracks.

Outside the barracks gate, Carver leaned against the walls and watched the dispersing clerks with some attention. He took notice of one or two men, and stopped a pair at last, darting sideward and presenting something with an open hand.

"What of the ring?" said the first of the two clerks, a portly man with no room left in him for breath or patience.

"Well, I won it at cards from a fellow who said he was a clerk in the government employ. And I thought, notwithstanding his losses, he might want to buy it back off me."

"Don't know it," said the first man. "It's a cheap gaud; no gentleman would hold such a thing in much regard,"

"Well, I thought it might be sentimental, like."

"Be off with you," snorted the clerk. "We cannot assist you."

But before Carver had turned away, the other clerk, who was younger and not so weary, laughed. "Pawn it if you want coin. Old Kennard will take such things."

Then the two clerks went on, and Carver closed his fist about the ring and glanced up at the high walls of the barracks. Impossible to know how many eyes looked warily back at him as he turned to go.

KENNARD, TRANSPORTED for receiving and forging notes, a lean, suspicious spider of a man, in no way reformed as a moneylender and money changer, glared at Carver and pinched the corner of his beard before he set the ring down. "You ain't come by that by way of a dead man's hand," he said, reluctant to phrase a question or statement.

"No," said Carver stonily. "Not yet. I don't want credit, only to know whose it is. Did you ever write out a ticket for this?"

Kennard hissed and clicked his tongue. "I've seen this ring, once or twice. Same fellow."

"Name of?"

Kennard barely glanced at his record book. "Sidmouthe."

"Where found?"

"How the Devil should I know? He clerks for the magistrate, Foyle, off and on. But he is a man with a habit as requires ready money on a regular basis, if you take my meaning."

"I'm not sure I do."

"The Chinaman's vice," said Kennard, with a grimace and a half wink.

"Thank-ee," said Carver. "I'll be on my way."

Kennard waved him off. He was already sorting through a pile of slips of paper before him, marking down little scratches in a ledger book. The late sun, yellow and dreary through the grimy windows of the pawnbroker's, gleamed in Carver's eye as he turned.

THE CLERKS AND COPYWRITERS, shipping agents and chandlers emerged at a certain hour from their dingy boarding houses and cottages about the cove and Darling Harbour, and, avoiding the barracks, the gaol, and the hospital, they traipsed along Princess and Fort Street, and lost themselves in lanes and public houses where the lights glimmered with a sheen of stale respectability. One such place was Mitford's, where the clerks played at backgammon and whist for pennies, often finding Dutch gilders or francs among the takings.

The night was well stewed when Carver entered. He lingered, eyeing the company and noting the comings and goings, before he made his way down the long room, past tables and settles, to a plain door at the far end. Carver did not trouble to knock but opened it and stepped through. There was nothing on the other side but a short passage and another door. No light had been set on this side, only a low glow beneath the other door. When Carver closed the door behind him, he groped, for a moment, to find the wall and guide himself to the other end.

He stopped and sniffed. There was something on the air other than the smoke of native ash, the aroma of boiled mutton and maize-meal. For a moment, in the dark, he looked down and breathed deeply, striving to piece together some recollection. Then the other door opened and a man in a threadbare coat brushed past him, muttering painfully, "...loose coppers, loose coopers, I had a few, but who calls?"

Carver stepped through the door before it closed. He was let not into another room but a courtyard or enclosure with a deep veranda. Stars and the partially illuminated moon hovered in the gulf between the wood-tiled roofs. Carver edged forward. The air was cool and still, but the thick, sweet, and cloying scent, like corrupted night-flowers, was strong and palpable.

A man sat on the top step, nodding, dressed half in convict weeds, but Carver ignored him. In the dim gap under the eaves, with only the odd gleam of a light behind a window to show anything, he saw a row of bodies, some reclining on their sides, some half-sitting, with tiny lights, reduced candles, flickering between them. A few filthy mats were also scattered across the planks. Close at hand, a woman crouched under a ship's lantern hung from a hook. Impossible to judge her age or height or frame, beneath a tangle of matted hair, but she gestured with a withered hand at a row of thin, long, clay pipes she had laid out on a bit of cloth. On her right was a closed chest, like an apothecary's.

"Light a pipe, dearie?" she said. "Forget yer troubles. Ginny will pack it with her special mix."

"I fancy I will," said Carver. He paused. "Is my mate Sidmouthe here already?"

The woman merely nodded down the row before she held out her hand. Once Carver had paid her, she turned to busy herself in her box. Only then did Carver realize that a baby was sleeping peacefully in a crate pressed against the wall behind her.

With pipe in hand, Carver edged along the darkened room, past soldiers and washerwomen, drovers, sealers, and labourers. His eye measured them and rejected them for their boots, their scarred hands, their stained shirts. But in the far corner, at ease, lay a tall man in the short, neat coat of a clerk, with loose white cuffs, dabbed with old spots of ink. He was of more than usual height, but with a heavy belly and spreading waist, so that his whole form, even lying on his side, tapered towards the head. His face was elongated, anchored by a pendulous, petulant lip. He put the stem of a pipe into his mouth and drew back the smoke.

Carver seated himself cautiously, with his back to the crumbling plaster. The opium pipe smouldered. He waited, marking the fluttering of the man's eyelids, the upward flick of the enlarged pupils.

"You're Sidmouthe, ain't yer," said Carver.

"A piece of him." The words rolled out, slurred and sonorous.

A dry smile touched the hangman's lips. "I have something of yours." He set the signet ring on the boards between them.

Sidmouthe's eyes widened, and then he looked away. "Oh. Is that mine?"

"I got it off a whore who said it was yours. Her man owed me."

"A Maid whom there were none to praise / And very few to love," Sidmouthe intoned.

Carver put the stem of the pipe between his teeth and stirred the scorching smoke in his mouth without inhaling. "You must have been sweet on her," he drawled.

Sidmouthe reached out and nudged the ring. His hand was limp, long fingered. *"But she is in her grave,"* he whispered, *"and, oh, / The difference to me!"*

"I didn't say you could have it yet," warned Carver.

"I haven't said it's mine yet," said Sidmouthe, drawing back.

Carver let the ring lie. The opium-eaters stirred around them. Carver heard a woman giggle, a man cough.

"Damnable hot," said Carver.

Sidmouthe shook his head. "Doggerel, sir," he murmured, slurring words. "Low terms, low subjects. Lacking the proper language of sentiment. I myself, sir, am a poet. My lines have appeared in the *Athenæum*. They were remarked upon. Remarked, I say."

"Pleased to hear it," said Carver affably.

"A low subject, all the same. I am not concerned with low subjects."

"But that subject told me a queer thing," Carver went on. "She had took it into her head that she was to go sailing home, when the time came. How could a common package like that think she could take passage from here?"

Sidmouthe sucked hungrily at the stem of his pipe. "Impossible. We none of us can leave here without the permission of the judges. We must escape in song, in verse, in dreams…in smoke, ha-hum, if you mark the conceit."

"She was most particular on this point. But that's what's peculiar." Carver leaned closer and his voice fell. "I had thought she had got the idea from her man, he being the boastful sort, and hiding from the constables on account of the suspicion that fell on him. But how could that be? He had once planned to escape, certainly, with a lady of my acquaintance, but no further than Port Middlebay. No. I think the girl gave the idea to him. But then, where did she get that, a street-walker?"

"It was indiscreet. She was too familiar. I had a fond thought for her, the maid, the winsome thing. Posies and ribbons and such. I gave her my ring to carry, for a keepsake. But she would speak to anyone." An oily tear rolled down the man's cheek. "Did I hang my little dolly for it? I can't recall."

Carver was motionless, wreathed in the smoke for a moment, but then he chuckled and moved to mop his forehead with his kerchief. "She was scorched in the fire after her man was hanged."

"The smoke, the lotus flower, makes these things seem so when they are not," mumbled Sidmouthe, turning and setting the pipe down. "The deed and the fancied deed are one and the same."

"Did you string up her man, though?' said Carver softly. "Were you jealous of your girl? Or was he too close to a particular truth?"

"Absurd," returned Sidmouthe. "We had an arrangement. Why, I let her keep my ring in token of my earnest affection."

"I don't believe you did kill him, or her. You don't have the hands for it. The rope would burn you. But you knew what she intended, who would get her onto a ship?"

Sidmouthe's pendulous mouth dropped into a frown. "It could not be done, the poor thing. The system would not permit it. The system is infinite, majestic, imperturbable. We are both men of the system. Let us not play false with each other, for you are Charon himself, the psychopomp, the shadowy usher."

Carver's head dropped. "I don't take your meaning."

Sidmouthe's eyes were closed, yet flickering and moving always. "I have seen you hone your craft within the walls of the old gaol, executioner. You are the fine point of the system, the shears that cut the last thread. All the rest of us line the path, but you open the trapdoor and Godspeed!"

"I don't take no notice of the system. I do the necessary, and a hundred other men make the choice before me."

"You hypocrite," said Sidmouthe, pushing out each word with his thick tongue. "You presume upon the system and set to its work. We all presume on the system. And make no account of how it presumes on us."

Carver eased closer to Sidmouthe, placed one hand on his shoulder and brought his mouth towards the man's ear. "Since you know who I am, I swear I will smother you right here, and not one of these lotus-eaters will raise a finger or remember who passed, unless you speak quick and true. Who do you clerk for? Whose work do you do, come to that?"

"I am clerk of the court to the right honourable Justice Foyle, of the New South Wales magistrates. Justice Foyle. *Pffft!* It don't help you to know that, but there it is."

"Froggy Foyle? Do you take me for a fool? A drunkard, aye, to sign anything you set before him. But who oversees the matter?"

"I cannot say."

"Think again. Remember what I may do."

"You are still in more danger than I. You have roused the serpent unawares, and its sting is working in you."

"I ain't got your precious book, if that's what you mean, and O'Doul knows it," rasped Carver.

"What book?" said Sidmouthe.

"Your 'leather book'; that's what the old woman called it."

"Ha-hee." Sidmouthe giggled. "Leather book. That's droll. The ignorant old crone. You wouldn't be here at this hour if you were the one who knew where it was."

"Wake up!" snapped Carver. "Shall I tell you what I know?"

But Sidmouthe mumbled, "A poet sir, poesy smothered under cerulean skies, verily, liberty's fair branch transplanted to dusty shores..."

Scowling, Carver sat up again. "Leather book she called it, but the old Irish dame is half-deaf anyhow, and just repeating what she heard without understanding. But what if I said *Lethe*? Is that a proper poetic figure?"

Sidmouthe opened one wondering eye. "Nonsense. Ridiculous."

"But near enough for a man of your temperament. The river of forgetfulness. Clerks and forgers, gentleman convicts. Hades, indeed!" Carver wiped his mouth. "It's you who turn the system. Ticket-of-leave, concession, assignment, pardon. All those slips of paper stronger than walls. A pardon, the right to return home, what would that be worth to a convict who had the means and the yearning to get away, who was cheated by the settlers and the soldiers and the governor? O'Doul is your smuggler, your voice among the convicts, but you are the systematic men, and the system is yours to turn to any purpose. So I hazard that you make note of all these names in your ledger, your precious Lethe book. But someone has taken it. The same one as killed Staines and hanged his man Devers, and you are all astir and all frightened, and desperate to have your secret record back, of all those you have spirited across Lethe."

Sidmouthe groaned and turned. "Phantoms, black phantoms, gathered to torment me!"

"Wake up, damn you!" said Carver. "Who provides you with ships, berths, captains who won't look too closely at one more passenger? Not the Irish, I'm sure. They send you the convicts, and you turned to them to help find your lost book. But who is it you work for, there?"

Sidmouthe reached for the pipe again, and Carver slapped it out of his limp hand. "I tell you," said Sidmouthe, slurring and drooping, "he don't know about it, he's too far away, and as long as he don't know it's lost, we're safe."

"Whom do you mean?"

"But the other one, he won't be stayed, resolution and ruin, madness and blood, he won't be stayed."

"Which other one?"

Sidmouthe's eyes opened, but he looked beyond the opening into the blank, hot night. "I expect we shall all be hanged for it. What an artist dies in me. I have no more particulars. Good night, good night."

Sidmouthe closed his eyes again. Carver shook him hard, but a thin line of drool descended from the clerk's slack mouth.

The hangman rose laboriously and reeled to the railing, famished for fresher air and a clear view. The luminous spread of stars above the courtyard dazed him. He stalked slowly back to the common-room, and the fug of smoke and salt-beef surrounded him. Hastily, he bought a tobacco pipe and a gill of rum, and settled himself at the back of the room, among the clatter of backgammon tiles and skittles. He lit the pipe and drew on it hurriedly, to cleanse his mouth, but the rum went untasted.

"I make no account of the system," he repeated to himself. But his thoughts roamed from the drowsing clerk in his poppy dreams to the black enclosure of the hulks, to an Old Bailey courtroom, and the scrawl of faces at the dock: brought to the system, rendered by the system, and set down in the lists of the system. For the system raises prison walls and gallows, and sets ships upon the sea and flourishes in thin soil at the edge of the world. Convicts and free men alike invoke the system and hold it in awe whether they respect or abhor it. And mark how it convinces us that the system alone is material, and we are but scribbles, annotations, and means to its ends.

• • •

IN THIS DOUR frame of mind, Carver watched an hour or more pass by the rickety Dutch clock hung over the mantelpiece. He heard the faint reverberation of the artillery piece at the barracks: it was after curfew, but no one in the room seemed inclined to finish their drinks, and the games, the flutter of cards and passing of coins, went on. As soon as the sound of the gun had faded, Sidmouthe appeared at the rear door. He had straightened his topcoat and put on his hat. The clerk slipped his watch into his pocket and settled the fob in place. Carver looked down, but the smoke was thick about him and he had little fear of being seen. After Sidmouthe left, Carver glanced out of the window to judge in which direction he started, and then followed.

At this hour the streets were dim and the moon a discarded section of orange peel. Carver sauntered uphill, with his eye on the elongated figure of Sidmouthe. There were still persons abroad: sailors; soldiers, some on horses; furtive convicts and their women. In the faint light their features blurred, became pale and grey as the moonlight reflected off the dust of the day. Bats fluttered overhead. A spider, with legs long enough to span a saucer, scuttled along the rutted road in front of Carver.

At the first corner, before an inn, Sidmouthe turned back to scan the road. Carver did not check his motion but walked on steadily, only veering a little to make for a side lane. He guessed that Sidmouthe, in the strong lights of the public rooms, could not see his features on the darker road. When they started again, Carver buttoned his coat despite the heat, for it was blacker than his shirt. In this way they went on: at the next corner, Sidmouthe paused again, and Carver drew back into the shadows of a stable doors. They left the region of warehouses and settler cottages behind, moving into the scatter of poor shacks on the outskirts of the town, where the dogs barked and red-brown mongrels roamed among the little gardens and fenced patches of earth.

Carver guessed which way Sidmouthe was walking. It was not the usual path, from the gaol or the hospital, but he was climbing toward the burial-grounds. Carver risked drawing a little nearer. Only starlight and the sickle moon gave a weak illumination to the road up here. A few scattered and immaterial clouds sometimes veiled the stars.

Sidmouthe slowed and became more cautious, checking his pace as the graves became evident, a jumble of rotting wooden crosses and rough-cut stones tumbling in prickly array down the even slopes of the hill. Carver shortened his step and fell back until he strained to see the other man, sometimes detecting only the flicker of Sidmouthe's shirt-cuffs. But the clerk's eyes were bad. Sometimes he kicked and stumbled over rocks; sometimes he paused, and Carver imagined he was repeating odd lines of poetry or elaborate curses under his breath. A low wind, freighted with the heat of the plains, shifted over the dry weeds and long grass, stirring fragments of bark and hard, withered leaves.

Sidmouthe turned along the dirt track, and Carver grinned to himself, for he was certain where the other man was heading. Before executions had been cooped up within the gaol walls, on account of the public disorder they provoked, the town gallows had stood on the edge of the cemetery, for the convenience of the magistrates, the gaoler, and presumably the gravedigger. Carver slipped away from the road among the gravestones. Loose gravel and leaves ground under his boots. He bent closer to the earth as he picked his way between the graves. Not far from him, he heard a snort, a yelp, and one of the wild dogs that lurked and scavenged around the town sent up a yipping howl.

It was too dark to read the inscriptions on the masonry and wooden markers as he passed. They died by all means here—by fire and flood, by fever and hunger, by the constable's bullet and native spear; they tumbled drunk into the sea or shuddered at the end of the noose, and made silent company in the hangman's mind. But Carver paused often and crouched when he heard leaves rattle in the wind or the dogs hacking, while he drew closer to the skeleton of the old gallows-tree.

Sidmouthe paced and kicked at stones by the rotting beams. Sometimes he paused and tilted his head back, and Carver speculated he was stealing sips from a flask. Clouds, thin as gossamer, sometimes crossed the path of the moon or dimmed a handful of stars. Carver eased himself down in the shadow of a tombstone, breathing softly. Peering out, he saw a sudden, quick flare of yellow light—the clerk had struck a lucifer to illuminate the dial of his pocket watch. Carver rested on one knee and willed himself silent and still.

A horseman came riding up from the town. The animal picked its way reluctantly along the track and snickered at whatever it sensed on the wind. The rider was briefly picked out, a shadow against the glimmer of the harbour and the sprinkling of ship's lights, now utterly unseen as he passed a stand of ragged red gums. Sidmouthe turned at the sound of hoofbeats, and then the rider dismounted: a grey incoherence leading the greater mass of the horse.

Carver heard Sidmouthe call a low *halloo*. The other man did not answer, but advanced nearer the ruined gallows.

Carver began to edge forward, crouched, placing his hands on the ground, his back bowed and his thighs tense. Grass rustled and the coarse stalks caught at him. He strained to keep low. Sidmouthe and the stranger were talking, but the wind faltered and suppressed whole phrases and brought odd words back to him: "—do you mean...book...all recorded—"

"She is not there!" said the stranger with a strange emphasis: sadness, anger.

"I cannot authorize a higher payment," Sidmouthe replied. His voice was rolling, almost mournful.

The stranger's response was broken by the yapping of a dog.

Carver dropped to the ground. The earth was warm and smelled sharp. There was no way forward for him but to cross a patch of open ground, but a cloud had moved away from the moon, like a lady's shawl slipping from her shoulder. Heat made him pant. His breath sounded raw and loud in his ears. Sidmouthe mumbled something, and the stranger spoke again in hard, emphatic tones.

Carver raised himself to run, and then he heard leaves behind him cracking and the rattle of long grasses disturbed. Startled, he jerked around. From between two graves slunk one of the yellow mongrels, the mix of English dogs and dingo, that roamed the margins of the town after dark. The beast cocked its head, and its blank eyes met Carver's. Carver gritted his teeth, almost in a snarl. The dog began to yelp, not bark, but a sound higher and quicker, and from other corners of the graveyard came more whines and bays. Carver fumbled for some stone to throw at it.

"Who's there?" he heard Sidmouthe call.

Carver looked back. Sidmouthe was a few steps away from the other man, staring into the dark. Then a light flared in the clerk's hand, for he had struck one of his matches and held it high, like a child seeking to illuminate the night.

The figure behind him hissed, "Liar—who's there? Police!"

Sidmouthe turned, stuttering denial, and the match went out in his hand. The other man stepped forward with a single, graceful skip as Carver rose to his feet and bellowed a warning—for which man he never knew: "Hold!"

Sidmouthe fell to his knees, and the other man separated from him like a shadow severed from the object that cast it, and something small and hard fell to the ground. Carver ran, heedless of the broken ground, but the shadow had already caught at his horse's reins and kicked up into the saddle.

The beast wheeled, whinnied, and jumped towards the cart-track. Carver stopped by the broken gallows.

There was a whimper behind him. "I am slain," whispered Sidmouthe.

"You are a damn fool," said the hangman bitterly, as he watched the horse gallop down the dark slope from the graveyard. "What possessed you to call out?"

"Have some pity, man." A groan, half-swallowed, squirmed out of Sidmouthe.

Carver turned. "A hangman's pity is a quick ending."

He saw Sidmouthe topple to his side, with his legs drawn up, as he had seen the man lying, hours before, in the opium den. Swiftly, Carver knelt. A knife gleamed darkly on the ground: a common sailor's thing. Sidmouthe held up a hand, as if to push him away.

"I am to die here," said the clerk in wonder and pain.

"Folly," said Carver briskly. "I have seen lashed men shed as much blood and more, and walk away."

Sidmouthe let his hand fall.

"Who did this?" said Carver.

"Hospital," croaked Sidmouthe.

"Soon enough. Where is the book?"

"He would not take it. They *are* all there," Sidmouthe added, petulant, like a student corrected in class.

"*Who* are all there?"

"All the names." Sidmouthe waved weakly at the ranks of the burial-ground. His mouth opened and closed.

"Did you know his face?" pressed Carver.

"She's not there," mumbled Sidmouthe. "Why did you interfere? I meant nothing by the light. All in order. Kindly fetch me my pipe."

"What name?"

Sidmouthe stared without expectation at the broken ground beneath the gallows. He did not answer.

The hangman rocked back and sat on the earth, and covered his head with his hands, and the dry wind from the plain pushed over him, and the stars showed him nothing.

CHAPTER II.

Before the Examining Magistrate

THE CELL WAS dim and sweltering, a void without time. Carver lay on the floor with his coat folded under his head and his eyes fixed on the ceiling, as though reading a text in the cracks and fly-spots there. Sometimes his lips twitched, as words and thoughts rose and fell. His breathing was low and rapid.

At length, he heard a key worked in the lock and the bolts shooting. Ellington appeared at the door, ill-defined in his grey uniform.

"Get up, man," he said. "You are called."

Carver scowled and raised his head slightly. Ellington had grown his beard longer lately and trimmed it square beneath the chin, rendering his tapered face more extensive and severe.

"Be patient, corporal," said Carver. "I'm known for my punctuality."

"That's sergeant," barked Ellington. "And I ain't known for my patience."

Carver hoisted his back off the floor and folded his legs. He looked up at Ellington with hooded eyes. "Promotion, is it? And all puffed up with it. But I recall where you started. You may set your sergeant's bluster aside with me."

Ellington glanced to either side, and let his voice fall. "I *am* promoted, and I mean to make a good by it."

"Fair enough. Every man must make his way by the rules." With a grunt of effort, Carver pushed himself to his feet and steadied himself by the wall. "Until he stumbles."

ELLINGTON USHERED Carver into the police magistrate's court. Fitchett was seated at his desk behind the long partition, and the clerk of the court was in the box to his right. But there was no bench for the jury, simply a bar for the prisoner, and a table with four spindly chairs in front. It was not yet midday, but the square, neat room was hazy with dust, darkened by the severe wainscoting.

Carver broke his step and halted by the doors. "Is this an arraignment?"

"In light of last night's events, you are to be examined before the bench," said Fitchett. His voice rang high and sharp in the empty room.

"Is this how you generally take evidence?" said Carver.

"It is how I shall take your evidence," snapped Fitchett. "You will be charged if you do not satisfy me."

Carver cocked his head. "Charged with what?"

"Murder."

"You mean the dead clerk."

"One of her majesty's faithful servants."

Ellington planted a hand between his shoulders, and Carver marched up to the bar.

"There's no charge to make," said Carver. "Good God, man! I raised the hue and cry myself."

Fitchett sucked at his front teeth and glanced at his clerk, a small man with a straggling grey beard, a stoop, and perpetual asthma. "I sent you forth," he said, framing each word for the clerk's busy pen, "as any informant should, to make inquiries respecting the deaths of two men, Matthew Staines and Ralph Devers, one of whom there were already witnesses to attest to an altercation and threats between you, and you were found, shirt bloodied, with bloodied knife in hand, two hundred yards from the gallows, where another man, stabbed, had breathed his last. I therefore advise you heed all my questions and answer most fully."

"If that's the way of it," returned Carver, "I had blood on my shirt because I tended poor Sidmouthe as he died. And I picked up the knife his killer left behind as evidence. And if your constable thought to look, my hand would cover the marks of blood on the handle, for my hand is broader than that of the man who struck the blow. So I say again, there is no charge to answer."

"How did the perpetrator get away, since you were nearby?"

"He had a horse."

"A gentleman's horse?"

"A horse that could be got from any stables along the way," said Carver, sullen.

"And thus he got away from you."

"That's the way of it."

"Three deaths, and your stamp on all of them," hissed Fitchett.

"Four," said Carver under his breath. "You do forget: four."

Fitchett brushed his words aside and leaned forward from the desk. "And while in my confidential service, it pleases you to meet with my wife and parade with her in public, among the highest society of our colony, and question a respected officer of the corps. My wife, on police business! With a felon."

"Who told you that?"

"An individual of excellent probity and standing."

"If it's a question of your wife," said Carver, "she is a great deal sharper than you are, sir, and therefore her opinions are worth standing by."

"You will strike the last reference to my wife. What I said as well," said Fitchett to the clerk.

Fitchett and Carver watched, with odd fascination, as the clerk dipped his pen again and drew four lines across the paper.

"I should have you flogged," Fitchett resumed wearily, "—don't write that!"

The pen paused. Carver looked up. "Would you know who the murderer is or no?"

"Do you have a name?"

"No name. But I can begin to describe something of the man now."

"Whom did you see?"

"It was too dark. But I make him out him all the same, and the little steps that led him there."

Fitchett rested his hand on his closed fist. "Do not prevaricate."

"I don't mean to trouble the bench," said Carver, "but hear me out."

There was silence in the dim, cool room. The clerk paused to blot his writing sheet. Men passed outside the courtroom door.

"I know what sort of man your murderer is. I know what he has done, and where he is going," said Carver.

"Pray continue," said Fitchett acidly.

"He's handy with a knife. A sailor's knife, mark. Knows how to cut a throat. And he knows how to tie a rope tidily, though he tried to trick us with a hangman's noose and the thirteen turns I don't use. Therefore, say a sailor, not a convict, a stranger in Sydney Cove. They picked a sailor for the task. Someone who has the power to come and go."

"Say a sailor, if you will. But a sailor for what purpose?"

"Because old Staines, maybe he thought to marry again, or maybe he just wanted to know, but he started to look into the business of his missing wife, the Irish political who ran away with a soldier—yes, the selfsame story I called on your wife to unearth—and he started to ask questions that folks here did not want answered."

"Such as?"

"How does a convict step on an English ship bound for London without being discovered as a stowaway? How do they escape this great prison at the end of the world?"

"Speak slowly, so that the clerk may make note of your words."

"Well," said Carver. "That's the matter. That's the question that got old Staines killed for his troubles. And the man he sent out to ask that question was a man he thought he could trust. A convict. A loyal servant. His overseer."

"I see," said Fitchett. "Then how did this other man, Sidmouthe, come into it?"

"He's the key to it, ain't he?" said Carver, warming to this task. "All your clerks and copyists and private secretaries. The invisible men behind the assignment system, writing it all down."

Carver paused. The clerk at the table serenely dipped his pen in the inkwell, and raised the quill again. The hangman looked down.

"Ticket of leave: they write it out; conditional pardon: they write it out; ship's manifest, the convict lists, death notices—from the colonial secretary down—they write it out and keep the copy fair."

Fitchett shook his head and drew up, as though a broad black spider had run suddenly across his desk. "You mean convicts are dealing in forged papers?"

"Aye, your reports and tickets and registers, heaps of papers, the whole colony cosseted in them."

Fitchett shook his head. "Impossible. If this were so, if this man Sidmouthe was behind it, why is he dead also?"

"He's dead because he's a secretary, not a cutthroat. He hired another man to do his dirty job with Staines and Devers. But the job was ill-conceived and the man left his marks everywhere, and so the magistrates decline to hang the wrong woman and don't stop hunting. Constables are asking questions. They arrest a clutch of smugglers. And Carver, the executioner, is on their trail. And your sailor thinks to himself that he can profit farther yet by two murders and a theft."

"A falling out between thieves," said the magistrate quickly.

"In my experience, it always comes to bloodshed between such men."

"And a theft, you say."

"A book. A record. The trail of a systematic man. A record of all the false names and false papers, kept by Sidmouthe."

Fitchett seemed frozen through the spine, but the sides of his nostrils twitched. "Stolen, I take it, by your murderer, in hopes of gaining a hold over Sidmouthe and his associates."

Carver tapped the side of his nose. "Your Honour has it exactly."

"There. Do not blot that last remark," said Fitchett. The magistrate leaned forward. "We must have that book. We must have every name therein."

Carver shrugged. "The murderer has it."

"And where is this murderer?"

"Gone, I expect."

"Gone. Where gone? Say at once."

"Think on it. Gone to his ship or another." Carver nodded towards the shore. "Sailed for England with his stolen book, I should imagine."

"Guesses. Speculation. How do you know?"

"What else could he do? He thinks he has been betrayed to the police. That's why he killed poor Sidmouthe, because he took me for the police. What would you do, except run for it?"

"Describe the man. He shall be stopped at his next port."

"I cannot."

"You are lying."

"It was dark. I could not see him."

"Fifty lashes will repair your recall."

"Make it a hundred lashes, and you will see your answer cannot be whipped out."

Fitchett clenched his fist and straightened the fingers one by one a moment later. His eyes remained on Carver, and his thin lips pressed on each other and retracted while he stared. The hangman faced the magistrate's chair with his head raised.

"I fail to see how you are any more use to this court," said Fitchett. "You will be dismissed from your office. You will return to your own company of convicts."

"I said I couldn't describe your man. But I have seen his frame. I know his voice."

"What do you mean by that?"

"I mean, if you give me leave to follow him, I will bring him down."

Fitchett shuddered. "Leave to follow. Leave to depart the colony, you mean. Leave to go where you will. You are mad. Take him back to the cells. I shall contemplate charges shortly."

Ellington, roused from his wait by the doors, stepped forward.

"But you want that book, don't you?" said the hangman.

Fitchett sighed. "You mean the secret memorandum that you claim the clerk maintained?"

"I mean the felons that escaped with false names; the clerks that wrote out papers for them; the magistrates that signed for them unawares; the ships they sailed on; the ports they went to. How many gone under your watch, escaped transportation, thumbing their noses at you? All the busy rats under the rotten boards beneath your bloody bench."

"We have only your testimony that such a book exists."

"That can be mended. I can prove that there was a book and a sailor, if you take these wretched shackles off."

"More boasting." Fitchett touched a fingertip to his temple. "I do perceive you lie more than any other convict I have ever had before me."

"Put it to the test, and you shall have the murderer and the book before this bench. And you will have some notice then, I say. Position, prestige, in the governor's eyes."

The magistrate looked down. Carver saw the man's eyes moving aimlessly along the papers before him. "I shall hold you in contempt if you withhold but one word from this court which is material to our ends."

"I withhold nothing. I can't find your book or your murderer from a cell. My hand is made, and now I must play it."

Ellington watched the two men. The magistrate, shifting on his bench, agitated and rigid in anger, and the hangman, outwardly composed as though standing on the gallows before the baying tribe of convicts and settlers. Yet the hangman's breathing was fever-rapid also.

"You will be remanded for one day. The sergeant will go with you everywhere. Bring me proof that will satisfy me on all points, or I will have you lashed to ribbons and you will answer a murder charge."

Carver nodded sharply. "That's settled." He leaned across the bar and offered his hand to the man behind the high bench. "My hand upon it. No? We'll set to it, well enough. Bustle! The dead will wait for us, but the tides won't."

Carver turned and hurried out of the court, drawing Ellington into his wake.

Fitchett rose from his chair, sighed, and then drew a thin hand across his scalp. "Have you written all that?" he asked the clerk.

"I did, sir. For the most part. He speaks rather fast, that hangman."

"He is too familiar by half," said the magistrate. He shuffled away from the chair, took a half pace back. "Too familiar. Give me your notes. I do not think it proper to record what has passed here. These are not commonplace matters."

CHAPTER 12.

Obsequies for a Clerk

CARVER STRODE ALONG the waterfront, and Sergeant Ellington dogged his heels.

"That was a fine farmyard tale you spun for His Honour," remarked the policeman.

"A farmyard tale," returned Carver calmly.

"Of a cock and a bull," snarled Ellington.

Carver looked up. A fresh breeze sported along the shore, and clouds mounted and toppled in grey hosts above the headlands. His pace did not alter a beat. "So you say. But all your police and informers are no closer to a murderer's heels."

"And all felons lie," said Ellington. "The only thing I can't fathom is why you're so set on getting yourself on an English ship, when you could stay ashore and sport with the magistrate's fine filly of a wife."

Carver took no pause but turned smartly on his toes, sure as a sailor on deck as a fishing ketch turns, and he punched, low and quick, catching Ellington under the chin, so the man cried out and stumbled backwards, to sprawl on the ground with a howl of surprise.

"Say those words again," said Carver, "and by God a grey tunic and red piping will be no shield from a drubbing."

Ellington pulled himself upright and cradled his jaw. "Lay hands on me again, and you will taste the lash, and worse. You may cozen Fitchett, but once a brute, always a brute. You cannot walk away from the gallows."

"Get up," said Carver. "There's work to be done."

"A fool's errand."

Carver crouched and looked at the constable as though to assess his handiwork more fairly. "Do you not see that there's a thread that binds it all, from the emancipist to the magistrate's clerk? Do you think that wily cove Sidmouthe provided his services free of charge? No. There's tin in this, a lot of tin, and if the dead don't interest you, then who's got the money should. For they'll all come, looking for a scent of the book. Or wondering who'll betray the other first. Sidmouthe may have spent the better part of his gains on harlots and opium, but they will come to spy on each other. Now, the day's turning, there's foul weather on the horizon, and we have work to do. This Sidmouthe, he clerked for a beak, did he not?"

Ellington lurched to his feet. "Justice Foyle."

"The same. And I expect they'll be burying his poor murdered clerk shortly, and he will have to pay his respects." Carver rose and shook his head as he rubbed his knuckles. "The Frog's man. See you, a drunken master and a clever servant. All the stamps, seals, and forms he would need. Well, there's one way into it."

"Your temper is still hasty," said Ellington. "I'll see you twisting under the cat yet."

"Devilish hot, ain't it?" returned Carver. "I doubt they will linger long about setting Master Sidmouthe to rest—let's go."

THE HEAT GREW as they trudged away from the waterside, until it seemed to hold the face as with feverish hands. Ellington, in his woolen suit, panted as he shuffled behind Carver. The hangman worked no less, and stopped periodically to mop his brow. The church stood to the west of the burial grounds, a heap of sandstone blocks and finials thrown up by the last governor in place of a rickety wooden chapel. Carver and Ellington gathered themselves in the shade of the little postern gate with its narrow canopy. The scene was silent, though insects buzzed in the thin yellow grass outside.

"We wait out of sight," said Carver. "Mark who attends."

"What for?"

"For the scroungers and schemers, for the rats and crows."

Carver tugged at Ellington's sleeve and they drew away to the scant shadow of a cottage on the other side of the crossroads. The hearse came first, from the hospital morgue. Black plumes drooped on the horse's head, and the beast plodded with its nose close to the dust. Behind came the mourner-in-chief, Justice Foyle, with his coat open and his neck-tie crumpled, disordered by grief and rum in equal measures. Foyle had been handsome and young, but now his nose and cheeks were blotched and his wide mouth opened and closed as if with a spasm. He leaned against a stout, red-faced woman clutching a parasol. Behind came half a dozen clerks of the Colonial Secretary's Office, in canvas coats with black crêpe attached to arms and hats, like so many grim little banners of a ragtag army, striving to be sombre and flagging in the heat. After this slouched a line of convicts and settlers, and some boys kicking at stones in the dust, drawn by the novelty, presumably, of a man murdered in view of the town and the culprit not known. A mournful band, led by a dismal clarinet, shuffled in their centre.

"Is that it?" said Ellington, spitting in the dust.

"No," returned Carver, leaning forward. "That old baggage there is Mother O'Doul. You have her favoured son in lockup for smuggling. Watch her closely. The O'Douls have a hand in this. Why would she be here elsewise?"

The old woman came hobbling at the back of the train, with a young woman to steer her. Carver marked Seamus a few steps behind.

The horses stopped, and the rest of the cortège stood coughing and wiping their faces in the roiling dust, while six clerks stepped forward to heave Sidmouthe's casket off the cart.

A fine carriage, with polished panels and two high-stepping horses, slowed and stopped in the road, but the window remained closed.

Carver edged forward. "I know that carriage. I have seen it before. Outside the grounds of Government House, I think."

With loping strides he crossed the dusty intersection and jumped onto the standing board of the carriage. The equipage shook, and Carver swayed, trying to catch a glimpse between the leather blinds. The driver shouted, and the long whip in his hands flicked towards Carver, who dropped to the ground and skipped away. Then, the carriage drew off.

"Who was that?" said Ellington, panting as he approached.

"MacNeish," said Carver. "An officer of the corps, retired, with no business being here. Let us get nearer."

The chapel bell rang, like a small boy banging a stone against a pipe. Six or seven women in dubious dress appeared and were frowned at by the verger. Carver pushed inside and forced his way to the front rows. O'Doul was seated on a little pillow, scowling rigidly at the Anglican hymnal. Carver caught her eye, and gave the old woman a tip and a wink. O'Doul did not nod back, but her mouth closed up by a degree.

The Reverend Honeychair presided, scattering platitudes while the streetwalkers and doxies in the last rows dabbed at their eyes. Ellington sang loudly and glowered at the hangman, who seemed perfectly placid and paid little attention to the congregation.

Outside, under a mottled sky befouled by clouds, they lowered Sidmouthe into the hard ground and scattered the red earth upon him.

"Have we seen enough?" whispered Ellington, wiping his neck with his sleeve.

"Not quite," muttered Carver. "There will be the wake, mind. Watch out for the ones that watch each other."

With the obsequies complete, the mob of clerks, law-writers, whores, and free-convicts, fanning themselves with hats and led by the clarinet, moved down to the last public house on Market Street, the Magpie, to a service of oysters, small beer, and sour rum. One or two half-lines of poetry were declaimed, to general approval. Ellington's cap had grown scratchy and his head ached. Justice Foyle waxed maudlin at the little table near the hearth. Carver talked for some time with a modest clerk, but all Ellington overheard was some chatter over the fine points of a ticket-of-leave, Certificate of Freedom, and the text and paper and seals of a pardon. The women became shrill. He could no longer see if O'Doul lingered. Carver sat at the magistrate's table and raised a tumbler to his lips.

The stale room roared and pitched like a ship at sea. A woman pulled at the front of Ellington's coat.

"'Ere, what are you about when another good man's been killed and the murderer ain't found?"

Ellington looked down. "We'll find him, never you mind."

But two others had pushed in around him. "How will you find him?"

"What's his name?"

"What right 'ave you drinking here, constable, while the fellow's barely in the ground?"

"I am making inquiries," he said.

"Questions, here? Why, he thinks it's one of us!"

"Mongrel!"

"Informer! Spy!"

Ellington put a hand to the shoulder of the first woman to ease her aside and was shoved in the chest for his troubles. He stumbled over a man on a stool behind him, and held up his arms to the angry women. Stepping aside, Ellington looked around the crowded room.

The executioner was gone.

• • •

IN THE MORNING, when the shadows were long and cool, and only the servants were stirring indoors, Mrs. Fitchett went into her garden. The garden was walled not against animals but as a deterrent to convicts. The paths were of coarse sand and crushed shell, laid out neatly and squarely, separating the banks of vegetables, lettuces, carrots, and tomatoes; the irises and marigolds that she loved; and the green kitchen herbs—parsley, mint, and lemon balm. Lemon and orange trees, and the rare, strange fruits her convict servants had brought her provided shade. Antonia passed between the towering foxgloves, and the air about her was fragrant and gentled.

A man was standing in the shadow of the ash at the far end of the garden.

"I am not helpless," she said. "You shall not offer me harm."

"Nor do I mean to." Gabriel Carver stepped forward.

She did not fall back. Her hands went to her sides. "What is this?" she hissed. "My husband and his men have been hunting for you all night."

"I must bring your husband a man and a ship. I cannot find either with a constable trotting at my heels."

"You lead them a merry chase, I expect."

Carver grinned crookedly. "I do."

"And am I to dance for you too? What tale will you spin me when you have gulled the magistrate and the sergeant?"

"There is no tale for you. A man must have a calm place to think. And I would see you again."

Her nostrils drew together. "You cannot stop here. Someone will see you. I was your champion. I persuaded Archie of your abilities. I took you into society, exposed myself to gossip and rumour."

Carver looked down at his black boots on the pale path, the scattering of petals. "Why so, I wonder."

"Why so?" she exclaimed. "It is so dull to be the sensible magistrate's wife, world without end. You present a conundrum, should I not take an interest and find a little freedom in that?"

"Then will you help me resolve it still?"

She faltered. "There is as close a watch on me as any convict under guard."

"Make your excuses. Come down to Cockle Bay, at midday, alone. I shall explain then, as well as I can."

"And how should I do that?

Carver raised his hand as though to touch her face, and she did not flinch. "You're a clever woman," he said. "I trust you'll find a way."

He moved quickly, for such a man. In a moment he had pushed himself up along a bent apple tree, thrown an arm across the wall, and disappeared.

"Well," she said, dabbing at her face. "'Clever woman,' indeed! Presumptuous man."

She looked over the lines of her garden and tried to order her thoughts and her racing heart. The English trees that she cherished were thirsty. The other plants gleamed and raised heavy leaves to the sun. Was it possible to imagine order without severity, discipline without brutality, here in the shadow of murder and the lash and the hangman's knot? *Make small things sensible*, she thought to herself. She wiped her face again and went to fetch the watering pail.

ANTONIA FITCHETT, who had once been Miss Fairchild, tripped down the dirt track towards Cockle Bay, and for this moment her senses dilated, expansive as the sky, and she thought that this was what it must be to be a prisoner released, to finish a sentence or gain the governor's pardon, and take possession of a few free steps. She was dressed in her oldest dress, like a colonist's housekeeper, and had taken a shawl even her maid thought too shabby to keep. The breeze was in her hair, and it lightened her.

At least a dozen small boats, some little more than cockle-boats or native canoes, were drawn up along the shore, boats the convicts and free settlers used for fishing, for trade along the harbour, and for outings. Near one of them stood a familiar figure, and she made for that.

"Good afternoon, Mr. Carver," she said.

"How d'you do?" he returned, with a tip of his head. He gestured to the slim boat behind him. "Will you come out with me?"

"I shall, though half the constables in Sydney are on the lookout for you."

"Only half?" he said, grinning. "That is not as flattering as I had thought. Though it is better we were away."

She picked up her skirts to step out to the boat once he had floated it. He offered to lift her, but she waved him off.

Rowing, he said, "You do not regret meeting me this way?"

"I don't believe I shall, if you answer me plainly."

His mouth quirked. "And what plain answers may I provide?" They were out on the great basin of the harbour. The waves shimmered, and the wind, hot and draining on land, seemed like a benediction here. There were no people on the shore except for a few natives foraging, and no sound came to them. "We may speak freely here," he said, "without fear of spies."

"What is it you mean to do? What is it you intend, with all these tricks and games, eluding the constables?"

His rowing slowed a beat. "The truth is I don't know. Day after day, I don't know. But I've got one end of it. Ruth Staines is at the end of it. And I'm drawing the line in, hand over hand. And I can see where it leads, though I don't know the shape of it. I can only guess, and it's a terrible thing, even to me." He glanced at his own, sunburnt hands, resting on the oars. "They make a theatre of the gallows, and they think death sharpens the moral. But death sharpens nothing; it makes you dull, dull, dull. And I must show the dullards what they think they want to see, so they will follow me onwards."

"And where must they follow you?" she asked, in a low voice.

"To the docks of London, if need be."

"You contrive your own escape. You mean to leave the colony—and me."

"That is where I am led. I cannot let it go, no more than you can. Look here. That sly old colonel, MacNeish, told us he had no notion of where Captain Pryor could be. But he sits every night on the club veranda and drinks and smokes good English tobacco, and he uses paper splints to keep his pipe alight."

"And should he not?"

"A proper thrifty Scotsman. He takes the paper from home, old letters and whatnot, from his desk if need be."

Suddenly, wonder replaced accusation in the blaze of her eyes. "You lit the pipe for him! You took his paper splints."

"It was a speculation, a throw of the dice. And yet I find a scrap of a letter. No date. No address. But the old man writes: 'my dear Pryor…the land disposed…four horses…tolerable cool…'—and there, out of habit and economy he is caught in the lie."

"Is that why you asked me about his business interests?"

Carver nodded. "And what's more, he happens to pass the funeral of a murdered clerk, who was deep in the matter, as the rest of us gather. So I thought it wise to follow him, and do you know where the old bird went?"

"I cannot think."

"Well, once I got away I could go and see. Up the hill to where poor Sidmouthe had his rooms. He sent his driver in to look, of course, while he waited. I caught them leaving. The colonel had the same thought I had, but he checked to see who was at the funeral, and then went to search the dead man's lodgings."

She said, "I asked about his interests and properties. He is mainly in the mercantile line, for the regiment and so on. Justice Foyle is a partner in the same venture, with Fordham and a few others."

"Fordham, you say!" exclaimed Carver.

"Everyone in our little society knows everyone else. The Currency prefer to deal with the Currency. And Mr. Fordham is cleverer and more serious than he seems. He joshes Archie so, but keeps the police magistrates on his side, drinks with Foyle and MacNeish at Kember's."

Carver's jaw tightened. "Fordham. Staines's neighbour. Does he profit by all of this? He's a good rider, also, with a stable of pretty horses, I reckon. But we know nothing else about him."

"And do you know MacNeish is a factor for a shipping company?"

"What company?"

"Jankle and Son, of London."

Carver slapped his thigh. "A shipping company! And Ruth Staines and Captain Pryor, gone by sea. What's more, when I searched Sidmouthe's pockets—"

"As he lay dying?"

"Aye, even then. When else? I found ship's passages, blank, but made up for vessels owned by Jankle and Son, Ports of London."

"You mean to go to London, then."

"I believe the murderer will stand there." Carver paused, awkward, and for a moment he seemed pensive and weary to the woman before him.

"And why should my husband agree to his? London is far, far away."

He shook his head. "It is not my will. It is the design of the system. New South Wales is a penal colony, but if we are right, how many have escaped it so? One, ten, a hundred? It cannot be tolerated. I imagine the governor's office is already asking questions. An emancipist on the outskirts of town is one thing, but more dead, and a magistrate's clerk killed in sight of the town: it won't be kept down. And besides, the magistrates will fear what this man could do if he gets away with his evidence. What if he tried to sell his proof? Who would pay for it in London: the Colonial Office, the minister himself? There are voices in parliament raised against transportation, the penal colonies. Your husband will be desperate to bring this crime and this criminal back."

"And is this your charge? Is this the task of the hangman of Sydney Gaol?"

"Who else, then?"

Antonia looked back at the golden shores of the cove, drifting by. "Who else? But you are not who you seem, Gabriel Carver."

He peered at her. "Who should I seem to be?"

"You play the coarse hangman, the grim clown, the jaded convict. You play it perfectly. You feign ignorance, but you can read and write, I know, and you follow the law as well as my husband, and do you think us all so dull that you can cast off fragments of Shakespeare under your breath and not one person will realize?"

He shook his head. "There's nothing in that. I know my letters and like a show. Every gaol contains a convict beak or two."

"But they do not take pains to conceal who they are, or drown their thoughts in rum, or hide in the gallows' shadow."

"You are too good," he muttered. "You cannot lie to an honest soul."

"Why did you take the hangman's office?" she asked hastily, reaching for his arm.

He flinched. "Why did you marry that scheming nincompoop?"

"Too tall, too bony, too poor, too old, too opinionated, until sensible Archie came calling one misty afternoon for a sturdy, sensible wife with steady nerves who would not wither in the feverish summers of the colonies!" she exclaimed.

She caught at his shirt cuffs and twisted them to hold him still. "That was my choice. What was yours?"

"What you say of me is true. I would tell you all, upon my soul. But to do so would put us both at hazard of the law: you to know who I am, and me to be so revealed. I am not prepared for that, yet."

"Is it that you have so little faith in my confidence?"

"I have all faith in your goodness and honesty. You have glimpsed the lost side of me. I had thought that left behind. I would remain the same in your eyes, a little longer."

Without pause, he leaned forward in the little boat, took her by the waist, and kissed her swift upon the lips. He felt her stays shifting beneath his hand. Her feet slipped on the boards underfoot. Her breath was cool upon his cheek.

"You are a changed man upon the sea," she said.

He drew back. His look was almost furtive. "It was the hulks that changed me," he said.

"No, not quite, I think. And I am different also, with you. A little more Antonia, a little less Mrs. Fitchett. Let us go a little farther, please, while we are free among the waves."

He rowed on, tracing part of the shore, until he found a small cove with flat, buttery rocks and green shade from the cliffs above. He landed the boat, and hand in hand they retreated to a patch of shade with only a view of the north shore, and no trace of the colony in view.

THEY RESTED BY the waves until the sharp calls of birds skimming above the rocks reminded them of the progress of the hours.

Carver stood and offered his hand while she pinned up her hair. She waved it away.

"You will leave me so, I know," she breathed.

"It cannot be helped."

"Is that the hangman's refrain?"

"It is so."

"You will leave me here, on this far shore, a prisoner like the others," she said. "I know it."

"Then why did you consent to meet me here?"

"You are a cypher, Mr. Carver. I thought I would discover your secret. Is that plain enough? You little comprehend the dullness and constraint I labour under. Grant that I saw in you and your task some escape from that for a lively mind. And I do care for you, whether you will or no! But I am mistaken. You will take no care of me."

"You are not mistaken," he said shakily. "But I must see it through. And whatever I hazard or do, the answer lies in London."

"And is it your task alone to settle this?"

"I wanted no part of this in the beginning. But if I abandon it now, then no one will remember or speak for the dead, and I will remain the cold-hearted hangman, nothing more, free to take myself to the Devil by the quickest pass. No one to recall that burned girl and no one to take pity yet."

She took his arm to help her rise, but when she had straightened her skirts she resumed: "You speak suddenly of pity and truth, but the convicts say you betrayed your own kind to step onto the gallows."

"So they say. But even you do not know the man who answered the call to the gallows that day. You see clearer than most." He bent and kissed her cool cheek, wet with salt.

"We must go back," she said, "and resume our duties."

"You husband does not know you are out?"

"He cannot know," Antonia hissed. "They would lock you up and ruin me."

"They will arrest me anyway." Abruptly, he winked at her. "But that may be the means. I shall contrive the proof your husband needs."

He steadied the small boat while she climbed in. She settled herself and looked calmly at the expanses of water and hills. "We have been at liberty, a little while, at least. I am grateful for this. This memory of our better selves will bear me along."

"You will hear from me. Somehow, I swear it," he said, as they slid out into the waves. "But, after we return, you may hear bad reports of me. I would rather you remember me like this."

She smiled, and against his will he thrilled at her regard. "Why, Mr. Carver, do you not yet see that being badly thought of frees a man to do what is right as well as wrong?"

CHAPTER 13.

Sent from the Fatal Shore

THE HOT WIND blew from the vast and uncharted interior, as though to prove that the world was forged in fire and sure to end in fire. In the cells of Sydney Gaol, the prisoners panted and groaned, and even the warders shuffled through the rounds and often paused to wet their hands and faces at the trough by the main gate. After dark, Wilmot idled by the gate when he heard the heavy-handed knocking outside. Snarling, he opened the door. First a man, heavily shackled, stumbled through, and then came Sergeant Ellington, haggard and red-faced, with an armed constable behind him.

"What's this, then?" said Wilmot.

"Brought your hangman back to you," croaked Ellington. "He's led us a merry dance these two days."

"He don't lodge in here," returned Wilmot.

"He lodges here tonight, on my chief's orders, to see how he likes it, and to remind him of his duty."

"Drunk, I suppose," said Wilmot.

The shackled man raised his shaggy head, and Wilmot saw that it was Carver, stooped by his chained hands, with blood above his brow, drying in a line, a swollen bruise beside his eye, and a thick lip, that gave a strange emphasis to his half-sneer.

"Aye, it's me," said Carver. "I am due a ration of rum, am I not, in the government service? Though I swear I am the only sober man on the gallows."

"Where did you come by him in this state?" said Wilmot to Ellington.

"Up on The Rocks. He gave me the slip once today, which I don't take kindly too, so I gave him a taste of the irons."

Wilmot hefted his keys. "They won't take kindly to him in the men's barracks. They have grievances aplenty there fresh in mind."

"I don't mind if he's ruffled a bit." Ellington sniffed. "He has caused me a heap of worry, and it will do him good to be reminded of where he comes from. As long as he's able to stand before the bench tomorrow."

"The surgeon should look at him," said Wilmot.

"Moynihan," croaked Carver. "I want Moynihan."

"He ain't here," snapped Wilmot.

"Just lock him up," said Ellington. "It's too late and too hot."

Wilmot took the swaying hangman under his arm.

"Yarra decent feller, fer a guard," said Carver.

THE BARRACKS OF the Sydney Gaol were crowded beyond endurance, dark but for the scant light that entered through the vertical slots high beyond the reach of any prisoner. Still, in the fug of dead air, the prisoners strove towards what little ventilation was admitted and clustered around the strongest and luckiest, who could raise their faces to the draughts from the outer walls.

Wilmot unlocked the door, and for a moment the beam of his lantern fell on the men massed inside. Then he pushed Carver through. The hangman was dusty and tattered, like a stockman's dog at the end of a long muster. Only when the door closed and the lock turned did he find his balance, and then his back and shoulders straightened, and his hoarse panting fell into slow breaths. He shuffled forward, kicked chains, boots, trod on a sleeping man's hand. Growls of protest and derision came back to him.

"O'Doul," said Carver, softly, to anyone near. "I want O'Doul."

A reedy voice rose close by: "What do you want with the damnable Irish?"

"Do you know him or not?" growled Carver.

"The end, by the last little window," said the voice, petulant. And then, "And who are you, calling at this hour?"

"I am the man who will kick you soundly if you do not stand aside," returned Carver.

He edged into the foul darkness, among men sleeping and sitting and turning unseen. Periodically, he called the same name and was greeted with jeers, or spat upon, or sometimes a hand tugged at the cloth of his pants, or he was pushed and turned from behind, and so he was passed from place to place inside the lockup. Meanwhile, the overcharged clouds brewed into a storm beyond the inner gates of the harbour, and thunder mumbled like a drunk in the street.

The wall loomed black before Carver.

"O'Doul?"

"He's here," growled another. "But who asks?"

"I'm a friend of his mam's."

Carver heard the men move. Something hard and sharp was pressed against his neck, cold even in the gaol.

"His ma is particular about her friends."

"So am I. And I saw her t'other day at a wake, in a foul mood, for the dead man has lost something, and I have a mind as to where it is. Do you hear me, so, Callum O'Doul?"

"Will you babble our business to the whole cell?"

"I will, if you're not sensible and make yourself known."

A figure rose suddenly before Carver. Lightning fluttered against the slots, like the tapping of a lover's fingers against a window. The knife was withdrawn.

O'Doul leaned into Carver's side. "There are twenty men in here who would kill you as soon as they guessed your name."

O'Doul heard the hangman laughing low and wearily in his chest. "Don't be so sure."

"Make your case or be damned!" hissed O'Doul.

"You know what's missing," said Carver. "The work of a clerk, taking names and dates and notes of ships and property given in exchange. Aye, enough to hang the lot of you. It went missing, and when Sidmouthe went to collect it he couldn't give the killer what he wanted, and he died also for his troubles. The killer will go on looking for what he wants, but he's done here. He's away across the oceans, back to England, leaving all this trouble behind. Sidmouthe and all the rest of them serve an English master. You know it too. But I'm the man to follow and fetch that book."

"You mean only to save your own skin again," said O'Doul, "and leave us to it."

"Well, I can't deny it suits my purpose. But if I am gone and the book is gone, and all the magistrates have left are a heap of bodies and their own confusion, would that not confound them and end your troubles?"

"You're full of tricks, aren't you?" said O'Doul.

"The question is, will you stand by, mewling about your misfortune in Sydney Gaol, while the old woman hobbles about and makes her own trouble, or will you take a man's part and set to?"

The lightning licked at the openings in the wall, and for a moment Carver could see Callum O'Doul's face, painted pale as though with white chalk, puzzled and suspicious.

"What would you have me do?" said O'Doul, at last.

"Bring evidence against a ghost," said Carver. "Tell the magistrates what I tell you. You must persuade them that the book is real, and contains what they want, and that it is gone. Then the magistrates will have no choice but to send after it, no matter how far. But the word must come from one of you."

"Why should I trust you, hangman?" whispered O'Doul.

"You needn't trust me, just say as I say. Turn over your evidence, and you will walk free, if you are canny enough."

Perhaps the wind shifted, for the air stirred, and the whole room of men, chained and burdened, shifted and began to murmur. O'Doul leaned closer to Carver. The hangman began to speak again, and the sound of the long pent rain hissed higher and higher.

THE GALLOWS IN the gaolyard stood unattended. Three guards escorted a single prisoner down the hill. The magistrate, Fitchett, hunched under an umbrella at the base of the wharf. A few steps away, Ellington stood to attention while water pooled and dripped from the visor of his cap. Rain and the swells breaking against the foot of the seawall made all speech dull and vague. Only when the constables came near with Carver between them did the police magistrate stir.

Carver's black hair was plastered to his head, but he did not stoop.

"You may choose to scoff at our methods, sir, but an informant has done you a good turn," said Fitchett.

"How so?"

Ellington stepped forward. "Informant presented himself. Informant has some standing among the Irish brethren. Says he met a man who got drunk and was boasting at the Killarney Races. Man hinted he knew who had conspired in the murder of an overseer on The Rocks. Furthermore, when pressed, claimed to have done work for a clerk with a prosperous scheme. Informant hears of the clerk being murdered later. Says he also heard this man at the races claim he had sure and certain knowledge of a register that an Englishman would pay good money for."

Carver absently rubbed his swollen and bruised cheek. "Name of this man at the races?"

"No names were exchanged. But the informant was able to tell us that the man in question had a berth on the Indiaman *Agatha*."

"I told you it was most likely a sailor," said Carver. He looked out along the pier and the oily swells. "Why trouble to bring me down here, if you go to arrest him?"

Water dripped off the sharp corners of the magistrate's umbrella. "You have indicated, in sworn deposition, that you could identify this man from his stance and voice."

"I could. I will witness before any court, and then you will have your three-fold murderer."

"The *Agatha* sailed two days since," said Ellington, winning an acidic glare from the magistrate.

Carver grinned. "Two days I've been in the cells."

Fitchett waved off the constables and leaned forward like the mast of a listing ship. "You will go now in the custody of Sergeant Ellington. You are to board the next vessel from this port, with all speed. And when you are docked in London, you will swear out a warrant and you will find this murderer and he will be brought here for trial."

"Find his wicked book of secrets, you mean, and whomever he means to deliver it to," said Carver.

Fitchett drew back, as if a snake had lashed at him. "There is no passage from this colony. There is no end to transportation. The Empire requires that."

"And if I am not inclined?"

"Do not hinder me, or think that you can brave the lash."

"And," said Carver, "does this mean you abandon all folly regarding Meg Harper?"

"The case against her is no longer sound."

"I owe that fellow who killed Sidmouthe a drubbing. You may rely on that," said Carver.

"You are a scoundrel." Fitchett sniffed and looked around. "The boat is here."

Carver walked forward, and Fitchett added: "And I warn you, if you try to evade the sergeant again, you will hang by British law. You are a convict and a transported felon. You have no freedom without his protection."

"I will set it in my remembrance," returned Carver.

But as Ellington and Carver turned to go, Fitchett stepped closer to the hangman, and for a moment both were under cover of the umbrella, and Carver could hear only the sound of the droplets pattering against the waxed silk. Then Fitchett hissed, "You were observed, in *my* garden, in conversation with *my* wife. It shall not be tolerated. Whether you return or no, there will be no further contact with my wife, in word or thought or deed, or I will not forbear to avoid her ruin, or yours."

Then the magistrate straightened and walked away, face set and stern, towards the muddled and indistinct heap of the town, against the streams of filth brought down by the rain.

CARVER SLIPPED EASILY into the prow of the boat, while Ellington fumbled and cursed as he lost his footing in the water collecting at the bottom. They pushed off from the landing, and the two sailors set to work with the long oars. The dory wallowed, sluggish. Sound fell away; the beach fell away; the light cleared and became even and grey.

"Can this thing go no faster?" said Ellington.

"Content yourself," said Carver in reply. "There's fresh water mixed with the salt to make us heavy."

The oars dipped and pulled and rose.

Carver was seated near the prow, facing seaward, intent on the open harbour. A ship stood outlined against the rain, a low, broad three-master.

"What vessel is that?" said Carver to the rowing men.

"The brig *Stella,*" said one of sailors. "Convict transport, returning with cargo for Jankle and Sons."

"There are some of us as will have no difficulty settling in to a convict ship," said Ellington, with a vile grin.

The hangman made no reply. He hunched forward and rested his hands on his knees. The convict executioner faded, utterly transformed: gone were his glances and black humour and bitter retorts; the man in the boat was pensive, like a scholar reading alone in a dark library. When the rowers faltered, Carver turned to look at their destination. The motionless ship, her yards hanging like shrouds, her spars stark as the gallows beam, was the only solid thing on a phantom sea.

PART TWO

THE HULKS

CHAPTER 14.

The Adamant

The Pacific Ocean, 1830

HE HAD NO BERTH on the *Stella*, only hooks for a canvas hammock among the foul-tongued seamen on the lower deck. The sailors avoided the hangman as a creature of ill-omen, and he was content with their indifference. At evening Carver stalked the forecastle and watched the great sea swells and squalls passing on the horizon until the darkness came and the stars returned. The lower decks were hot and stank of seal-skins and whale oil. Later, in the dark, his mind ran back with dull persistence to the hulks, the perpetual, breathless gloom of the orlop deck, the lapping of slow waters, and the drag and click of chains. But as the Pacific Ocean dilated into an eternity of salt water, he snatched at glimpses of London again: the bluster and muck, smoke and spires, ragged children ducking among the carts; lanes, courts, and gates; and the graveyards and rookeries, the pleasure gardens and theatres. And, inevitably, into his recollection of these old scenes rose the faces, the principal actors to their parts: Susan Vale and Oliver Kempe, Simon Chalke and Darren Hardacre—and the Carver that once was.

The Prison Hulks, Off Chatham, 1823

GABRIEL CARVER had a bullying swagger even as he walked in fetters. With his jutting head and heavy labourer's shoulders, he strutted along the deck, grinning at the diffident wraiths of men confined to the prison hulk, which had once been the ship-of-the-line *Adamant*. The *Adamant*'s splintered oak beams, loose nails, and warped planks had endured war with the French, but the warship had been anchored on the Medway off Chatham, in sight of the vast estuary flats, not long after the era of "Campbell's Academy" (when the hulks were a terrific novelty to the public press, and most transported prisoners were set down for the Americas). Now it leaked, and listed, and grew dense with slime and white barnacles.

The first rule of the hulks was never to ask a convict to put a name to his crime. Carver, though, had a quick tongue and saw no ill in spinning out a tale to impress the others locked close under the decks with him. He had been a footpad, he said, and later a highwayman on the Stepney Turnpike. He had been prisoned in Airenchester for theft, and later taken and tried in London. Close enough—no one knew that in London he had been one of a crew of Resurrection Men (for this was before the Anatomy Act), where he had been engaged in dragging fresh corpses by lamp-light from the thin coverlet of soil afforded by the crowded, unguarded parish graveyards of Rotherhithe and St. Anne's. For certain, he had married by stepping over the broom—no parish registry had recorded the alliance—to a brisk slattern called Meg Harper. All these guises he put on and off at need, as another man dresses for dinner, court, or the hunt. The only man who troubled himself to listen to and untangle his various tales was another prisoner: Oliver Kempe. What Kempe took to be true or otherwise he in no way showed, but guilty men are tenacious in their secrecy.

Kempe was of a similar height, and likewise broad as Carver, but on the day he arrived he had also a clerk's thick waist and pale jowls—acquired from coffeehouse dining and perching at writing desks. When the skiff drew up against the *Adamant*, wallowing on the river, he stepped to the platform bolted to the mouldering hull easily enough, but there was an air of defeated fastidiousness about him. Kempe and Carver were assigned to the same hard berth, with ten others. Perhaps his gravity and manners interested Carver, for out of mischief, or more likely boredom, in the black passes of the night, while the prisoners were locked in, he resolved to needle the new bird into a confession.

"I know you," Carver whispered.

"I think not," came the soft, weary reply.

"But it's true. I seen your face about the Old Bailey."

"You may have." When Kempe spoke there was still a fading Southeastern inflection in his words.

"Lawyer's man, ain't you?"

"No more."

"Been about the courts then. I knew it!"

"Stryver and Dearden, I clerked for."

Carver grinned in the dark. "All well," he said. "But how did a fellow like you come to stand before the beaks, on the wrong side of the lawyer's benches?"

Kempe shook his head. "I should have lived quiet," he said to the dark. "I should never have come near the shows of London."

"Oh," said another man, lying nearby scratching at the eternal lice, "but the shows of London are devilish grand!"

THE OLD SHIP, masts hewn to stumps; boards splitting; gates, pens, and watch-houses stacked above the decks, groaned and creaked as the tide turned on the low, flat river, or the winds pressed inland off the salt marshes. Those who were fit were taken off by day to work along the shores and at the naval yards, like so many grey scarecrows. The lowest deck, the orlop, would not give a marine room to wear his cap when he stood upright.

The prisoners were roughly segregated by a few low partitions, more like cattle pens than walls, and slept in hammocks, which were stowed during daylight. The warder of the *Adamant* maintained this bracingly old-fashioned view of their safety: at night, men and women were bolted in below decks with a handful of armed guards above, and endured as they could in the cold and dark and the stale, reeking air. When light came in by the portals, they gamed and gambled, picked at the vile food, and haggled over soap and stockings, tobacco and weak beer, needles, and combs to catch the swarming lice. And later, in the night watches, there were scuffles and cries of pain, lust, and confusion. The hulks were a black space, neither land nor sea, home nor exile, but assuredly the limbo in between.

THE JOCOSE CARVER and the reserved Kempe were not natural friends, but they were near enough in age to make common cause to guard against the assaults and petty thievery that infested the below-decks of the hulks. Besides, educated men, Carver had heard, were often assigned special duties on the hulks and in the colonies, and so accrued special privileges, and he thought it politic to make an ally of the disgraced solicitor's clerk, once he had drawn out some splinters of his wretched past. That was before the day that Sergeant Hardacre stepped on board to take his first watch.

THE GUARDS WERE held by general consent to be louts, subject to near the same corporal punishments, little better than the prisoners they looked over but for their red coats and muskets. Sergeant Hardacre had a smooth schoolboy face, round cheeks, a creased chin, and a dip in the centre of his upper lip that gave him a perpetual smirk of humour or contempt. He took crisp, short steps on deck, and never raised his voice, though every second or third word he spoke was a casual blasphemy. When he fell in for the night watch as the prisoners were being rounded up, counted, and led below, one of the old hands, who had been laid up before in the hospital ship, paused to spit. "'E's put a musket ball through two men already, as they tell of. The first was swimming for it, and would 'ave been picked up by the long-boat any moment. The other he said was standing too close by the rail with a yearning look, and so he shot him through as well."

"Were there no charges?" said Kempe, shuffling nearby.

The old hand shrugged this away. "One dead man makes room for another."

Carver looked back at the sergeant in his crisp red coat and scowled, biting the inside of his cheek.

Most of the night guard preferred to doze or slouch under the awnings on the top deck at night, or in the wardroom knocked up over the poop deck, and let deviltry reign among the prisoners. But from the first, Hardacre showed no fear of going below, and brought with him neither musket nor pistol, only his notch-handled bayonet, which he swung like a country gent's riding crop. He gambled with the prisoners for their meagre possession, stockings and wool caps, razor-blades and snuff-pouches. He cheated them at cards and dice, and when one man made a remark on this, he closed the matter by pinning a marked card to the man's face with the point of his knife.

There were forty-six women assigned to the hulk on the upper deck. Many of the guards held them as whores regardless of their crimes, and traded favours with them accordingly. Some guards had been lashed for sleeping among the women. Yet Hardacre made them his especial prey, and having the keys to the gates on the ship's gangways in his possession, there was no way to stay him, and no officer would dare take him to task. His attentions were vile. None of the women he chose would say more, but that he battered them, and smiled, and turned his glowing face to the shore as the boat pulled away at the end of the watch.

Among the girls he had picked out was Dot Tucker, a pretty, frail wisp with fine, pale hair. Another prisoner among the male convicts, a long-limbed boy with a crooked face called Stanton, who had been a printer's assistant, was sweet on her. They exchanged secret notes and long looks between the bars that divided the poop deck where the prisoners took their scanty exercise.

Stanton's hands twisted, he shuffled from side to side like a bated bear in the pit, when he saw Hardacre leaning against the railing and Dot with her lips swollen and blackened.

"How can he smile, the brute?"

"He may smile and smile," said Kempe through clenched teeth, "and still be a villain."

"I will 'peach on him," hissed Stanton. "I will inform on him to the superintendent."

"Don't be a damned fool. That man holds life and death over all of us."

"It's not right!"

"Who said there was s right or wrong to be found anywhere in the matter?" snarled Kempe.

The boy sidled to the bars, and the girl's name he whispered was like the sound of raindrops beating on canvas: "Dot, Dot!"

The woman looked up. Her hand covered her mouth. Only Carver had the will to act, jostling and tugging Stanton away from the partition. The boy's hands remained tight on the bars. Hardacre glanced over sleepily, and yawned, but he saw the tall boy, panting, on his knees on the deck, with Carver standing over him.

The sergeant ambled along the barrier. Stanton shuddered; Carver plucked at his collar.

"What's this?" said Hardacre, slowly and coolly. "There's no conversing between the bars. That's a day in the hole."

"He don't mean nothing by it. He's weak-minded," blurted Carver.

Hardacre did not trouble himself to glance at Carver, but said, "Do you question my judgment?"

"No. I do not, only—" began Carver.

"Then you object to my authority," continued Hardacre.

Kempe drew a sharp breath in through his teeth. Carver shook his head, like a dog in the gaming pits, harried.

"I don't mean nothing," he said.

"Of course not," said Hardacre. "Your sort never do. All cock-of-the-walk until you're set against it."

Carver squared his shoulder, and a faint shudder seemed to pass through him. For the first time, Hardacre shifted his gaze to him. With a swift motion, Hardacre drew back his hand to strike, and Carver winced, twisting. The soldier's grin was savage, but the blow did not follow. Instead, he kicked at Stanton, who was still kneeling on the planks, casually, as if he were batting a stray chicken out of his path.

"You ain't got the backbone to say yea or nay to me," said Hardacre. "None of you. A hard man, a stone? You're sand, crumbs, dust, nothing."

The prisoners stood motionless in an arc around Hardacre, Stanton, Carver, with their heads bowed. Carver panted, and clutched at the hem of his tunic like a defeated schoolboy.

"Two days in the hole," said Hardacre. "Thanks to your mates here." He hauled Stanton up to his feet, and then shoved the boy towards the hatches. The rest of the prisoners fell away from him, obscurely defeated, and then resumed their weary shuffling around the deck.

AS THOUGH TO ADD savour to his inviolable power over the girl, Hardacre began to torment the boy. The sergeant inflicted pain with the lash and the butt of his musket, but seemed to no more regard it than a gamester at a cock-fight would feel for the scuffling and squawking of harrowed birds, other than as a curiosity or show. Only despair interested him; all other hurts were incidental to his humour. The prisoners were accustomed to cruelty and indifference, to rages and curses and arbitrary blows, but

Hardacre's calm smiles, his winking and wheedling familiarity with the officers, frightened and appalled them.

The bite of a rat below decks could infect and rankle, and breed a fatal poison from a trivial wound. And so, Sergeant Hardacre had offered Carver no hurt at the exercise pen, but the guard's contempt and his own weakness grew rancid in Carver's mind. Other guards were as free with the lash as Hardacre, but their punishments were more tractable, consistent with their word and the mad patchwork of rules that bound the prison ship. But the sergeant would whip a man for no reason: for losing a boot in the mud, for stuttering during grace, for looking at the deck during roll call. At other times he would ignore infractions, treat informers or murderers with solicitude, and his arbitrary choices did more to discomfort the prisoners than any rage.

"What's his business?" complained Marsh in the mess. "He's got no business with the boy, or any of us." He prodded at a hank of grey salt beef in his bowl.

"He does what he pleases. That's his business. And it ain't to be borne," said Carver, who was hunched over the bench opposite.

"Well may you say that. You talk a heap of great talk," returned Marsh, "but what do you mean to do about it, aye? What can you do?"

Carver chewed and grimaced.

"There's nothing to be done," said Kempe. "It may be beneath your notice, but we are prisoners here."

Carver turned to him. "That's meek talk, watery talk. Where's your spirit, man? I don't care for a man without spirit."

Kempe grunted and crossed his arms. He was picking at his poor rations, not eating some days, and his face had started to lose its padding.

Chalke had come last to the bench, and now he leaned across. "But that's the question: what's to be done?"

No one thought, or cared, much about Simon Chalke. He had been a ostler, an oysterman, a petty thief, a familiar at the gates of Newgate: a lean slip of a man, twenty-five years old, with a pointed chin, hollow cheeks, elongated ears.

"We're not slaves, are we?" said Carver. "Nor chattels. We're men still, and may have our way." He eyed the deck, the rows of hunched backs.

Marsh shook his head; Kempe snorted; Chalke grinned and drew back, but Carver still scratched his cheek and brooded.

CONFINEMENT, THE LONG wait for transportation, stretched out in a series of hideous days, exhaustion, worry. Stanton began to cough. At night he would shiver, and the sound repeated as a toneless chime through the links of his fetters. Still, when the prisoners were exercised, the girl looked back to her trembling boy, slumped on the black tar deck, with her faint blue eyes. One evening Carver prowled over to Stanton, while Stanton was shivering and trying to hold up a book to the one lantern.

"What's that?" said Carver roughly.

"B-b-bible." That was the only kind of book the prisoners were permitted on the hulks. But this one had the cover torn off.

"No, it ain't." Carver plucked the volume from the boy's grasp, and as Stanton reached for it, he thrust it over into Kempe's hands. "What is it?"

Kempe frowned. The book was still open at the page Stanton had clutched at.

"Well, you can read it, can't you? Gives us a passage, man, if you care to."

Kempe licked his lip and read:

I dreamed my lady came and found me dead—
Strange dream that gives a dead man leave to think—
And breathed such life with kisses in my lips,
That I revived and...

Kempe stopped. He pushed the book towards Carver, but his face and eyes he covered with his hand.

"Well?"

"Angel protect us," said Kempe, under his breath. "You read it and you will know it, you damned brute. Let the boy have it."

The rest of the prisoners looked on but would not meet Carver's eyes. Without speaking again, Carver pressed the book into the young man's hands.

But it was not for this breach of the rules that Hardacre sent Hugh Stanton to the lash: it was for his dropping his bowl and spoon in the mess.

RAIN SPREAD DARK shrouds along the edge of the sky, rendering glimpses only of the church spire and roofs of the serene village on the other side of the river. The ship's company, prisoners, and marine guards were arrayed on the deck. Without masts or sails, there was no protection from the wind or the icy drizzle, and the men and women in their drab prison weeds huddled and paced and shivered.

They had strapped Stanton to a useless capstan, and the lasher stood nearby. The boy was no more than a collection of bones within translucent skin. Hardacre unravelled the lash. His guards lined up behind him like neat red pegs.

Near the front row of prisoners, Stanton's mates had gathered.

"Look to him. He won't make it," said Kempe, through clenched teeth.

"The lad is sound," growled Carver.

"He ought to scream," said Chalke. "That's the thing. He ought to howl and beg for pity. The lasher may go easy then."

Carver jostled him hard with his shoulder. "He's no coward, no worm squirming before the guards."

The prisoners on hand murmured approval, but Chalke edged away, rubbing his upper arm.

The lasher drew back the cat and shook out the strands. These were limp as rags in the rain.

He began with an easy stroke. The prisoners stirred, but to this rote demonstration there was no sign of horror. The punishment, like privation, fear, and disease, was but the due course of the system.

Sergeant Hardacre spoke: "Set to, man."

The lash made its marks: a welt, a weal, a wound. And the rain became steady and pattered on the boy's back, disrupting the trickle of blood. Stanton coughed, and coughed harder with each fresh strike, and a sort of burble of half-words and moans escaped him, but he did not cry out.

"Hold on, lad. Hold on," hissed Carver.

The lash marks multiplied and the blood ran. Stanton slumped against the mass of wood and steel he was tied to.

"Twenty," cried Kempe. "For pity's sake. Where is the surgeon?"

The lasher paused. The lieutenant glanced at Hardacre, who said, "The full measure."

More strokes in the rain; the deck was tainted with a thin pink froth of blood.

The boy ceased to moan. His head turned and his feet slid and failed to find purchase.

The mass of prisoners constricted and edged forward. All turned to the ragged figure pressed against the capstan. Even the lasher shook his head.

"The surgeon," a woman blurted. "For God's sake, fetch the surgeon."

From the side of the ship, beyond the forecastle, came a harrowed shriek and a splash.

AN OFFICER RATTLED out the order. With shrieks and bellows the prisoners were herded below deck. Many stumbled on the slimy steps and fell in the press, to be tangled among jerking limbs or trampled. The soldiers followed, shoving and cursing.

Down on the orlop deck, the men were barged and beaten into their partitioned rows.

When Kempe staggered in, Carver watched him lean with his fists against the hull and raise his head, as if listening for something above the waterline.

"A lasher," hissed Kempe. "A damned butcher!"

"Murder," said Carver, crouching and crossing his hands over his knees. "In plain daylight."

Then Kempe looked back. "He has done for the girl. Do you not see? She has gone overboard."

"What?" said another man, rubbing his head.

"Did you not hear the fall? The poor girl went over the edge." Kempe slapped the timbers. "They must put out the boats."

They heard the voices of the guards raised. The count was being taken. And down the centre of the deck strolled Sergeant Hardacre, with an easy grin.

"Do you think she meant to do away with herself?" whispered Chalke.

"He thinks Hardacre set her over," said Carver grimly.

Chalke hissed. Hardacre's pale face, with its round cheeks and jaunty side-whiskers, appeared at the opening of the partition. He glanced around, but his eyes carried no more sympathy than those of a hack mouthing the words of a pantomime for the third time in the night.

"You'll be pleased to know your precious sleep won't be broken by coughs any longer."

"You dog," husked Carver.

"What's that?"

Chalke sidled to the sergeant. "We all had a liking for the lad, and it goes hard with us. We don't mean no disrespect."

Behind Chalke, two of the others were inching towards Stanton's little pile of possessions.

"I don't care for your respect," said Hardacre cheerily. "You might as well pray to me and hope I listen, because I am all the god you will know until your transport sails."

In the dark corner of the deck, Carver kicked at one of the other prisoners and stooped to snatch something square and hard from among Stanton's things.

"Did they put the boats out?" said Kempe. "Someone has gone overboard."

"You have sharp ears," said Hardacre. "So do I. But anyone who swims for it will drown or be shot. I'll see to that."

"Yessir. Plain as day," said Chalke.

Still grinning, Hardacre slipped away. They heard him sauntering down the rows.

"It ain't to be borne," said Carver, in a low voice. "It ain't discipline, or even punishment what just happened. It's low murder. The boy, and the girl too, I expect. We ain't none of us safe, I say. He could come for any of you next."

In the perpetual gloom of the under-decks, only the eyes of men showed as white points. The words came back: "And what would you propose to do?"

Carver edged forward in a low crouch. He pointed to Kempe. "You, lawyer's man. What will we do, under the law, like?"

Kempe turned back, shaking his head. "Summon twelve free men, and appoint yourself bailiff."

"Aye," said Carver. "And are we not men, capable, not rats and baggage? Therefore we must be a law among ourselves."

"Sedition!" whispered Chalke.

"No. We must be deliberate and of one mind if we are to be rid of Hardacre," said Peterson.

"Just cause," said Carver. "True men together."

"What cause?" said Kempe. "Will you draw up the charges? Submit evidence? Call a jury?"

"Do you doubt the need?"

Hardacre was returning, slow boots on the planks. The hulk groaned as it turned under the shifting tide, the overburdened timbers flexing as the whole mass strained against the anchor lines and the chains grated. No light came in at the portals. Rain enfolded the shore and swept across the tethered ships. The grey-green estuary and the vessels set there became indistinguishable.

CHAPTER 15.

The Lottery of Lost Men

CARVER WEDGED the end of his tin spoon between forefinger and thumb and thrust it under the edge of the head of a nail in the soft wood of the deck. He grimaced, and pushed, and the old nail shifted minutely but did not come loose. His fingers ached and were bruised with the effort of prying up the nail. He looked up. This was the short hour when prisoners gathered in the mess before being confined in the lower decks, cramming slop into their mouths, gaming, or bargaining with their sparse possessions. The nail, if it came loose, would at least cost nothing.

Carver gritted his teeth and worked at the nail again.

He became aware of a stir along the deck, and with a true prisoner's instinct he covered the nail and spoon with his hand and looked up, unhurried.

Hardacre came swaggering among the benches with his bayonet in hand. He looked about without urgency, but Carver realized that the guard's hard unsympathetic eyes were fixed on Kempe, who leaned over his tin plate a few yards away. Slowly, without undue care, he moved his hand to his side.

The guard stepped into place before Kempe's downcast eyes.

Hardacre bared his teeth. "It's Kempe, ain't it?"

"Yes, sir. It is, sir."

"Would you care to come aloft for a breath of air?" said Hardacre, pleasant as a country squire to a hunt guest.

"I expect I would," said Kempe, though he felt fear, a parasite, coiling and coiling about his heart.

"Then step lively, man," barked Hardacre.

A hundred hooded eyes marked them as they went, but only Carver watched the guard and the prisoner, shuffling in chains behind him, and did not look away. When they had passed out of view to the topside deck, Carver frowned and stalked to the base of the ship's ladder, gazing up into the dark with his head cocked.

ON THE DECK of the condemned warship, among the ramshackle hutches and awnings and gates, a cold wind blew, and the shore was a mere fold of darkness under a frigid half moon and a sweep of clouds. Hardacre nodded to the lone guard on the deck, who was seated on a barrel and idly rolling dice for his own diversion. Kempe moved towards shelter from the wind, conscious of the weight and drag of his shackles and the fouled, dark waters beneath the hull.

Hardacre, as if reading his thoughts, leaned towards him.

"Here," said the guard, "take some 'baccy."

"I don't have the habit," returned Kempe.

"You'll need it where you're going, if not for recreation, then for barter."

"I don't mean to be ungrateful," said Kempe.

Hardacre grinned and turned his head to one side, digging for a flask in his coat pocket. "At least take some grog. It will restore you better than the weak beer they pass below deck."

The grog burned at nose and throat, but Kempe felt readier. "I don't understand," he began.

"Oh, I don't expect you should," said Hardacre serenely. "But I've been looking at your entry in the superintendent's book. I've been chatting with my mates on the Newgate lock. I know a thing or two about you, old chum." He winked. "You're a sly one."

"Am I? I don't mean to be."

"It says you're a lawyer's clerk. That makes you an educated man. A man who can read and write. Clerks are of use to the officers and captains on the river. Clerks get good berths and easy jobs, better than cutting ditches and building dykes for the navy. But you're a sly cove. You keep all that quiet, and muck with the common scum, the Newgate filth and all."

A lone glimmer in the distance was but the stern-light of another prison ship. Kempe choked down a shudder of cold. "I don't mean to be. I don't like to put myself above others."

Hardacre nudged him in the belly. "Oh, but you're a curiosity then, a reg'lar mystery. Maybe you mean to report yourself to the colonial secretary when you come to the other side. Maybe you mean to report on us all."

"No. Nothing of the sort."

In the gathering dark, with only a few caged lights to see by, Hardacre's face was reduced to a few pale strokes, the grinning mouth, the empty eyes. He moved again, setting his back against the rail, and Kempe winced.

"Another mate of mine," Hardacre resumed, "told me an interesting tale. A real eye-opener."

"Whatever it concerns—"

"Concerns a lawyer's clerk. Like yourself. Perhaps you know it. It was in all the broadsheets. Great amusement to all sides. Came out with the trial of a Ewan Vale. A slovenly, directionless youth, said to have murdered a well-to-do city man and owner of a small glassworks, who had lent him monies on account of his infatuation with Vale's sister."

Hardacre looked aside at Kempe. The prisoner was breathing heavily, his eyes fixed on the deck.

"And here, on the third day of his trial, Vale is exonerated by a witness, a grocer's assistant who claimed to have met him in a public house on the day in question. But the grocer's man turned out to be an opium-fiend and, when pressed on the stand, indicated the defence solicitor's clerk had invited him to speak before the courts, with inducements. Now what would you make of that?"

"It was folly," said Kempe dully, "in the extreme. If you ask my opinion."

"Well, you're right. Quite right. When the beautiful sister (if sister she ever was) was not to be found, the solicitor's clerk was brought before the King's Bench in disgrace, and then the charge was brought down, he was sentenced to transportation and hard labour. Pity, poor fellow. Took down for suborning perjury. That's the phrase, ain't it? An educated man, like yourself."

Kempe raised his head and looked at Hardacre. And through his naked fear there rose a deeper horror, striking beyond wariness and disgust, as though the sergeant had conjured before him a legion of old ghosts, fears, and illusions.

"What do you make of it?" urged Hardacre. "A pretty tale, you think. And why did the lawyer's clerk stoop to lies and obstruction? Turns out he himself was also in love with the beautiful sister, and she prevailed with him to arrange a false witness. But that's something a fellow might like to keep from his chums, lest he look like a liar and a gull."

Kempe forced the words with a dry throat. "I suppose he might. What of it, then?"

Hardacre shifted again, keeping one hand on the rail and facing Kempe. "There's some unfortunate words going about, regarding myself and that boy who died under the lash. This business puts me out of temper. I shall stamp it out."

"And what of the girl?" blurted Kempe.

"Silly bint. The poor fool couldn't take it. Pitched herself off the edge. No business of mine."

Kempe winced at the leer on Hardacre's face.

"But what I want," continued Hardacre, "is a clever fellow to help me keep order underneath. You're chums with that hothead, Carver, ain't yer?"

"We're not confidants, if that's what you want."

Hardacre raised his fist and casually battered Kempe over his left ear. "It ain't smart to lie to me!"

The sound of the blow rang as hot as the pain. "It's the truth. We muck in together. I don't know his mind on all things."

"That'll do. You keep a weather-eye on all of them. You talk to me and none other. No officers. There could be a good berth waiting for you, an educated man. But you know what comes of those that cross me." Hardacre's boot shifted, raising the edge of the chain that joined the shackles on Kempe's legs.

Kempe moved his tongue in his mouth. "I know."

"Good man. Good man. No harm in a friendly chat, is there?"

"No harm in the world," said Kempe, lowering his head.

"Go in, then. Jack there won't stop you."

Kempe shuffled away. He did not look back at the shadow of the guard, leaning against the high ship's rail with the black sky behind him.

CARVER WAS SEATED on the lowest step of the companionway as Kempe stamped down. Carver turned his head but did not meet Kempe's eye. Kempe stopped when his boots were on the deck. His mouth was set and dour.

"You say we must make common cause together against Sergeant Hardacre," said Kempe under his breath. "What had you in mind?"

"Twelve men and twelve nails, and a quiet place we can meet, clear of eyes and ears. Then we shall see what we can devise."

"Twelve nails?"

"For a lottery of lost men."

"I will present myself," said Kempe.

Carver turned the ship's nail in his hand over, and closed his palm about it.

SUMMON TWELVE FREE MEN, Kempe had said. It was a bitter joke; perhaps the twelve complacent faces in the jury box had recurred to him as an image of futility. But an ironist is not of a mind with one who still clings to an illusion of himself, no matter how obscure. And so Carver seized on the idea without reservations.

Carver's reasoning was sound in this: Hardacre had his enemies, for the true wellspring of resentment is not fear but contempt. Carver carried his plan up and down the decks. It was his signal cause, his mark, and the whispering that went around him carried it farther. Even the thought seemed to fill him with a new sense of himself, a prideful expansion. Many grinned, shook their heads, and drew a line across their necks. Yet the rumour of defiance gained weight and persistence, as the hulks gained weeds and barnacles at anchor.

THE UNDERDECKS of the *Adamant* after dark were dim as the tomb but in no way as restful, unless the churchyard be infested with rats, squirming and scraping, and gnawing at each other. After sundown, the braces were hung with canvas hammocks one atop the other, creating a dense weave of sagging sheets. Only a few lanterns were attached to hooks between them, and apart from the bins, privies, stores, and the solitary cells, there were, in the decrepit vessel in the old days of misrules, few secure barriers between the general mass of prisoners. Those who attempted to move about the underdecks found a maze of ropes and chains, ship's timbers and boards, hammocks, and men.

Gabriel Carver rose, and groped along the planks in the half-dark, sometimes kicking or being kicked at by squirming figures, towards the ship's stern.

"You will find the tiller there—what's left of it," Kempe had said. "It's as good a place as any to gather."

"And how would you know?" Carver had retorted.

"My father was a seafaring man, after a fashion."

Eleven men had gathered in the tiller room. The tiller itself had long since been hacked away, and the boards of the deck had fallen through. Black, reeking water slopped below as the hulk swayed. One man lit a stub of a candle, blowing softly on the glowing wick. A fugitive light, unsteady, touched the beams of the ship. Eleven men, bearded, lean, and haggard—for to feed a man on the hulks was to cut into their profit—resembling so many goblins gathered in a ruined palace.

"You know my mind on this," said Carver. "King George and his courts may deem us so much trash, suitable to be cast to the ends of the earth, but are we to forbear the work of this brute among us, this Sergeant Hardacre, and not make common cause against him?"

"We are one short," said Kempe, in a low voice.

"Short of what?"

"A jury—if you mean to pass judgment in this place."

"It ain't a matter of judgment," said Harkness, creeping forward into the thin light like a lizard. "We all seen what he did to that lad, and Jones before him, and Hibbert before that."

"Here," said Carver. "Write it down: there's the charge." But no one heard him.

"And the girl," added Kempe.

Hibbert shuddered. "There was no call for that. I've seen men die under the lash before. I've seen cruel punishment and worse. The guards are bullies and the officers are profiteers. But none of us are safe under this Sergeant Hardacre. Not a one. He will do murder as easy as a man squeezes a louse."

"And did you see Hardacre push her over the edge?" demanded Carver eagerly.

"I did not. All I know was that he was by the poor boy's side and drove the torment on, and he was not there when it finished."

"She went over the edge," said Kempe. "She knew too much. What else is there?"

"And what should we do about it, convicts and lost souls all?" said Chalke, who was seated like a tailor cross-legged on the deck.

"That's for us to decide," said Carver.

"But he's right," said another man, Gaines, a heavyset Essex horse thief. "What business have we with a guard? Why, we have all got lashes and worse to show. Breaking regulations is one thing, but this has the stink of mutiny about it."

"There is no mutiny where there is want of proper authority," said Kempe coolly.

"Preach all you want," retorted Gaines, "but answer me why."

"We don't need to account for ourselves. We are all convicts here," said Carver heavily. "Thieves and blackguards and murderers, liars and perjurers, one and all. Some of us have done murder and desperate deeds. But it does not mean we must take our lashes meekly, or let the Devil himself lead us a dance. I would take to the gallows rather than be proved less than a man."

Gaines looked down. "Strong talk. Then say *how*, rather. What do you intend?"

"It's folly, this," said Chalke. "Worse than folly. Damned sedition."

"Then why show yourself here?" snapped another man. "Scurry along, you rag, if you don't have the liver for it."

A hiss ran along the foredeck. A guard was moving above with a heavy, staid tread. All the men gathered by the stump of the tiller shrank and cowered, like rats discovered in a corn bin.

"My answer," said Chalke, in a whisper, "is that Hardacre has cheated me and robbed me to my face."

"We must all be in, or none," said Carver. He edged forward. The stump of the candle was guttering behind him, making his face hooded and black.

"If we are of one mind," said Kempe, "we may proceed against this beast."

"*You* have changed your tune, then," said Carver. He twisted his back to look at Kempe.

Kempe drew a long breath; his nostrils flared, but he said only, "I grant you this, we are none of us safe until we either take ship for the colonies or this man is removed. He watches us all. If he knows or guesses what we suspect, how many of us do you think will set foot on Sydney Cove?"

Water slopped and sucked in the scuppers. The deck was rancid with human filth and crawling vermin. And the circle of men, shoulder to shoulder, leaned closer.

"Here's the way of it," said Carver, "each man brings a nail."

"We did that," said Gaines. "What follows?"

"Hand them in."

Ship's nails, rusted, twisted, were passed from hand to hand, and Carver gathered them up. Then Carver, London thief and resurrection man, bent over the ruins of the old ship's steering and all present could hear metal scrapping across metal.

"I mark one, so," said Carver. He had scratched a circle around one length of iron.

"A lottery," breathed Edgecombe.

"A lottery for lost men," said Carver. "A lottery proof against informers and back-sliders, for none is to know who is chosen until the deed is done."

Kempe shook his head. "You set us at great moral hazard."

"Do you object?" hissed Carver. "Do you have reason here to object?"

"I only see that we all want an executioner," said Kempe. "And not one of us wants to take the task. And by setting us to game for it, you get us to wager our souls on what each man's conscience would not accept alone."

"If there is a man here who would step forward without prompting, let him," snarled Carver.

There came no answer, until Chalke piped, "And what is it to be done?"

"Don't speak of that!" said Kempe sharply. "We all know."

"There are many accidents a man may come by, guard or prisoner, in these rotting hulls," observed Gaines.

"Now, every man draws." Carver held up his fist, clutched around the nails.

The brown light of the candle was almost too dim to make out what he held. Each man in turn reached in and with stiff fingers drew out a splinter of metal from Carver's grasp. Gaines clenched his heavy fist, but his hand was firm. Chalke plucked out a nail like a pickpocket. Kempe's hand shook and he almost dropped the nail he took. Carver pulled the last nail to himself. He did not look at it.

"God have mercy on us all," whispered Edgecombe.

The candle went out, as Dean smothered the last of the wick between his fingertips. One by one they departed, creeping and sliding between the beams and bars and hanging berths, into the cluttered chaos of the prison ship. The hulk groaned and dead water shivered in its bowels, like a leviathan of the deep with poisoned dreams.

CHAPTER 16.

Night and Foul Weather

"FILTHY WORK," said Kempe, "leaves foul stains."

He tugged at the scarf knotted around his neck. The scarf was thin, knitted out of a coarse wool, and immeasurably stained.

With knotted shoulders, tearing backs, and burning hands, they were hauling the mud they dredged out of the channel off a naval barge. Hunched, smeared with filth and slime, the convicts were indistinguishable, and even the lasher, sliding on the gangplank, hardly knew who he was whipping.

"If you mean our lottery," returned Carver, as the two of them stooped to drag a barrow, "you need not be fastidious—unless you chanced to draw against the odds."

Kempe panted; his words came rough and thick. "I curse the folly that brought me to this place. But I have only myself to blame for that. Go hang, I say! You have made us all party to murder and mutiny."

"Do you doubt the need?"

Kempe staggered. His hand slipped on the handle. "No, I do not."

"Then it is easier to say a thing's to be done than step forth and do it."

Kempe paused to wipe mud away from his mouth, but succeeded only in spreading it to his lips, leaving him coughing and spitting. Between hacks he said, "Perhaps you drew your own marked nail. Perhaps you would rather do it yourself."

"I would," said Carver quietly. "I would rather be a man. Aye, I would rather my Meg said I strove against difficulties than fell under them."

"Pah! Boasting talk. You puff yourself up out of nothing, so. The hulks bend a man's mind that way."

Kempe glanced at Carver. The other prisoner's mouth was set in a grim half-smile, mixed of pride and contempt. Chalke was trudging towards them pulling an empty barrow, and he met their eyes and nodded diligently.

"What if he had your precious nail!" hissed Kempe.

"He's not the man for it. You would have heard him squealing and weeping in his berth if he had," said Carver. "Now hush. Little jugs have big ears."

They emptied the mud beyond the shoreline. As Kempe straightened and squared his burning shoulders, he fingered the coarse scarf and looked out on the marshes, the banks of green reeds, the maze of dikes and the low, pale heaps of clouds. A breeze moved from the land. Behind them, a guard barked and the lash cracked.

THERE WERE ONE or two men among the mass of prisoners who might be relied on to procure certain items for barter or otherwise: playing cards or gamester's dice, soap, buttons, and thread, stockings, boots, combs—and razors. Whickham was one such. The guards favoured him, for he traded with them also. And he berthed on the upper deck near the infirmary, and had mess duties. It was said that he had once been an officer who had dealt corruptly with the quartermasters, but since corruption had little tenure as an offence within the king's army, this was an unproven speculation.

Carver approached him in the galley, a dim, hot space of banked fires and clanging kettles. There was little said between the two men; only the prisoner's wary nod, one to the other. Carver held something out: a silver-plated watch chain, with a few dangling mementos that he had taken from Stanton's berth. Then the two men shook hands. Only a pickpocket deep in the craft would have seen the straight-razor pass between them in that gesture.

Carver turned. Chalke was shuffling up behind him with a tin-pot and a sickly grin. Carver nodded. Whickham had returned blithely to his business. Great pots rattled and the sweating cooks cursed.

"IT'S BEEN NIGH on two weeks, and still the thing ain't done," said Chalke, with a mournful shake of his head.

"There may be some who are called to do a thing and lack the spine to do it," said Carver, rubbing his chin.

"Who would you mean by that?"

"It's not for me to say. We all swore to it. We must keep it a secret. But what do oaths matter to a lawyer?"

Chalke tapped the side of his nose and winked. Carver also smiled, a lazy sidelong grin.

AFTER NIGHTFALL, a wind blustered off the mudflats and marshes, bringing charges of rain, icy sharp. The hulk, top-heavy with gates and walls, rolled with the buffeting of the wind and strained at its rusted anchor chains. The soldiers hated to step out onto the upper decks and face the claws of the squall, and the three on duty had settled into a crouch behind the watch cabin. The prisoners were rolled up in their hammocks below.

A lantern descended from the top deck to the orlop, drifting down through the dark like an allegory of Lucifer's Fall. Shuttered, so that a mere glimmer showed between the slats, the lantern travelled between the prisoners until it reached a certain row.

Oliver Kempe was woken by a hand on the stays of his hammock, shaking the cloth back and forth. As men do, he gave a cry and reached up, but his arms were trapped inside. The lantern angled towards his face. Into its sparse yellow circle came the pale features of Sergeant Hardacre.

"Up," said Hardacre, "and shut yer trap."

Kempe began to form words, and Hardacre stopped this with a hand on his throat. "Follow me, or suffer for it."

Kempe rolled out of the hammock. His shackles pained him, and his feet scrabbled uncertainly on the boards. He saw Hardacre's lantern retreating from him, like a miner's light in a pit. Kempe fell to his knees to crawl out and pursue the guard. As he hobbled forward, he passed Carver's berth. A hand clutched at his elbow and for a moment he fancied he saw a gleam, as of a tooth in a grin, down in the dark.

Dazed, he followed Hardacre. The guard was pacing towards the bow of the hulk and the old sail lockers, the solitary cells now: the coffins or the black-trap, the convicts called them. Kempe crept past the stores and the wind wailed along the water and whistled in the few tiny vents in the prow. Hardacre had opened one of the cells, and thin lantern-light bloomed inside. With his tongue thick and his gut grinding, Kempe slipped inside. Hardacre set his light over a hook.

Hardacre turned on Kempe at once, his usually smooth face scowling and contorted. "What's it about, then? Speak or I'll gut you."

"What's the matter?" began Kempe.

Hardacre darted at him, had him by his rough prisoner's tunic, both hands bunched and his smooth forehead gleaming. He shook Kempe with every word: "We had an agreement, you and me.

A nice understanding. Now weeks go by, and you sulk and hold silent, and I hear that prisoners mean to make mischief with me!"

Hardacre pushed his thumbs up to Kempe's face, pressing beneath the eyes. "You lay out the whole business, or I will cripple you."

"Who told you this?" said Kempe.

"Don't you try me with that," grated Hardacre.

"Prisoner's plots," gabbled Kempe. "All words and boasts. Belling the cat! None of the mice dare do it alone, but it is all they can speak of."

Hardacre's thumbs settled, resting on Kempe's cheek, but his hands still pressed on his jaw. "I am the cat, aye? And who is to do it?"

Hardacre scanned Kempe's face, avid in his attention, as though searching a fine bowl for some fault or flaw. Kempe shuddered. His hands were free against his sides and loose. He considered all possible lies, and the consequences of each deception fled him.

"I am chosen," he said. "I drew the token. And therefore you are safe."

Hardacre extended his arms, and Kempe stumbled back from him, knocking his head against the back of the cell. The guard raised his chin, grinning and exultant. "You damned Judas," he said.

But in the dark of the prison-ship behind Hardacre, stooping and scuttling forward, caught for an instant by a stray beam of the lantern, came Gabriel Carver, with his right hand raised high.

There was but an infinitely fine sliver of time in which to think, to deal with each impression. Kempe grasped at the sleeves of the soldier's coat as if in fear, but his hands were grown broad and strong, hardened to the convict's pick and shovel. He clutched at the wrists, and for a moment Hardacre was held immobile.

Carver slammed against Hardacre, and his left arm came down across the man's shoulder to steady him. The right hand flew up, but it struck a beam even as it swung down. Carver made a hasty slash, drawing the razor in his grasp up from the side of the neck, but he was a labourer, and burglar and bully, no slaughterman, and he drew the keen blade through the pocket of soft flesh beneath the jaw, from hinge to hinge, but missed the vital blood vessels beneath.

Blood flowed nonetheless, a gout that wet Carver's grasping arm. Hardacre roared with rage and surprise, and turned, his arm swinging like a flail, beating Carver down so that he staggered, hampered by his leg-irons, and fell.

Hardacre turned on Carver. Bloodied, his throat stinging, but taking no mortal hurt, he reached surely and quickly for his familiar bayonet. His back was toward Kempe: he had no cause to think of him.

Yet Kempe had undone the sailor's scarf he kept around his neck, and he dropped the scarf with a simple motion over Hardacre's bloodied neck, closed the loop, and pulled.

Hardacre was choked, hauled off balance. His voice stifled, he fumbled with his knife and tried to strike over his shoulder, but Kempe, still tightening the cloth, eluded him.

Carver, on his knees, lunged and pinned the soldier's flailing legs together. Kempe stepped back and yanked the scarf tighter and closer still, winding it for purchase about his hands. They had Hardacre writhing between them, almost off his feet. Kempe groaned and snorted, grinding his teeth. His hands burned, and he saw nothing; not the ship, not the cell, not the other prisoners, only the one man twisting and jerking within his grasp, as air and life were throttled out of him.

Hardacre shuddered, kicked, grew weaker, and still Carver clutched at him.

Then there was but a dead weight, and still Kempe held the knotted scarf steady, until the strength of his arms gave and his knees buckled, and he fell.

"You damned fool," whispered Kempe. "You damned fool. What have we done?" His voice was curiously calm, flat.

"Surely we are quit of this man."

The hulk shifted again in the squall. Canvas awnings creaked and the anchor lines thrummed. Hardacre's head lolled on the boards.

"He's dead."

"We must put out the light," gasped Carver.

"No. Shutter it. We will need it presently." Kempe's breath rattled in his chest. "What did you tell this man?"

"Nothing." Carver caught his breath. "I sent Chalke to tattle a little. To say that the prisoners had hatched a plot against him, and that you, Kempe, had special knowledge of it."

"What?"

"Only to spur you on. I saw you talking to Hardacre. I knew what he would put in your path, to betray the rest of us."

Kempe sat back upon his heels. "And you thought to run me out as bait. That if Hardacre took me aside you could come upon him nearly alone and do the deed yourself."

"Why should the honour fall to you, when you dithered and delayed?"

"And you thought you would make it your honour? Well, you have missed your mark. Do you not see? Chalke is an informant. You did not use him: he wheedled and guessed and got the truth out of you. And Chalke will be the first to speak when this is discovered. He will name me to the guards as soon as the hue and cry goes up, and then one of us will hang for sure."

"I struck the first blow. I lured him down here. It was me." Carver sounded sullen, a child deprived of a prize.

"And I finished it," said Kempe quietly. "I have carried a weight of anger and shame for a near eternity, and it all falls from me and leaves a species of nothing."

There were more sounds: boots or feet shuffling along the deck above. Carver started and Kempe looked up.

"Who is on watch?" said Kempe.

"Purvis."

"Then he will not come down unless he is disturbed. But we two are dead men, as soon as the watch is over."

Carver crawled forward. "What do you propose?"

"I? I did not set this trap. Did you give no thought to what would come after?"

"We must get off this ship," said Carver.

"How?"

"Can you swim?"

"We are in shackles, man. We will surely drown."

"Then we must take a boat."

Kempe hunched over, drawing harsh, sharp breaths. "Only officers and guards can get to the boats. We must gain the top-deck and risk everything on reaching the shore. Night and foul weather are our only friends."

"What of him?" said Carver, pointing to Hardacre's lolling corpse.

"I would have dropped him in the bilges," said Kempe. "Perchance they would have believed he fell in by chance and drowned. But now there is a great gash across his neck and no hope of that. Leave him here. Lock the door. There is no better place for him. But wait!" Kempe laid his hands on Hardacre's oilskin and drew it back. "The red coat may serve us for once. Get it off him."

In the half-dark, with cold fingers, they stripped the slick wet cloak and coat off the corpse, fumbling over Sergeant Hardacre's neat brass buttons.

"Who will wear it?" said Carver.

Kempe began to draw the soldier's coat over his ragged convict tunic. He could not pull it closed around his shoulders, and the collar choked him. He put on the tall cap and the cloak. "Walk before me," he growled. "We must dare it all, or perish."

Kempe ran his hands along the sergeant's flanks. And, as he'd thought, he found the keys to the gates between the decks on the ring there, for Sergeant Hardacre had set about the ship with no obstructions or permissions save his own. Their chains would not come off so easily: they were riveted on.

Then Kempe pushed Carver out of the cell, and he raised the lantern and partly drew back the shutters. The long, dim reaches of the hulk were before them, packed with sleeping men.

"Huzzah!" cried Oliver Kempe. "For the South Seas and mutiny!"

An answering roar went up among the men so disturbed, a bedlam racket. Carver scuttled through the uproar, and Kempe paced behind him, settling the soldier's cap about his head. Prisoners squirmed and shook in their berths. As they passed their old place, Kempe glanced sidelong and thought he caught Chalke's long, pale facing peering across at them in cold wonderment.

Kempe's chest ached and his throat closed, as though he himself were subject to the noose. Afterwards, for long years, he would have no recollection of the walk along the deck of the *Adamant*, except for the breathless haste of it, and the clamouring of the disturbed prisoners.

Carver scurried up the ship's steps. The gate at the top was locked, but Kempe undid it with Hardacre's own keys. He was lucky: the second one fitted, for his hands shook. So too the next gate on the upper deck. Then there was only the hatch to the quarterdeck to go, but the air here was fresh and cold and bitter.

The hubbub and shouting followed them up. The hulk seemed alive with scratching, complaining devils.

The last hatch was thrown open. A light appeared between the bars. Kempe leaned forward and hissed something to Carver. Then the guard appeared, swathed in oilskins, for though the running rain had passed, still spray was hurled by the wind across the ship.

"What is that damnable strife?" bellowed a voice from the deck.

Carver stumbled forward into the barred light. "Don't let him take me up there. He will throw me over the side!"

The guard, looking down, saw only the prisoner in chains, and the sergeant's cap and cloak in the shadows behind.

He laughed. "Haul yourself up here. A dousing will cool your head." The heavy grate rolled back.

Then Carver climbed towards the rocking quarterdeck, and Kempe came up behind him.

The guard retreated into the lee of the superstructure. Chains and gates heaved as the gale beat around the top-deck of the hulk.

"Come," said Kempe. "They may realize their error at any moment."

The deck of the *Adamant* was a wasteland, shuddering as the hulk rocked, swept by spray. Ghost-light flickered behind grates in the super-structure, made vague by the mist and cold.

Carver shrugged—he was starting to shiver—and shuffled towards the rail. "All or naught," he said. "We must try and swim to shore."

"Not unless you want to spare the Crown the cost of a shroud. You will drown for sure," growled Kempe.

"Then why did you bring us here?"

"For a boat."

Kempe clutched Carver by the shoulder, and in a rough dance they reeled towards the side. Twice, Kempe made a show of beating Carver around the head with the flat of his hand. Then, Carver was leaning over the rail with Kempe behind him. The water was all darkness, a void filled with the sweep of the waves.

Carver recoiled from the oily chaos of the river. On the side of the hulk, over its mass of makeshift shutters and boarded gunports, a sort of gangway had been constructed, reaching down to the cutters and jolly boats that ferried prisoners to their labours each day. The whole thing shivered and wobbled. Carver clutched at the rail.

"We must go quickly," hissed Kempe. "And leave the lamp, or they will surely guess their error."

"You cannot mean to go down there," said Carver.

"I meant to do all this in silence, and conceal the deed, but you have set all that at naught, so we must dare an escape. Perhaps they will think we drowned."

"We will be swept out to sea and drown in truth," said Carver.

"All the better."

Kempe hung the lamp upon the rail and then slipped over the edge of the planking, dropping over the bulging side of the ship to slide nine feet to the platform below. He staggered, fell on one side, and clutched at the slick planking. The soldier's cap was lost. Carver toppled after him, landing like a sack of laundry, almost spilling into the water as the hulk rolled. He stopped himself only by clutching at Kempe, who clawed at a gap in the boards to keep his place.

They had fallen into utter darkness. The mass of the hulk was one black shape beside them. Water sucked at the ragged, crusted side of the hull and waves gulped and broke beneath them. All else was grey and incoherent. There was no chance of standing, so for an infinite age they crawled and groped downwards, sliding and rolling as the ship shifted.

The bottom landing was inundated, and cold waves shifted and soaked them. Carver's hand smacked against the gunnels of a longboat. His fingers were raw and icy.

"No!" bellowed Kempe, "too large for us."

Two jolly boats, used by the officers for mail and incidentals, were tied up at the end of the platform. Drenched and sputtering, the prisoners crawled towards them. The smaller boats skittered against the hulk. Carver merely pushed the first one away and fell head first into the water when he first tried to get into it. Retching at the silty water, he finally scrambled over the edge. The little shell was already part filled with water. Kempe dropped in afterwards, and Carver could hear him fumbling for the oars.

Kempe pushed away from the hulk.

"Which way?" shouted Carver.

"Into the wind. It is blowing offshore. I can smell the fens."

Fumbling with the heavy oars, finding the oarlocks by touch, they brought the jolly boat about.

"Pull!" bellowed Kempe. "And pull for your life!"

The boat wobbled, and waves smashed over the side. The shadow of the hulk seemed immovable, an island of stone, and for a long time nothing seemed to shift and all their efforts were futile. But then the darkness about the prison ship became absolute, and the sound of the wind stronger. Suddenly, they were in a frail cup, a dainty thing, on the lightless and restless surface of the river.

CHAPTER 17.

Two Gone Ashore

KEMPE HAULED at the oars. The little boat rocked dizzyingly. The lights of the hulk drifted behind them.

"Which way?" said Carver.

"The current will take us out to sea," grunted Kempe. "We must land as best we can on the edge of the salt marshes. Hide. Wait for morning. Find a blacksmith or a forge, I suppose. Starve and freeze, and wait to be captured, I expect."

"What matters it? We are dead men, both."

"The man that killed Sergeant Hardacre is for the noose. What did you think would come of cutting his throat on the deck?"

"I thought the man that did for Hardacre would be a hero, not a beaten dog." Carver looked down to the water between his feet. "In truth, I did not think much on what would come after." He clenched his hands. "If you should get clear, do think on my Meg Harper."

"Bah." Kempe let the oars rest and looked about. The clouds had lifted fractionally. He could smell coal smoke, but the little villages along the foreshore were clothed in darkness. "At least we may choose our own course for an hour or two."

"You are pretty crafty in a boat for a city man," said Carver, with a touch of bitterness.

"I grew up by the sea," said Kempe, after a long pause.

Carver shivered and tried to shrink below the gunwales out of the bite of the wind. The clouds began to rise and break, and now and then the muzzy sheen of the half moon was revealed, a smudge on the sky. Kempe looked about. The river widened greatly as it drew closer to the sea and the mouth of the Medway, and a sluggish flow had taken hold of the little boat. There were no means to judge the hour, or how near the dawn could be. Kempe thought he might hear a church-bell tolling, but it may have been his imagining on the open water.

"You don't talk like a country man," said Carver, muffled, from the end of the boat.

"I set all that aside when I was articled in London. My father, you see, had a great need within him to make his son a respectable man." Kempe laughed, but the sound caught and emerged harshly from his throat. "A respectable perjurer, respectable escaper, and soon to be a respectable murderer."

"Well, we don't have to dwell on that," said Carver.

"What's the use, out here, whether we do or not?" replied Kempe.

"And your father was a clergyman—no, a schoolmaster—I'm sure."

Kempe flexed cold and aching hands on the oars. In a low voice he said, "No. My father was a fisherman. I spent a good part of my boyhood on boats. Though it was smuggling good French wares that made him wealthy, a respected man in the village, who could sing as loud as he liked in the chapel and entertain the rector in the parlour. The only thing we feared, besides storms at sea, was the excise men knocking at the door. My father thought to set that right by making me a proper London lawyer."

Carver turned uneasily, trying to draw his legs up from the water that lapped at the bottom of the boat. "A man should have a trade," he mused. "Even the hangman has his calling. I had thought to go into soldiering, but I couldn't tolerate another man telling me what to do."

"What trade did you take to, then?"

Carver grinned to himself, unseen in the dark. "I was a pretty fair resurrection man, though the stench was something foul. Good money in that also. There's always a call for a man who'll do what others won't."

At that moment a burst of noise, like low thunder, rolled across the water towards the vast, imperturbable circle of the night.

"What's that?" said Carver. "Is it a storm? Will we go under?"

"No. We are discovered. Chalke has got the ear of a guard. They are firing the cannons on the ships to warn the villages. We must get off the water before dawn: it will be too easy to see us then."

THE BOAT GLIDED in near silence. Carver sulked in the bows, sometimes moving to hide from the wind, sometimes chaffing his hands and arms, or bailing with a cracked bucket when Kempe directed him. Kempe hauled at the oars, cutting across the current as he could best judge it. But convict work, long enclosure in the dank hulk, had worn and wearied him, and at the end of each breath came a sharp, deep rattle in the lungs. He kept his head high, though the cold stung his ears, searching for the lights of other boats. Then, he would breathe deeply through his nose, trying to detect the odours of mud and grass and rotting weeds that would tell him the shore was close by, and listen intently for the rustle of reeds, or the lowing of cattle along the dykes.

Perhaps the moon had shifted somewhat in the sky, for Kempe, turning back, glimpsed a slick shimmer, glassy and still. The little boat shuddered and then ground to a halt.

"What is it?" said Carver.

"Mudflats," Kempe returned grimly. "The tide is out."

"Do we wait in the boat for morning? Will the tide carry us off?"

"No. We must try for the shore and make what distance we can."

"You are damnable sure of yourself," said Carver.

"It is hopeless," said Kempe. "But the tide may take the boat further away when we're out, and confuse searchers."

They tumbled out into the stinking, foul-smelling mud, which sucked at their boots and clogged their fetters and chains. Agony to walk in, with aching shins, forever sliding and swaying and losing balance, as the whole force of the mud sucked them down. Almost blind in the night, with only the faint sense of the grasses piled against the dim line of the land and the sound of small wavelets lapping behind them to guide them away from the river. The extension of time was interminable, a hell of stumbling, mud-coated, stinking, shivering, worse than any forced labour on a treadmill.

At last, the ground became marginally firmer, the air fresher. They staggered against a low bank of sand and mud and thick-stemmed sea-grass. Kempe was hacking, retching; Carver reeled and his sinews burned.

"Hide. Rest. Dawn." Carver ground out the words, as though crushing shells for lime.

Kempe had already fallen to the ground beside him.

The weakening of the quality of the dark, like ink fading in water, revealed the river as a vague band and the edge of the sky. The breeze freshened, and the ranks of grass and reeds hissed. Carver stood up, swaying, and looked around. A low exhalation escaped him.

"What's the matter?" said Kempe, who still crouched on the mud.

"Four years on the damned ship, worse than a dog in the kennels, ordered here and there, whipped and bated, and forever waiting to sail. Now, leg-irons or not, I choose which way to walk—for this little while."

"But which is better?" said Kempe quietly. "Free for an hour or a day, or fettered safe and sound?"

Carver spat on the ground. The taste of mud was thick around his mouth. "I wish to God that my hand had gone true. My conscience is clear on that account."

"Are we to go together or apart?" said Kempe.

"It don't matter to me, as long as it's away from the river. I can't bear the sight of it."

Kempe rose. The two men, slimed and bedraggled, in heavy prison tunics, with wild hair and tangled beards, were indistinguishable, gaunt as scarecrows, pale as the revenants of drowned men. They set off, shambling. Great bands of grey cloud gathered and grew distinct behind them, but there was no colour in the dawn.

FETTERED AS THEY WERE, they could go no faster than a weary shuffle, and all thoughts of freedom were mere daydreams, tatters of mist. The marshes, fields, and ditches, the raised paths and fences, were an open maze to tempt and harass, leading from nothing to nothing. Kempe scanned the misty stretches of land for columns of smoke, thinking to find a farmhouse with perhaps a workshop, clothes, food even, but Carver thought to avoid all meetings and spoke of wandering overland to the mouth of the Thames, for his notions of most regions outside the great city were hazy.

Instead, they crept along muddy cow-paths at a mean pace. A cloud-shrouded sun loomed on the horizon, but they had been walking no more than an hour when they heard dogs barking and men calling behind them.

Kempe let the red coat drop to the ground; it was too heavy, bloodied, and too bright for concealment. "They have found the boat," he said. "We must hide."

There was nowhere to hide, just a path across acres of green, sodden field, a scattering of copses in the distance, a church spire, the high path along a dyke half a mile distant. They ran painfully as they could, though their shackles bruised and tore at their damaged shins. The barking of the dogs and the voices of men grew distinct behind them.

When Kempe looked back he could see the soldier's tall caps, muskets, and bayonets scoring the air above them.

They ran on, and did not look back again—three hundred yards more, grinding out the last minutes of the escape. Kempe could not have thought his body would burn so, his head be so foggy, his mouth so dry, his heart race so fast, ears ringing and seething, and his arms and feet and shoulders so heavy and inflexible, like bands of iron riveted to his flesh. His run became a shambling, his thoughts as harrowed and dull as everything else.

Then there was a *hiss-crack*, like a great stone falling from a column. A musket ball ploughed into the dirt before them and threw up fragments of mud. Kempe registered it, dazed, as though it were a fact with precedent. Two more cracks, soldiers bellowing orders, the dogs in a frenzy, and Carver fell flat upon his belly in mid-stride, as if clubbed down by a giant.

Kempe stumbled to the earth. His forehead touched the ground, and his sight drew in around a blade of green grass, all the sensory universe compressed to that point of contact. The dogs surged about him, snapping and worrying at the rags of his convict weeds. A soldier pulled his head up. He was panting, senses reeling, drunk on terror and fatigue.

He looked aside. They had kicked Carver onto his back. His mouth and eyes were open without staring and without breathing.

"Who is this man?" barked a corporal. He was holding a piece of paper: a description of the escaped prisoners.

And all that Kempe could see was the blood dried and set under Carver's chipped nails, the razor rising and falling in the lamplight.

"That is the man that killed Sergeant Hardacre," Kempe said.

"Which man is that?" said the corporal carelessly.

"That is Oliver Kempe. God rest his soul."

"Well," said another soldier, prodding the dead man with his bayonet, "he's dodged the noose."

Cape Horn, South America, 1830

WILD SEAS AND crags of ice in the distance. It was too cold to stand long on the deck, as immense surges of saltwater broke over the prow. Kempe, who had so long worn the name Carver as to regard his former self as an actor might an old character, prompts and costumes now discarded, lingered in the dark below decks. The last morning of his first escape, the colourless, dim dawn over the empty road, the open field, and the dogs, baying at him while he covered his head and Carver lay dead, three steps from him, the scene he had buried in rum and heat, seemed a distant thing, a vapid melodrama, all wooden lines and stiff gestures.

London, 1823

THE SOLDIERS DELIVERED him to the county lock, limp and heavy, like a body in the shroud. When the constable asked for a name, the marine sergeant said, "Gabriel Carver, escaped the hulks." Then he was transferred to the sepulchre of Newgate for trial. By then the convicts on the *Adamant*—with the informant, Chalke—had been rowed to their transport and dispatched to the prison colony. Kempe wondered idly how those who had drawn from the clutch of nails in the lottery of lost men had divided out the meagre possessions he and Carver had left, perforce, behind. Chalke's face, staring out from among the bunks, eyes wide, sometimes returned to him.

Kempe stood mostly silent in the dock, with shoulders bowed, and spoke only twice to say nay to the charge of murder, and aye to escaping. There was little evidence to call: the trial lasted until luncheon. The chief warder stood in the box to tell that an informer had come forward (the prisoner bent his head at this; there was invariably an informer) to warn that certain prisoners had taken against the sergeant of the watch, who had a reputation for harsh treatment, and one of their own, named in the affidavit as Oliver Kempe, had certain knowledge of the plot against the sergeant.

Did the warder propose that the prisoners had conspired severally to murder a guard, His Honour enquired, with a sour glance at the prisoner.

The warder coughed behind his hand. The prisoners were subject to many wild notions, which came to nothing. It was not to be thought that they would ever muster the means to accomplish such a thing. In any case, none of the convicts would say anything on the matter.

And yet, remarked the judge, unmoved by this comfortable fiction, the dead prisoner had plainly got the better of one of his guards.

The warder supposed that in this case Kempe, the man found dead with blood still upon his prison clothes, had been confronted by an angry Hardacre, struck out in terror with a hidden weapon (the prisoners were, regrettably, very skilled at fashioning such things) and carried the moment. Hardacre was notoriously loose in discipline and incautious in his dealing with the prisoners. Besides, he had been seen on deck talking in private with the prisoner before.

Under oath, the prisoner spoke a few words, hard and curt, never looking at the judge. Kempe had come to him with blood on his hands and the sergeant's coat and keys. Blamed him for his difficulties; then demanded his help. Threatened to impeach them all for what he had done alone, otherwise. Fearing sudden discovery and a charge of mutiny, Carver had agreed, helped to take the boat, and they had landed together. Nothing else to say.

The judgment was handed down without delay by the grizzled judge, half-dozing and winking in the dim courtroom, while London smoke and London rain pawed at the windows. A sorry matter, altogether. Gabriel Carver was guilty of escape, an accessory after the fact of murder. The crime was punishable by death, the sentence commuted to transportation for the term of his natural life. The main actor in the crime was dead before he could be brought to trial. The man in the dock lowered his head, and smiled grimly, and no one in the court marked it.

PART THREE

CROSSING LETHE

CHAPTER 18.

The New Police

London Docks, March 1830

SMOKE AND RAIN, mud and the stench of foul water, the roar and clamour of the streets, and the vast forests of masts and church spires and black belching chimneys closed in about Carver as he stood on deck, and he breathed deep of the smoke and river and smiled, a quirk of the lips, in remembrance, wonder, and glee, all unseen.

Sergeant Ellington shivered. He was lean and diminished in a great grey woolen coat. "Foul place," he growled. "Noisy. Dirty. Freezing."

"Heart of the Empire," returned Carver. "Your courts and judges, kings and queens, governors, and Parliament, your jurors, lawyers, and scoundrels: all seated here. Your convict ships and regiments and settlers all set out from this port."

"Don't get prosy with me," said Ellington. "Once we're off this ship, one wrong step and I shall swear a warrant against you."

"Don't it strike you as impressive we've just come a mighty way for one wrongdoer?" said Carver.

"You just stay with me, before and after. And don't speak until you're spoke to."

The ship edged towards the docks, slower than a shackled prisoner, under the guidance of the pilot. The air burnt the back of Carver's throat, and he felt the familiar prickling of his eyes and nose. He had no coat, but he had been colder before. He began to laugh, and ended by coughing instead.

"Well then, sergeant," he said, "what do you propose?"

Ellington looked out at the city with wide eyes, but his shoulders sagged. "I am instructed to report to the Colonial Office."

Carver coughed into his hand again, but his eyes were merry. "Lead on, sergeant. I shall go in your custody."

THEY WERE DELIVERED from the ship to the docks, and left to tramp upwards from the shore, among heaps of ashes and street-muck, drays and carriages, the crush of labourers, sailors, and clerks. Dull April cold lingered over everything: the sun was smothered. Ellington dithered, scratched his head; could find no one to give him directions, and eventually Carver took him by the arm and drew him towards Whitehall. Men and women cluttered the footpaths and jostled in the streets. Reeling and footsore, unbalanced by months at sea, they came in among the heaps of monumental marble, columns, and soaring porticos of the War and Colonial Office. Half-dressed children fluttered and squabbled and picked at scraps along the gutters like hungry sparrows.

They got in, were stopped by a hall-porter, sought directions, and were lost again among the sterile corridors, the grand flights of stairs, milling petitioners, and scurrying secretaries. Ellington handed over his letters, was ignored, laughed at in astonishment, harried along. Carver dogged him and ambled after. They were instructed to wait in a dusty, unheated anteroom, with tattered maps pinned all over the walls.

Ellington beat his heels on the patterned tiles. "Our man could have gone a thousand miles by now. He could have taken another ship."

"No," said Carver. His throat was dry. "He sailed to London for a reason: he has something to sell here."

A dapper gentleman in a neat black coat and neat pointed shoes came out to them. By then the bells were ringing four o'clock. He bent over Ellington, took his letters, and clucked with his tongue against the inside of his mouth.

"Highly unusual," muttered the neat young secretary.

Ellington scowled. "We're here to arrest a murderer."

The secretary smiled thinly. "M'dear fellow, your function in its *entirety* is to keep the murderers and other sorts on your side of the oceans."

"If you don't want us here…" began Ellington.

"It don't make a blind bit of difference to me whether you're here or there, but the governors, you know, don't want trouble. *Highly* unusual. Who's to keep you, aye? Who's to report on the matter? Under whose authority are you?"

Carver, hands behind his back, was studying the gilded finials on the ceiling.

"This murderer could have been here a month or more already," said Ellington sullenly.

The clerk whistled through his teeth, and wrote something in pencil on the back of one of the letters. Then Ellington and Carver were ushered out into the hallways, jostled and turned, and deposited on the streets.

They went at once to the magistrate's court, for that was what the neat man had written with a brief note, but they were turned out at the door by the bailiff, for the day had grown thin. Ellington brought them to an alehouse and ordered chops and porter, but he was surly and silent, and frequently counted out the few coins in his possession. Carver did not bother to engage him.

"TWO PRETTY LITTLE parrots far from home," said the magistrate, scratching his razored scalp, for his wig was on the desk.

They were in chambers, before the first case of the day. Gaslight squeaked and popped behind the magistrate, a thick-set, square-jawed heap of a man, who had dispatched a thousand bodies or more to transportation with the same slow, rough speech and pretence of common sense.

The magistrate turned over the letter before him again. "I cannot quite make out why you have come so far, and at great expense no doubt, to contrive the arrest of one man, a sailor on the *Agatha*. No name. Precious little description."

"This sailor has murdered three men. One of them a clerk to the colony, another a respectable free-convict."

"You have lost him," said the magistrate. "He will have disappeared in London. He will have taken another ship. This is a fool's errand, and you expect me to make myself fool enough to join your chase?"

"He won't have gone yet," said Carver suddenly. "He has something to sell."

"A list of returned convicts. All condemned before the law. A list that only this man—" the magistrate scowled at Carver, "a convict executioner, no less—claims to have knowledge of."

"We can lay hands on it yet," said Carver, "if we are quick."

"Hopeless folly." The magistrate flicked at the letter with a blunt fingertip.

"We have our duty," said Ellington dully.

The magistrate harrumphed and ground his teeth together. The gas hissed and jumped. "I shall send you to these new police of the Home Secretary's, who are perpetually underfoot and making everyone's business their own. They can make of you what they will. Now get out."

"Sir—" said Ellington.

"Get out!"

• • •

THEY WERE DIRECTED by a bleary-eyed clerk of the court to Whitehall Place. The new police station was calm and well-lighted, with mud near the doors and a tall sergeant at the desk, who inked their names in a register and took them in to an officer. Inspector Meade looked at their papers, listened attentively to Ellington, and all the time kept his small, dark brown eyes on Carver. Meade was a hale forty years old, as wide through his chest and girth as he was about the shoulders, with thick whiskers, curly hair, and the watchful manner and sharp habits of a man often about the streets.

"Well," he said, "it's a rum story and no mistake. A fiend gone to ground in London and you two colonials on his trail. Sailor, you say?"

"We do."

"What sort of sailor: Englishman, Irishman, American, Lascar, Tahitian, Chinaman?"

"Englishman—Londoner. I heard him speak," said Carver.

"Colouring, height, distinguishing marks? Come man, we have precious little to get on with."

"About my height, loose framed, not heavy: eleven stone."

"Eleven stone, you say?"

Bashfully, Ellington said, "Mr. Carver is a hangman by trade."

"Is he so?" said the alert inspector.

Carver nodded. "Eleven stone, I would drop him for. I saw him in the dark. When I hear the voice, I'll know the man."

"In going to and fro, from one office to another," said Ellington deliberately, "we have lost precious days."

Inspector Meade charged out from his desk with no significant effort, and commenced buttoning his coat. "You'll want the docks," he said. "And if you want a sailor, we'll want the Marine Police as well."

They were marched to the docks by the tireless inspector. Down among the shoremen, wharves, and ships, with the constant rattle of wheels and creak of cranes, and porters hunched like crabs under great weights from all the far ports of the world: tea and furs and horn and sugar, cloths and china-wares. There they were cast into another smoky station-house.

"Marine Police," said Inspector Meade. "Been here longer than our lot. Patrol the docks against theft and pilfering. Know every ship and sailor and labourer."

The inspector barked at a sergeant; the sergeant shouted at a constable. Registers and newspapers were pulled out. Inspector Meade scanned the columns.

"There." His broad thumb stopped on a row. "Your ship: *Agatha*. Docked at Rotherhithe these two weeks ago, with a cargo from Australia."

"Two weeks!" exclaimed Ellington.

"You have been lucky. Now." The inspector's thumb traversed the table. "There. Provisioned. Departed for Newfoundland three days ago."

"Damnation." Ellington's head drooped. He was shaking with fatigue. "Our ship is gone."

"But not our man, most likely," said Carver steadily. "He has business in London. We must get the ship's manifest, and see who came off before she sailed again."

"Yes," said Ellington. His voice was dull and dry. "We must make the attempt."

"Jankle and Son," said the inspector. "Prominent firm. Offices not far." He clapped Ellington on the back. "Buck up, and we will try it."

Ellington gulped and nodded, and tried to wrap his coat closer over his lank frame. Carver grinned, like a man at the theatre pleased with the ending of the first act.

AT JANKLE AND SON, tottering heaps of crates and bales were erected along the dockside and in the warehouse. Carts were being loaded from above, ropes creaking, patient horses held steady while they lowered their lugubrious heads to their feed-bags. Inspector Meade, a corporal of the Marine Police, Ellington, and Carver, pushed their way inside, among many stares from the stevedores.

"Peelers!" ran the cry before them.

There were five clerks in the office, with their coats off and ink creeping up their elbows, and one small coal fire popping by the far wall. One man, lean, fifty or so, his face composed of frowning vertical lines, slipped off a stool and pulled on a black coat.

"You're not wanted," he announced. "Everything is in order."

"Now, Mr. Gally," said the corporal, "this isn't a customs matter. This is the Metropolitan Police. A serious matter. Murder, or so I gather."

The clerk looked around. "No one murdered here as far as I can see. This is a private business."

"Mr. Gally," said Inspector Meade, offering his hand, "we are making inquiries, only, of the crew of the *Agatha*."

"Well," grumbled Gally, "we are a private firm, and the captain don't care for snooping and questioning."

"Where is the captain?" said Carver unexpectedly. He had detached himself from Ellington and strolled behind the row of high clerks' desks.

"Not here," snapped Gally.

"Surely the owners will want to show a proper public spirit," said Inspector Meade.

Carver tapped on a ledger, shifted on his feet, flipped a couple more open pages.

"The captain don't take kindly to peekers and prowlers."

"Well, then," said Meade. "We can wait till he's called. We'll endeavour not to get in your way."

The clerk sighed. "Purvis, if you please, the copy of the particulars of the *Agatha*."

A ledger, thick with ruled sheets and India ink, was brought out and opened. The policemen crowded in. The clerk took his ruler and ran it down a column. Inspector Meade had his notebook ready and whispered with the corporal. Slowly, as if browsing in a bookstore, Carver stalked nearer, nodding at the other clerks. Ellington stood near the little coal brazier and tapped his feet.

Eventually, the inspector hurried over to Ellington with his notebook open.

"One man died on the voyage. That's neither here nor there. He was Irish. Too old to be your fellow. Two got off in Buenos Aires. No matter. Three cashed out and left in London. Of the three, one a Black. So, two left. We have the names, and we shall put them out to the stations. Sailors don't go far from the ports, on the whole. There are boarding houses, public houses, flop-houses. We shall pick them up, by and by, and then we shall make progress. Don't be disheartened!" Inspector Meade clapped Ellington on the back.

They withdrew, leaving only Carver, who had meandered over to the ship's record and now ran his blunt fingertip over the paper, pursing his lips, breathing softly. He stopped only once, but his face did not change. Ellington called. The clerks glared. Carver winked once at the puzzled senior clerk, and hurried after.

MRS. PEAT'S Lodging House was a diligently genteel stop for ship's masters, mates, and officers, on a corner in a ragged and transient neighbourhood close by the docks. The mistress kept a dark parlour near the street with grimy windows, for the use of her gentlemen. The dirt on the glass leant the room a perpetual fogginess. Ellington and Carver were installed here by Inspector Meade and told to wait for the next day—or the next. It was after nightfall, and a faint drizzle streamed over the port. They had ordered chops and greens and porter from the public house on the corner. Ellington had barely touched them, scowling at the plates, while Carver set to with a brisk appetite. Now the sergeant was hunched in one of Mrs. Peat's covered chairs, face pinched, sniffing and staring out onto the street, where vague forms passed and intersected.

"Cheer up, man," said Carver. "Everything is in hand."

"You're damned sure of yourself," said Ellington. "But we are cast-offs on a wild-goose chase. There are too many people and streets and voices here, and it does my head in."

"You ain't seen London before. It does rather impress."

Ellington scowled. "I was born in the colony. I never left it before this."

"Your parents were convicts," noted Carver.

"My parents were servants and croppers," snapped Ellington.

"Of course, no offence in it."

The sergeant rubbed his face. "It seemed like a fine, clever thing before we set sail, to follow the murdering bastard back to his hiding hole. But he's given us the slip, lost in a sea of faces and names. I think the whole aim of this business was to send you away before you could cause more confusion. Out of sight is out of mind to Mr. Fitchett."

"Well, that's a high estimate of my abilities," said Carver.

"We shall go back empty-handed, and both of us will look like fools. Put that down to your abilities."

Carver put his forearm on the table between them. "No need to paint it so black. I said there's a reason why our man won't have gone on yet. That's his little notebook of names. Every man jack wrote down there will have reason to keep it quiet, and will pay for the pleasure. But think it through a little more. Sidmouthe said he didn't have authority to pay more for the book. So that must mean that someone here, at this end of the Rats' Line, has the say-so. And that person would pay whatever they could to protect all the names in the book. Who it is, I don't know. Sea captain. Ship owner. Lawyer, even. But that's the person our killer is here in London to find."

"What of it?" Ellington smothered a sneeze.

"So, if we find that person first, our killer will come walking to us. No waiting and brooding in this musty lodging-house. And then Sergeant Ellington looks like a clever man. A decisive man. An officer who won't be out-foxed."

Ellington settled back into the stuffed chair. "What do you propose, then?"

"Call on Jankle and Son, while Inspector Meade is set about his business of rounding up the sailors. Perhaps it's not by chance our man sails on one of their ships. If you had bad work to be done quiet, wouldn't you start looking close by for a likely man?"

"You always got a question in your head and a place to go, don't you?" said Ellington.

"So? Your policeman has his informers. And your lawyers must make a case before judge and jury, by the fine old English rules of evidence. But all I have are these particulars and a thousand questions, and a thousand guesses more at the answers. So I worry at a question, I hunt it and I bring it down. And at the end of one of these questions, I will find my answer, by chance if nothing else, and then I shall know."

Mrs. Peat, being thrifty in her housekeeping, had few lights in the front parlour, and the hour had grown dark. The gaslighters had passed in the street, and now figures were filtering through the mist, resolving and dissolving as they drew near the glass and then departed.

Ellington had trimmed his new beard and whiskers before leaving the ship, but his sun-browned face looked dark, drawn, and weary. "When we have him, I expect our man will hang for what he's done. Whether he's been cheated or used. And others besides, if we lay hands on that list."

"Others besides," murmured Carver. "I expect so. Yes."

"How does that sit with you, hangman, to make work for the gallows? It don't seem to bother you much."

Carver stirred. "A hangman does not choose who walks to the gallows. That's for the judge and jury."

Ellington's face was almost lost between the high wings of his chair. "But putting a man—or a woman—to death. You must have an opinion either way."

Carver turned towards the glass and folded his arms. "I know that there are brutes who walk this earth and would be better off out of it. But who is to mark them and pluck them out with a perfect eye? There's too much to that, when every soul is a mystery, even to itself. And mortal judgment errs. We are in a state of dreadful error, and when we snuff out a life we snuff out also hope, and help, and restitution. It's a grand show we make of the gallows, and then a show of hiding it, but one hour there on the planks would reveal that it would be better to stay our hands and resolve to prevent what harm we could, than let the gallows make us dull and cruel. But being done, it's done. Let us not lie to each other. There's no hope for it."

Carver was not sure the policeman was still awake. Steadily, he set about gathering up the cold plates to set on the sideboard, and then went about the dim room, searching for more coal to put on the fire.

CHAPTER 19.

A Respectable Firm

THE CLERKS AT Jankle and Son put out the lights at half-past five in the evening and went out into the gathering dark. Their head, Mr. Gally, emerged last from the counting house and turned his key in the lock. He stopped on the bottom step of the warehouse to straighten his hat and tug on his kid gloves, and sniffed twice, without pleasure, for the street was bad that evening. Then he strode off.

Two men—one tall, lean, and unsteady, the other trim and quick—detached themselves from the empty carts and drays and crossed the clerk's path. Gally eyed them and drew himself up.

"Sergeant Ellington, I perceive. I am afraid I do not know this gent's name."

"Carver. I'm not a constable, though I am sometimes a servant of the law."

"Mr. Carver, pleased to meetcha, I'm sure. But I had thought our business with the police was over."

"It ain't quite," said Ellington, and then he stopped to cough.

"The sergeant means that there are one or two matter more," said Carver. "Come, let's take a mug of porter's ale. It's brisk out here; awful brisk."

He sidled neatly to the clerk's flank and all three walked on.

• • •

IN THE BOISTEROUS public room of the Gull and Cockle, Gally put down his mug and said, "It is best if the other clerks don't see me. My position, you know. Jankle and Son is a respectable firm."

"Which is plain to us," replied Carver, "and we don't want to go bothering anyone, or making a scene. No. Nor give the police reason to enter your office again."

The lines descending Mr. Gally's face deepened, like cracks in an old pier-post. "But I suspect you have business of your own with the firm."

"Well," said Carver. "Suppose you tell us what has changed of late?"

"Has anything changed?"

"No prowlers and peekers, you told the inspector. But who put *you* on guard against *that*, and when?"

Gally tipped his head fractionally towards Carver. "Instructions from the head of the firm."

"Unusual?"

"I should say so."

"And any unusual visits since?"

Gally sucked at his front teeth. "Apart from your peelers? One man, in a sailor's coat and a sailor's cap. Said he had a communication from the colonies. Wanted the owner's home address. Wouldn't leave his letter to the office. Most presumptuous, if I may say so."

"Did you give him the address?"

"Certainly not!"

"When?"

"Two weeks or so."

"No strange business since then?"

"Two more watchmen put on the warehouse and office at night. And then you fellows, the other day."

Ellington blinked and said. "We need to speak to the head of your firm."

"He is not in. Not expected."

"At his home then," said Carver sharply.

"Under no circumstances. *Express* instructions." Gally took a long sip from his hot rum.

"Police business!" barked Ellington. One or two of the drinkers clustered around him edged away.

"Forgive me," said Gally primly, "but I doubt very much you colonials have any authority to act here."

Carver nodded. "If you have a mind to spare the firm further trouble, you'd do well to cooperate. There is a reward for information leading to the arrest of this fellow. But he's cunning and determined, and not to be put off. We have reason to believe he'll be darkening the owner's door before long—if he ain't there already."

"Reward or not," said Gally, "I like my position and prefer to keep it."

"Of all the pig-headed, bloody—" sputtered Ellington.

Carver laid a heavy hand on the sergeant's sleeve. "You're a prudent man, Mr. Gally, loyal to your firm. But you haven't seen the blood and havoc that follows this man we are after."

Gally began to pull on his gloves. "Nevertheless, I will keep my own counsel on this. I thank you for the refreshments."

Gally rose from the small table. Ellington pulled on his own tankard and frowned. When the clerk had been lost in the uproar and press of the public bar, Ellington spoke: "Well, you made a bloody mess of that. Tight-lipped bastard."

"Never mind that," said Carver. "There's a dog that hears his master's voice even when the master ain't near. Let's see where he runs."

Carver slipped out of his seat, but did not raise his head high. Ellington grimaced, took another gulp of small beer, and stood, wincing as he elbowed the dock-labourer behind him. Carver was already making for the door, and the policeman traipsed after.

• • •

OUTSIDE THE Gull and Cockle, smoke and fog had set about smothering the streets and muffling up the souls who walked along them. Ellington bent at the waist and began to cough into the cuff of his coat. Carver drew him closer to the wall, but his eyes were on Gally, who was peering at his pocket watch nine or ten paces away.

"It's late," murmured Carver, "but will you go, regardless?"

Gally snapped his watch case shut and set off with his stiff, cautious gait. Carver waited for the space of five deep breaths and followed. Ellington pushed out from the wall and went after.

Gally did not return to the counting-house, but hastened away from the docks. He stalked up by Limehouse and Stepney, towards Bethnal Green. The streets were never clear, a rolling display of strollers and streetwalkers, flower-sellers, carters, and vagrants, and the furtive children, begging for pennies and digging for scraps in the trash-heaps. Warehouses and taverns in collusion gave way to shops and tenements, and then the streets widened into terrace rows, brick walls topped by iron rails, and hard footpaths.

"That's it," whispered Ellington. "He's going home."

"Go a little farther," said Carver, "and we shall see."

They walked on, with Gally pacing before them, straight as a stick. The fog and the coal fumes came down farther to caress the roofs of tall houses, heaps of new brick with towering, pompous iron fences with dire spikes. There were slender plane trees close by the gutters, and near the open roads Carver stopped in the shadow of one of these, and waited for a short time before peering out to see how far Gally had gone ahead.

Impossible to tell how much they had walked, or the time of night. Gally turned sharply into a curving street that ended in a dead end and a single, square house, dim, with clustering chimneys, patterned brick, and many narrow windows. Gally went at once to the gate, but it was shut and locked. Carver stopped, and

Ellington halted at his shoulder, as Gally pulled at the bell beside the gate. Almost at once, a man appeared on the other side. He turned his capped head to the clerk. The gate opened, silently, and Gally slipped inside. The head clerk hastened to the house while the gate was shut. For a moment, a crack of light opened in one of the front windows in the house. Gally scraped the mud off his boots by the door, which opened enough to illuminate his face, and then he stepped inside. The door was shut fast. All was close and quiet again.

Carver rested. His shoulders moved as he drew a deep breath.

"Is this it?" said Ellington, hoarse and low.

"Aye, the clerk has run to warn his master. Jankle and Son are at home, but they're not accepting visitors. They keep the gate locked but well-oiled. They are afraid of something, or someone. This is the place, sergeant."

Ellington rubbed his hands together. "Well, I'll try them in the morning. No need to skulk about here like thieves in the night."

"As you say, sergeant," said Carver, but his eyes were still on the dark house.

Another gleam came at the windows, as if a hand moved there and someone peered out. Carver lurched back, and Ellington, huffing, stepped off sharply down the street. Their boots slapped against the damp paving, and the air scratched at eyes and nostrils as they walked.

WHEN THE CHURCH bells were counting off the morning hours, they returned under the cover of drizzle through muddy streets. Ellington pulled on the bell at the gate, and a squat figure appeared, obscured under a heavy rain slicker and hat.

"The trade's entrance is round the back," this heap opined.

"Police business," croaked Ellington.

The man in the coat eyed Ellington's uniform and stripes. "You're not wanted here."

"Would you rather we came back with a police inspector and a pack of constables, to hang on the bell?" Carver enquired.

The man jerked his head, but did not touch the gate. "Round the back, if you must. Durkin will see to you."

Around the back there loomed another gate with a guard, dust heaps, and washing lines. At the kitchen door they were met by a scowling butler who did not stir until Ellington had shown him a letter of introduction from Fitchett's clerk. They were admitted through the rear of the house, into the cold and musty hallway, where they were abandoned for many minutes, and then the parlour door opened and they were ushered inside.

The curtains had been thrown back and hooked up, and a fire stirred into bright, spitting life in the hearth. On old man with fine white spindles of hair about his seamed head was sitting by the fire, hunched in a quilted dressing gown. Opposite him, by a wide fire shade, was a stout woman with a round face, broad mouth, and brown eyes. She had been watching for the door to open, but looked aside then.

"Sergeant Ellington, of the New South Wales constabulary, and Mr. Carver, officer to the superintendent of prisons," announced the butler.

"Father!" said the woman, suddenly, in the high tones of one used to addressing the half-deaf. "The policemen are here!"

The old man stirred and blinked. "How do ye do—sergeant, was it? How do ye do. I'm afraid I cannot stand. My legs are not so steady. I am Mr. Jankle, senior, of Jankle and Son. What may I do for you?"

Ellington slid his cap off. "We are here, sir," he began, "owing to the murder of a clerk in Sydney, who was known to your office, by the name of Sidmouthe."

"Aye? What name?"

"Mr. Sidmouthe, father!"

"Sidmouthe. Poor Mr. Sidmouthe. One of our captains brought us the news. But I did not correspond with him. I do not take much of a hand in the business these days."

"But you have since taken precautions, or something has alarmed you, so that you guard your house and office," said Ellington.

"Hmmm?" returned the old man.

"We have been told that a murderer may have travelled on one of our ships, even as part of the crew," said the woman. "We are an established firm, and we take care to protect our interests. Beyond that, we are utterly in the dark as to the meaning of this, or the interest the police take in our business—I say, we are quite in the dark, father!"

"Mad fellow," said Jankle, "aye? Grudge against the firm, grudge against his captain. Could come here, for all we know. Can't see why we should just leave it to the police. 'Get some men on the door,' I said, didn't I, Marion?"

"We are alarmed," said his daughter. "Greatly alarmed."

Carver had kept silent, folded his hand behind his back, and stepped away from Ellington, and seemed content to study the row of paintings suspended along the back wall of the parlour.

"All the same," said Ellington. "If anyone should approach you, or if you have received any threats—"

"We shall inform the police directly, of course," said the woman. "But we have nothing else to tell you, in that case, I am sorry to say."

"One thing I should ask," said Carver, turning from the wall. "Am I right in thinking you are a married woman?"

"You are."

"And your husband has a hand in the firm?"

"He does."

"And what, if I may, is your husband's name, since he is not here this morning?"

"My husband rides to the office this morning. His name is Pryor. Captain Pryor."

"Thank you," said Carver. "I'm sure the sergeant doesn't want to trouble you further."

"What's that?" said the old man, leaning towards his daughter.

Mrs. Pryor clasped her hands in her lap. "The sergeant and this other man are going now!" she bellowed.

SWIFTLY AND FIRMLY they were precipitated into the London smoke, through the same back door they had come in by. The door was shut hard behind them, and then the bolt shot.

On the bottom step, Ellington put his hand to the rail and coughed, half bent over. When he had finished, he spat into a grate, hacked, and straightened. "Well, that was a bloody waste of time," he said. "They don't know nothing."

"Come on," said Carver, through gritted teeth. "Not here."

Out on the street, Ellington's breath was ragged. "What a pair of bloody fools you made us, harassing an old man and his daughter. They don't know nothing."

"They made a great show of that," said Carver. "They set the scene most carefully."

Ellington wiped his mouth and sniffled. "What was that business about the lady's husband?"

"Did you not mark the portraits on the wall?" said Carver sharply. "Jankle and Son, says the sign. And there is old Mr. Jankle himself set up in his warm parlour to answer us, his daughter beside him. A fine, harmless, doddering old man. So where is the son? There on the wall is a portrait of a young man, with a mourning ribbon pinned to the frame. Dead, I should say, one way or t'other. And there is his married sister, with her husband. It's her husband that runs the firm, be sure of that. That's the man we ought to catch sight of."

Ellington stopped sharply. He turned to face Carver. He was the taller by two inches, and looked down in the hangman's face. "You and your damned schemes and speculations. You rattle us like dice in a cup, to see which way things fall. Well, I won't have it. We won't go hounding a respectable family because you have a notion off some portraits you seen. We've come far enough already. The bills are out and the reward is posted. We wait for Meade and his men to bring in the informers, then we go and collect our man. That's all. No more of your foolery."

Momentarily, Carver's mouth was drawn back, flat and hard. Then his shoulders fell and he blinked twice. "As you say, sergeant," he said mildly. "It was but my fancy. I had a thought they could tell us something."

Ellington tapped on Carver's chest with one finger. "You are here on sufferance. Don't you forget you are a convict in my charge."

"Oh, I shan't forget," said Carver, with a smile.

"We wait, and then we will see," said Ellington.

They walked on. Water dripped off the bare branches of the trees along the street. The drizzle lifted, became inchoate, as though mixed with smoke and the weak rays of the sun. Ellington began coughing into his sleeve again, and dragged his feet on the path.

BY LATE AFTERNOON of the following day, the sergeant was sitting and shivering in a patched armchair by Mrs. Peat's meagre fire, with faint drops of perspiration starting on his forehead. Ellington shook and squirmed, sometimes bumping his chair closer to the embers, sometimes moving away, but Carver was the more restless, leaving the room to sweep through the kitchen for a penny-loaf and toasting fork, or darting to the windows when heavy footsteps went by.

As the drizzle thickened and the day deteriorated, the landlady glided in with a tray, cups, and a pot. She set a full cup and saucer at Ellington's elbow.

Ellington sipped and wrinkled his nose. "Can't taste it properly. Something bitter, though."

Carver grinned, pulled the corner of a copper flask from his pocket. "Something stronger there, to burn the fever out."

Ellington frowned, but reached for the sugar bowl.

An hour passed, while Carver brooded at the window, listening to the church bells and sometimes glancing back to the policeman. Ellington set his head back, his eyes fluttered, and shortly he began to snuffle and wheeze. When the sergeant was quite asleep, Carver crossed to him, bent down, and sniffed at his empty tea cup. His face did not change. The parlour had grown dim.

Carver slipped out to the hallway, taking his coat with him. He winked at the landlady, and held a finger to his lips. Then he opened the door to the closing afternoon and went out.

AN OSTLER LED a fine carriage with two glossy horses out of the stables on Perry Lane. The woodwork was polished, dark, with no trace of insignia or crest, mostly free of mud, and the leather well-oiled. The driver clucked at the horses and they paced down the lane and turned by habit towards the quays and the warehouses. Cold drizzle fell from a roiling, sunless sky. At the corner, one of the usual dockside loiterers in cap and coat detached himself from an animated conversation with a passing harlot and fell in behind the ambling carriage at a steady lope.

The carriage turned into an unpaved alley behind a broad building. The straggler hesitated at the turn and then followed, almost brushing the wall, with head down. Ahead of him, the horses were reined in sharply, snorting and tripping back.

A door opened in the building. One man stepped through, looking both ways, and another came quickly behind him, making straight for the door of the carriage.

A shout rang between the close walls: "Oi! Captain Pryor, no time for your old mess-mates from Sydney Barracks?"

The first man, who had opened the door, started forward, fists closed, shoulders raised. But the other man, stopping with one foot on the carriage step and the other on the strap turned his head and called, "Who's that? Make yourself known!"

"You don't know me, but I'm well-acquainted with you. Colonel MacNeish sends his regards." The man stopped short of the carriage.

"What do you want?"

"You're in some bother. I'm here to bring you out of it, if you'll listen."

"Get in then. I can't abide delay."

Pryor lurched up into the carriage. Carver came on at a half-run but held his empty hands out before him. The other man came forward, flicked open Carver's coat to glance at his belt and pockets, and then Carver tumbled inside. The horses were already roused and started moving.

Carver threw himself onto the narrow rear-facing seat.

Pryor was watching him with heavy-lidded eyes. Nothing remained of the dashing captain of the colonies. Steeped in claret and pipe-smoke, Pryor had turned pale, heavy, and suspicious. His thick neck rolled over the sides of his high white collar. He had cultivated his whiskers, partly concealing the veins on his checks, but his nose was red and puffy. There was no enthusiasm in the eyes, neither humour nor fear, but they did not waver, resting on Carver while the older man wheezed and rocked, and the carriage gathered speed along the dockside lanes.

"Well, man," said Pryor, "make yourself known or I will shoot you through and throw you into the nearest ditch."

"I'm no soldier," said Carver. "Nor a policeman. But I called with a policeman yesterday, and I know you have unwelcome visitors. I go by the name of Gabriel Carver."

"Don't blather," grunted Pryor.

"That's nice," said Carver, shifting along the seat. "You're in a stew, and I'm here to pluck you out of it, if you'll listen."

"What stew?"

"Your little scheme, your interesting business in imports from the colonies, has sprung a hundred leaks and looks ready to sink. The Sydney magistrates have wind of it; the peelers have wind of it; and you've been threatened and asked to pay by certain party, and you're not sure who or what to trust now."

Leather creaked and the steel springs groaned under the carriage. The driver shouted at the street. Pryor's jowls shook and his breath rattled shallow in his deep chest. "I don't like your manners. I don't like your insinuations either."

"You did pretty well," said Carver, "throwing in your commission. Married the daughter of a prosperous house. Took a hand in the business. You've prospered, sir, prospered."

"Merit. Mine own merit. Steady, hard work. A prudent hand, sir. That's the sum of it."

Carver leaned forward, to be heard above the rattle and creak of the carriage. "And now that's floundering, and the noose looms before you, and you're dreadful afraid."

"I'm not afraid of dogs like you," growled Pryor. "When a dog barks at me from the gutters, I kick it." He glared at Carver, but in the dim cab the eyes were bleary and he could not hold them still.

"But you are afraid," said Carver. "Your wife is frightened. Your house is locked and guarded. You must have got a mighty fright when your ship docked and you got the news: your pet magistrate's clerk murdered."

The horses stumbled and slipped. Pryor steadied himself. "Before we go another hundred yards, you will tell me what you mean. I'm in haste, and I don't suffer fools or rogues."

"But you're a man as can give a fellow a chance to make a new life on home ground again, and I can bring you out of these present troubles."

Pryor grunted. "I can bring myself out. I am not easily turned."

"If you could, you wouldn't be hiding at home and skulking in the back of this carriage."

"What would you do? I don't make out what you say to be true or false. I only ask what you would do in this case."

"If I can put my hands on the man that's hunting you, I can have him arrested for murder and his little book of names will disappear from everyone's thoughts."

"That damn fool." Pryor's lips worked together. The words came out low and quick. "Against instructions, you know. Without my authority, entirely. Do you understand? Without my knowledge. All insolence and pretension. Making a book of his own? No doubt he thought to grind me, the miserable cheat. Be plain! How will you retrieve it?"

Carver nodded, as though setting out a hand at cards. "Make me your go-between. You have had the threats, so you must be in communication somehow. But you don't want to go yourself, because you don't trust in your safety and you know that blackmail's a thing that doesn't stop with one payment. Consequently, you wait, and make excuses, and try and think of what to do. Well, I'll do it for you."

Pryor glanced at the small slit of a window he allowed, for the daylight was fast running out of the streets. "And why should you succeed, a common convict—for so I take you, and I know the type well—with no friends or influence in this great city?"

"Because I know your man, no one better. I have followed him half the world."

"And how will you get to that man? He's outfoxed you already, or else you and your sergeant would not be here."

Carver grimaced. The carriage was closed and almost airless. "I have the measure of him now. Besides, he wants something of you, and he has risked a great deal to pursue it. And he's afraid of the law. Well, I can get him closer to you and away from the law. And for that he will have to trust me."

Pryor drew his bulk forward. "Do not think to play false with me as well. Cross me, and you'll turn up with the rest of the offal on the river bank, and none will know how or by whom."

Carver opened his hands. "Why should I? You're a respectable man, head of a respectable firm. You have a considerable position.

I'm thinking you would be grateful, and generous, to have this cloud removed."

"I see. And if you get that book, what then? You know the firm is suspected, or else the police would not be here."

Carver clasped his hands together. "When the book is in your hands again, the proof is gone. For the rest, you're a clever man, and you know how to scheme and conceal. Put it on another man. Put it all on Sidmouthe. He's dead and won't quibble. It don't matter to me."

"And again, how should I know to trust you?" said Pryor.

"Why, you oughtn't trust me. But I like it here, the climate suits me, and I don't mean to go back to heat and flies and lashers, and I know you can arrange that. We need each other, if you take it that way."

Pryor grinned, though it was more a gritting of the teeth and raising the lips beneath the florid nose. "Tarry's Theatre. To be called for. Under the name of Jackson. That's how I am instructed to communicate with our pest."

Carver unclasped his hands. The carriage jolted over some obstruction on the road and the horses whickered. "I'll call again, soon," said Carver. Then he added, "We don't have much time. The police are on the trail, and my sergeant suspects. I have given him the slip, since he's not well. We must act fast."

Pryor thumped with his fist against the side of the carriage. "Get on, then. But I don't know you, unless you can show me results."

"One thing more," said Carver, not moving.

"How now?"

"I must steer clear of my sergeant. He's a millstone for me. I need lodgings and fresh clothes. Five pounds, in earnest."

Pryor snorted, but he reached for his billfold. "I thought we should come to that. Well, I don't trust a man who won't work for money."

The horses shied and the carriage rocked on its springs. Carver stumbled, lurched forward and plucked up the offered note, but Pryor was immovable, fixed in his seat. Pryor flicked open the little carriage door. Carver nodded, touched a finger to his nose, and then slipped out into the mud and chaos of the street. He had only just touched the pavement when the carriage lurched away into the soft spring rain.

CHAPTER 20.

Walking Shadows at Tarry's Theatre

MANY STRANGE BIRDS fluttered in and out at the stage door of Tarry's Theatre, brash and chattering even in the muddled grey rain that had fallen since midday. Carver looked on, dressed soberly in a new hat, coat, waistcoat, and boots, like a junior solicitor or grocer. He lingered over the stalls outside a bookseller's, yet his eyes flicked to the stage door from moment to moment. Six hours before he had sent up a boy with a letter to the backstage booth. Two hours before, the answer had come to his lodgings. Now he watched while actors, dancers, and musicians, stagehands, and dressers paraded through the doors. No other onlooker would have thought him anything but an idler. Eventually, he adjusted the posy pinned to the front of his coat and went around the corner to the small, bustling square that fronted the theatre. The doors were open for the first evening show. The new lamps flared bright inside and cast their garish and varied reflections across the filthy puddles that had collected outside.

The audience pressed in, clerks and shopkeepers, labourers and gentry, men in black coats or checks and stripes, and women in feathers and bustles, among the hawkers and beggars churning the square. High lights, gilt, mirrors, and red brocaded curtains everywhere, dazzling and baffling to the senses, enveloped Carver as he slipped through the circling crowd. He presented his ticket, shuffled past the pit, and made his way to the hard wooden forms of the stalls. The arch of the theatre soared above him. Under the blaze of the chandeliers he would be clearly marked by anyone in the boxes that ringed the space above. He glanced up, shading his eyes, into the whorls of drapery and ornament. A lady's gloved hand on a cushioned balustrade, a flutter of white playbills, but no face he recognized looking down. The audience filled in.

Carver sat, and the lights were taken down, and somewhere the ropes and pulleys worked to raise the curtains with a whisper of folding cloth, and from that moment the theatre filled his mind, and for a time there was no Gabriel Carver, only Oliver Kempe, and no shame and transportation, no cruel, swift struggle in the blackness of the hulk, no passage of the ocean, no colony perched on the edge of the world, no woman screaming in the cells, no scaffold, and no rope, only the painted scene, the roar of the audience, and the play, that most terrible, original illusion to which we are prone, that art may give form to chaos. Inevitably, the old man on the stage turned his back on the truth and the hangman whispered at the same time, "Nothing will come of nothing," and all things ran dark from that first error.

During the interval, the fruit sellers came down into the stalls, and one beckoned to Carver. He shuffled over and set down tuppence for an orange, and in the same transaction the girl passed a note into his palm. There was a box number on the paper that Carver screwed up and let fall to the floor. Carver stalked up the sets of alternating stairs to the dress circle with a heavy tread. Some gentlemen were smoking in the passage and flirting with breathless girls. He dodged them, came to a door, and opened it without knocking. There was a small, high box beyond, with a fair view of the stage and the stalls. One man was sitting alone in a corner, shaded by the drapes. Carver stepped inside without haste. He shut the door and the cheap latch clicked softly.

"Are you alone?" said the man by the painted rail.

"You've had enough time to watch me and see that I'm true to my word," growled Carver.

The figure paused, inhaled. And then Moynihan turned from the brightness of the stage to the shadow at the door. "Curious, that it should be you after all."

"Not so strange," said Carver, "for you saw me coming long before I knew it was you."

"How did you know? Your system of detection eludes me."

"I didn't, for sure, until this moment. I had hoped it were not so. Yet I saw your name in the register of the *Agatha*, and I had my guesses well beforehand. It had to be someone like you, and it could only lead somewhere like this."

"Then you know my business here?"

"I do."

"And do you mean to help or hinder me?"

"Neither. I'm here to make a reckoning, and how I weigh it all up depends on what you tell me."

The surgeon cocked his head. "I see. Then you'd best sit by me."

Carver shed his coat and hat, and sat comfortably by Moynihan on the plush velvet chair, and for a moment the two men, observing the stage, were alike in posture and interest. Then Moynihan looked down and muttered to himself, "Where to begin, precisely? It is all so very long to tell. I am afraid to start, it seems."

"Ruth Tremaine," said Carver.

Moynihan drew a startled breath. "You know that as well?"

"What else could it be?"

"And would my reasons matter much to you in that case? Has your executioner's heart ever sheltered a scrap of love?"

Carver glanced at Moynihan, and his frown was cold and angry. "Speak to it, then. Ruth Tremaine. The name everyone would prefer I forgot."

"I do not forget," said Moynihan, in his precise way. "On the contrary, after she was tried and transported, I would imagine meeting her in all manner of circumstances. I would mistake other women for her in the street, see her face glancing at me in crowds, at balls, on country paths, as though it would be commonplace to meet her any day by chance. That, I think, persuaded me beyond all else that I had been in love. I could not forget."

"How did you know her?" said Carver, composed again.

"I knew her since childhood. Our families were of the old, sprawling, Anglo-Irish cast, with high connections and low. We had some distant, distaff relations in common. We played together as children. She had the quick temper, the passionate sense of injustice. When I came back from my studies and medical school, she had joined the movement. She believed not merely in common justice for the Irish, but in the poet's dream of a better, truer world. I could not persuade her to set aside her protests, her agitation, her sympathy with rebel plotters." Moynihan arched his neck, as though scanning the shadows of the proscenium. "Would to God I had had the courage then to stand beside her. Then we might have been taken and tried together, at least. But I maintained my small, poor practice, and avoided politics. She scorned me for it. I was too meek then, I know."

"She was transported, a political."

"And I remained. And for that you may rightly call me a traitor to my own dearest heart."

"But you knew what happened to her, and what she devised out in the colony."

"Yes. There were a few letters, over the years. She knew they would be opened and read, but some of the brethren, the Irish politicals, had access to smugglers and private mail. She married, a damned brute of a convict, but a free convict. I perceived the outline of her intentions then. She was unshakeable in her determination. By and by, she let it be known that, by means of a liaison with a certain marine captain, she believed she could contrive a passage home. A return to the struggle, as she said. I believed her, that she could make it possible."

Carver raised his chin, as though looking not at the stage but a more distant scene, framed by brown grass and drooping gum trees. "And then you waited for word again."

"And no word came," said Moynihan softly. "I waited for a letter, a meeting, a memento, a sign that she had returned to her family or resumed the struggle, though that would be death to her, and there was nothing. And nothing will come of nothing."

"Perhaps," said Carver, "she would prefer to remain secret and unknown."

"Not to me," said the surgeon, quick and emphatic. "At last I secured a position as surgeon on a transport, and I travelled with one hundred and eight souls to the place she had been, and saw the hardships and punishments she had endured, and steeled myself to endure more, for her sake. My skills were in constant use. I believe I saved a good few lives on that voyage."

"Do you plead for clemency on those grounds?"

"No. Not at all. Not for myself. I only plead that you hear me out."

Carver shifted and hunched his back. "Every convict trusts a ship's surgeon. That is how you gained access to so many things. That poor scorched girl trusted you. She told you much more than you told me. She told you about Sidmouthe, and you used what she knew to throw me to the Irish smugglers. But when you made that trap, you also revealed your hand."

The action on the stage had resumed. The audience quieted, the houselights dimmed. Moynihan went on, but his reply was perfectly audible to Carver in the confines of the box. "So I did. And you yourself sent me to her. Can you imagine my perplexity and alarm, when you came so close upon my heels? If you suspected me then, it was cruel of you to send me to her. I did try and ease her pain."

Carver made a swift, impatient gesture. "Staines. You were determined to find your old love, so you went to Staines."

"Yes. He was a sly, suspicious cove—and my only link to Ruth. I persuaded him that I had some intelligence of his missing wife.

I played upon his damaged pride and his convict's passion for secrecy. I rode out to visit him by night, with no one else by to know or see who called. He agreed to all this." Moynihan's shoulders in his fine black coat fell in a suppressed shudder. "That was an evil hour. There is all my shame and folly."

"Come to it, then," said Carver tautly.

Moynihan turned to the hangman. "Do you know he beat her and misused her? My beautiful Ruth. Lashed and set to labour like a slave for that damned brute. All for the privilege of taking his name and going off the store. He boasted of that to me."

"You dosed him with laudanum from your doctor's bag," said Carver gravely. "Of course he talked. You wanted him to."

"I did. A little at first, and more as he grew drunker and the opiate worked on him. I wasted a good brandy in that. Well, he hardly knew what a fine brandy would taste like. He had pickled his tongue in rum."

"That was my first clue," said Carver. "The spilled glass, the smell of brandy, and something else that I recollected later, that sickly sweetness of the opium den. Well, the brandy alone told me the visitor had to be a gent, a man of means and connections."

"And then I made a dreadful error," said Moynihan, "and left this mark on my soul."

"You thought he had murdered his wife, your Ruth."

"He spoke of her plans to escape him as if he knew them. And then lapsed into spiteful rambling. Wishes and actions all mangled. Eventually, he nodded and dozed and fell asleep. It was very dark, very hot, very late. I had come a great distance, all for nothing: I could not find her."

"And all your fury and remembrance came to a point, and you made yourself judge and executioner. No doubt you had your bag at hand, a selection of suitable blades."

Moynihan bent and clenched his fist before his eyes. "May God forgive, for so I did. But how did you guess?"

"There was no guess to it," said Carver. His voice became hard, distant. "Your common criminal, your convict, they brawl and rage, pummel and slash, with whatever weapon is to hand. Nine times out of ten, they strike for the heart or the head, but the ribs and skull are hard and leave behind great gashes or wounds. Or if they cut the throat, they cut wide and wild. But you were precise. Meg Harper saw it: a nick in the right place, and the old fellow died in his own fireside chair. So a true killer or a murderer of many men, or something else. You made a neat cut, but you didn't steal much, didn't riffle the body. Too genteel for that. And though the cut was skilled, the rest of it was intemperate, hasty. So no bushranger but a gentleman, with a knowledge of anatomy."

"I was dazed, frantic, weary when it was done. And there was blood in plenty, as much as I have ever seen."

"Death isn't tidy. Not even the scaffold makes it so."

"I recall looking about, going through the old man's desk in search of traces of letters, some of the correspondence between us. I went and stood outside, trying to think of how I might stage the entry of a thief."

"And you picked up the glass you yourself had been using, and tried to wipe it clean, though you left a trace of blood thereby, and put it back with the others."

"Staines dropped his own glass in the struggle. I thought it best to let it lie. But I had a confused notion of concealing my own visit. Is that one little smudge all my error?"

"No. It was everything that came after."

"I don't doubt that Staines lived a mean and repugnant life, but I regretted my actions as soon as I fled the house. I had still not found my Ruth, you see, which I had resolved on before leaving home. The old man's death was a fearful mistake, if Ruth was not dead or died elsewhere."

"A mistake," hissed Carver. "A whole life snuffed out on account of your mistake."

"As you say," said Moynihan, shaken. "A mistake is too facile. My guilt forced me to run again and again over everything that had gone between us. And then, of all men, they set the hangman of Sydney Gaol on my trail. I could see that you would not let the matter rest, and besides, I had a dreadful sort of pity and concern with the woman, Harper, who stood accused of my crime. She mentioned Staines' right-hand-man and overseer, Devers, and the fear of discovery made me wonder what you could learn from Devers himself if you brought him to ground."

"You decided to find the man yourself."

"Meg Harper had a sound idea where he might be, and, as you say, every convict trusts a surgeon from the transports."

Carver grinned without pleasure. "But Devers thought he had the better of you. That was why he was so damned smug when I came calling afterwards."

"He was pimping, drinking, smoking. He guessed at what I had done and determined that I would pay for it."

"So you decided to do away with him as well. You were better prepared the second time. You took a rope from my shack. You throttled him and strung him up."

Moynihan shook his head slowly. "He was half stupefied already when I called. A simple length of cord was all I required, but hauling him up by the rope was wearisome work. I only got him part way. I never intended what happened to that poor girl. If you believe nothing else, believe that. I left a lamp on the floor to show up the dead, and in her haste she must have knocked it over. Her death is another black mark against my soul."

"But no such pretty scruples about throwing the same death on me," said Carver steadily.

"We two were playing fox and hound by then, though you knew it not. The fox set out to muddy the trail. It was easy enough to steal a length of rope from you: you were sleeping in a sodden dream. But you had your own revenge. You sent me to that poor girl, and her suffering wrung my heart."

"Then you contrived a better trap with the Irish smugglers. But you gave your hand away in that."

"I do not justify myself. It was the girl who led me to Sidmouthe. I watched him, coming and going in the opium house. He kept that memorandum book with him at all times. Do you know he scribbled little scraps of maudlin verse in it, besides his list of names? He made little effort to hide it. I followed him into the den several times. Then, when he lolled in his stupor, babbling of visions and flight to the Orient, I stole the book out of his coat pocket. But there was one name there I sought that I could not find."

"And to terrify him and push him to respond, you threatened to set it all before his paymasters."

The audience murmured, as the gaudy figures shifted and declaimed on the stage.

"I did. I even took out my passage on one of their ships. I knew about his scheme and his employers. And even that wasn't enough. When you came upon us under the gallows, I was certain he had betrayed me to the constabulary, and the only thing to do was silence him."

"And besides," said Carver, "by then there was so much blood on your hands, returning were as tedious as go o'er."

In sudden motion, Moynihan twisted and caught at Carver's forearm. The surgeon's fine fingers dug in like parrot claws. Carver started, and looked for the flash of a scalpel in the dark. But no blade came. Instead, the other man searched his features with the analytical passion of the anatomist. "And who are you, to quote tragedies like scripture? No common convict or scoundrel turned hangman. You shed your dullness and inattention by degrees when the magistrate called you out, and I knew I had to flee the colony and seek my answers here. And here I find you again, against all reason."

"You did it yourself, man." Carver threw off the grasping hand. "You left such a trail of blood that not even the Sydney magistrates could let it lie. And you have the notebook, still, and that is what I want."

"I do not justify myself," Moynihan muttered. He faced Carver again. "But yes, the book. I don't have it here. But there is something you should see first, master hangman, and then we will speak of the book."

Carver leaned back, and the light chair shifted. "What's there to see?"

"Have you ever paused, with your hand on the lever, about to send a soul to perdition?"

"No. That's not my function."

"My soul is lost, but there are others you may consider."

Carver exhaled. "Very well."

Moynihan stood, reached for his fine white gloves and his tall hat. Two figures capered on the stage below. "Then come with me. You are alone? We may leave unmolested?"

"I am alone," said Carver. "But if you want to come close to Pryor and get an answer off him, then no ill must come to me."

"Of course." Moynihan set his hat upon his head. For a moment, his attention rested on the distant stage. "She hangs in the end. A true, precious soul. The author could have chosen otherwise, and yet she hangs. What do you make of that?"

Carver stood. "Happenstance," he said. "Happenstance checks us all. At least, the playwright knew us best of all, and that's what he says. The readiness is all. How I came by that is too long to tell here." He turned aside from the stage. "A prisoner I knew had that book, once, but he died under the lash. Another man took it, and then another. And by this strange path it came to me."

The two men walked down the stairs of the dark theatre like old friends, and no one marked their passing, for the business of the stage was all before them.

• • •

BEFORE HE OPENED the theatre door, Moynihan said, "I must return to your assurance that no one is waiting out here—we will not be followed or interfered with."

"Of course. And I should ask the same as you."

Moynihan raised a faint smile. "Naturally, for I believe we both have something the other wants."

Carver and the dapper surgeon stepped onto the street under the glare of the lights, and then wove their way among the theatres, coffeeshops, public houses, clubs, and brothels. The bright, lively women who lingered at every corner appraised them as they went by. Only Carver responded with a grin or a wink; Moynihan was serious and subdued. Then, in a cobbled lane dimmer and more noisome than most, they drew near a crooked public house, taller than it was wide with overhanging box windows. Moynihan ushered them inside. The common room was crowded, but the surgeon did not pause, mounting a flight of bare steps towards the private rooms upstairs. Higher up, only a few dim candles illuminated the warped panelling. Moynihan went to a closed door, tapped three times—soft, sharp, soft—and stepped in. Carver paused, as though to brace himself, and with his hands free and shoulders squared like a boxer he followed.

The room was wide, low, closed, and curtained against the night, though the lamps were poorly trimmed and flickering. The wainscoting about the room was close and murky brown, as though seasoned in secret dialogue. There was but one long, thin table and numerous chairs in various antique styles. Gathered about the table were several men and women—enough, to Carver's mind, to fill a large cell. Yet they were silent when he came in, and regarded him gravely. Some were meekly and respectably dressed, some arrayed in their Sunday best, but there was no show of wealth or finery. The faces, yet, were familiar. Lined, hard, watchful: the faces of the transports, the barracks, the marshalling yards, and the manifold prisons of the colony.

Carver drew his head up. "How now, what's this?"

Moynihan said, "These are but some of the names in the Lethe book. You cannot object to making their acquaintance, as you have hunted them across the seas. These are your returned convicts, perpetually under the shadow of the noose." He stepped to the other side of the table, and put his hand on the shoulder of a stooping man. "This fellow here killed a gentleman in a gambling den brawl, but his son married an innkeeper's daughter and grew rich enough to support him." Moynihan moved on; touched another. "This woman had three daughters when the magistrate sent her away. When she came back, two were yet alive. This man here ran three-hundred head of cattle on the Cumberland Plain, who in his youth went thieving."

"Reformed characters all, I suppose," snarled Carver.

"Too many of us present have blood on our hands, God knows," said Moynihan softly. "But these few agreed to gather here, to show that they mean to go by honest means, and not to look back to lost sins."

A company of ghosts, therefore. The ghosts of pride, and rage, and longing, of drunkenness, of gentleness, of boldness, determination, guile, thrift, and labour, thievery and despair, banishment and home-longing, sent back to haunt the shores they had quit under the weight of crime and judgment. Pale and steady, utterly silent still, they looked on the hangman.

"What of it?" said Carver, but he was subdued, all his bluster and fierce manner discarded.

Moynihan said, "If the evidence you seek is given up to the authorities, all these souls you see here will be forfeit. Whatever doubt and trepidation they live under now will be as nothing when their true names are revealed. Then they will be hunted and harried and brought in to the slaughter like loose cattle."

Carver seemed to tip forward. He did not look away from a single glance that met his, but he paled, and his mobile face was set and grim as on the scaffold. "This isn't my concern. They knew what they were doing when they came back."

"No, sir, with respect, we did not." The speaker was a woman, standing not far from Carver. She was lean, and her skin was weathered and grey, but she spoke firmly. "We came back to live quiet, or to die at home, or to go back to our old ways, but none of us bargained on what Captain Pryor intended for us."

"Pryor, you see," added Moynihan, "has perfected his unique scheme for all of us."

"He grinds us," said the woman. She put her thumb to the table and turned it. "Pennies and pounds, he grinds us. 'Stay close by,' he said to me, when I came off his ship, 'for I know your new name as well as your old. Don't think to fly me.' And then he takes his fees to advance every new venture or scheme of his. We're none of us ever free of the man."

"Aye," growled another man, "regular as the rent-taker he bleeds us. And if you can't pay, there's always some other service he can contrive. Contracts to arrange for him, shipments to pilfer, contraband to carry, rivals or union-men to beat and harry. We're no angels, Mr. Carver, as right you know. But Pryor is a black-hearted devil."

Carver stood silent, frowning, his jaw working.

"I have a wife," said another man, "and children, and Pryor's black hand is above them all. The last one of us they caught, he died in prison of fever and despair before they could hang him. Did I hazard all for my bairns to see that?"

"It ain't material," said Carver, with an angry shake of his head.

"On the contrary," said Moynihan, "this is the heart of the matter. Here is the Rats' Line you are tasked with undoing. The rats to exterminate."

The assembly stood, silent still. Carver looked along them. The room was too close and too quiet, the long table set as if for a dusty banquet in Hades. "I've heard enough," he said. "Let them go their ways."

One by one they passed out, and Carver marked each face as they went for a flicker of appeal or defiance. Then he was alone again, with Moynihan.

"You see," said Moynihan. "We have travelled the same course all this time, and it ends here."

"It's plain enough what you want from me," said Carver.

"Is it?"

"I should spare you to spare them."

Moynihan blinked. "My dear fellow, are you that dull? I took you for better. No. I do not expect to be spared. My sins, at least, are too heavy."

"Then what?"

"You are in possession of all the facts." Moynihan spread his fingertips on the long table. "I should like to know what you intend to do."

"I intend to take a drink," said Carver. He strode to the door and called for the pot-boy. When he returned, Moynihan had snuffed out all the lamps save the one at the end of the table, and drawn up a chair by the coal-fire in the grate. Neither man spoke until the boy had brought in the bottle and glasses, with a plate of crackers and a bowl of walnuts. Carver watched closely as the bottle was opened and poured. He took his glass quickly, swallowed the brandy, but then grimaced as at something bitter, and set the glass down. He did not reach for the bottle again.

Moynihan sipped at his own glass, but his gaze did not vary. "You are a cypher, Mr. Carver," he said.

"How so?"

"Here you are, met with your quarry and a room full of escaped convicts, yet you forebear to raise the hue and cry. You are alone, so I fancy you have slipped your leash, but you know as well as I do what it means to be hounded by the law, and yet you are not in my estimation prepared to go into hiding and spend the rest of your days looking always behind you quite yet. Are you the hangman still, or the magistrate's man? Will you stay in England a fugitive, or return to the colony, a functionary? You had few enough friends in Sydney. You are an enigma. I have always suspected that you bear a double mind in a single habit. So do I now. You know what

I have done, and why. You know what sort of man this Pryor is. I tell you frankly, you will not take me back until I have concluded my business with him. All comes to this point: will you help or hinder me?"

"I don't see that it's a matter of one or the other," said Carver slowly. "I want your confession. I want that book. You want Pryor, and though he won't trust me, he is content to use me to get to you."

"And do you think Pryor will then give you a new life, like these others, knowing what he does? I say again, what do you mean to do?"

Carver leaned back in the deep chair and turned the glass by its stem, catching a glimmer of the crumbling coals in the grate.

"Here is a thing a wily old Newgate solicitor once told me. It concerns a sly cove, who is to be hanged, and the hangman, who happens to be an upright, pious sort of man despite his trade. On the Sabbath day, the sly cove is told he must be hanged by the next Sunday. So he says to the hangman, 'Well, I will consent to be hanged by next Sunday, and I will pray for my soul until then. But that my prayers are genuine and not merely expedient, you must swear that the hour of my execution shall be unknown to me, and that the time and day you return will be a surprise.'

"'It shall be a surprise, I swear,' says the righteous hangman.

"Now the sly cove begins to think on what has passed, and he begins to reason that if the hangman has not called before Sunday, then he will know Sunday is the appointed day, and therefore he cannot hang on Sunday. But he thinks that, if that is so, and the hangman has not called by Saturday, he will know that is the day also, and by the same token, the day before, and the day before. And so, if the hangman is true to his word, the sly cove will perforce not hang at all."

Moynihan blinked. His lips were dry. "I see. A very neat line of reasoning. And what became of the sly cove and the pious hangman?"

"Having argued so finely with himself to this point, and being secure in his reasoning, when the hangman knocked at his door the sly convict was mightily surprised, and so he hanged, at the time and the place appointed."

Swiftly, Carver rose. He put the empty glass on the mantelpiece and wheeled away from it, and just as quickly he was at the door, and then gone. The surgeon did not stir. The room was mostly dark, and all the noise and heat was outside. He sat and watched the ashes flaking and settling for a long time.

CARVER WALKED, and for a good time he was heedless of his speed and direction, for thoughts, instances, and speculations whirled in his mind. He stopped before a wall plastered with bills and notices. "Found Drowned," said one. "Wanted: Reward," announced the others. Carver leaned in, flicked at the edges of the papers, and among the pasted bills he saw a description of himself. He snorted. Constable Ellington had not been slow in this. But as the drowned and the wanted garnered little attention from the rushing crowd, he walked on.

He paid scant attention to his route by Lambeth and Southwark, turning often, sometime pausing to look down on the river. The hangman did not brood much on those that were hanged and past: let others take the death-mask and mourn. But the faces of Pryor's ghosts were before him, and though he knew not why it should be—for memory and attachment are terrible mysteries to those who possess them, and there is no judge so practiced that he can read his own mind with perfect knowledge—he saw often the face of Antonia Fitchett, and imagined her before the bright line of Sydney Harbour at the lowering of the sun, and recalled their last afternoon, her last words to him. And so he brooded, and made the case for this course and that, for the guilty and the innocent, and raised them up and struck them down again.

Eventually, he found himself on London Bridge, and among the ceaseless press of humanity making their way across, he caught sight of one that Oliver Kempe had known. Surely this was Susan Vale? His heart halted in his chest. Her beauty remained: the thin nose pinched slightly at the bridge, the high, fine cheekbones, the hint of a golden curl beneath the line of her cap, but she saw him not in the crowd, but walked on with the gentleman at her side, and Carver knew he was too much altered for her to recognize even if she would, and some pasts were better left behind. He lowered his head and squared himself against the crowd.

CHAPTER 21.

An Agreeable Murderer

CAPTAIN PRYOR SAT at his desk again this morning, with a misty view of the docks and no particular business before him on the great swathe of English walnut. His thick hands tapped the blotter, took up and set down a gleaming pen. Then he folded them together.

"You have met with the man, then," he said.

Carver nodded. "I have. He is willing to oblige us, for a substantial sum, and with certain precautions."

"An agreeable murderer," rumbled Pryor.

"Desperate as he is, he is eager to be rid of Sidmouthe's notes. They are sure evidence of his guilt when it comes to the murders in Sydney, and he was horribly vexed to learn that the constabulary had sailed all this distance to retrieve them. No. He would be quit of them. That is your advantage." Carver stood, straight and composed, by the far end of the merchant's desk.

"And you did not work this advantage to lower the price?" said Pryor.

"In my experience, it won't do to bargain too finely with desperate men."

"I suppose not," said Pryor slowly, sketching lines with his fat fingers on the wood. "We deal as we must. Only a fool thinks that our trade is not taxed in blood. Prisoners to transport. Whale oil and bone returning. Muskets to the savages in New Zealand, to stoke their wars, flax and wool returning. Opium for tea and Indian cotton—armies to march, there's our commerce." Pryor's hands paused and flexed. "What's he like, this man?"

"A common sailor, but a crafty brute. There's one of them in every cell. No moral sense to him, but his type will dodge the noose again and again."

Pryor clicked his tongue behind his teeth. "His description, I say. How tall, how dressed?"

"Do you mean to trap me, or search for him yourself?"

"I mean your story of meeting him is a touch too glib."

"As tall as I am. Lanky. Dresses like a sailor. Bad teeth. Brown eyes. Broken nose, turns a little to the left. English. Londoner. You won't get the better of him on these streets."

"And how did this damned rogue get himself mixed up in my business?"

"Your man Sidmouthe brought him into it. The first victim, a free convict name of Staines, went looking for his long-lost wife. Sidmouthe meant to head Staines off, and ended by murdering him. After that, the two could not agree and the scheme unravelled."

"Damn fool," said Pryor under his breath.

Carver eased his stance, shifting to one foot. "And the woman, Ruth Staines, what became of her? She helped you hatch this scheme for returned transports, didn't she?"

Pryor looked away, towards the distant cluster of masts and the vague edge of the great river. "That was another country. The hoyden went back to her own people. There's no more to say of her."

"You went on with it without her—this trade in returned convicts, I mean," said Carver.

Pryor blinked and turned to his desk. "There was a measure of profit in it, I grant you. If you are willing to take the trouble. One handful a year, well chosen, but never too many to arouse suspicions."

"Well, it will cost you to continue."

"That is what you are paid handsomely to oversee."

"Then," said Carver carefully, "if you agree to the terms, there are one or two things to make ready."

THE GREAT CITY sighed as evening closed in, and the church bells, from Westminster to the slums and rookeries of Limehouse and Rotherhithe, began their tolling for evensong and repentance. Carver slipped into the Jankle and Son warehouse by a side door and skirted the walls as he walked up to Pryor's office. Inside, the captain was seated still at his desk, with a flat packet before him. Gally loomed at his shoulder, with his hands tucked behind his back.

"I did not specify that you would bring a second," said Carver sharply.

"You cannot expect me to draw out such a sum without a trusted man by me," returned Pryor.

Gally returned a watery smile to Carver's frown.

"Very well then," said Carver. "Make yourself ready—and leave him behind."

"Where, pray, are we going?" said Pryor.

"You follow me," said Carver. "That's what we agreed."

Pryor shrugged, put his weight on the desk, and pushed himself up. He lumbered over to collect his overcoat.

"A moment, if you please," said Carver.

"What is it?"

"I will inspect your coat."

"Bah! You seem to concern yourself more with this rogue's safety than my own."

"You want to get your book. I want to be rid of the both of you. Every man must play his part."

Pryor passed the coat to Carver, who worked methodically through the pockets. He plucked out a stumpy pistol.

"Is this for him or me?" said Carver.

Pryor shrugged and bared his teeth a fraction. "Would I not be a mighty fool to trust myself with a large sum and two felons?"

"You would be more fool to risk a commotion and blood on your hands with the police on your doorstep."

Pryor reached for his coat. "Very well."

Wordlessly, Carver passed the pistol back to Gally. The clerk glanced at his employer, who gave a quick emphatic nod, and then turned for the door.

"Sir," hissed Gally.

"What now?"

"You must not forget this." Gally darted out from behind the desk with the soft leather packet.

Pryor wheeled and took the packet. Briefly, Gally clasped his employer's hand. "Good luck, sir," he whispered.

Carver sniffed and glanced at the lean clerk. For a moment, an odd speculation pricked his thoughts. "Are you one of them, Mr. Gally?"

"One of whom?"

"Former convict—on the straight and narrow, of course."

Gally remained still as Pryor slipped the packet into his coat pocket and strode to the door. The deep creases about the clerk's face were set and inflexible.

"Wouldn't do to ask, would it?" he said.

CARVER WALKED SWIFTLY, while Pryor puffed and lurched behind him. Carver had turned, north and then east, but now he led them towards the docklands by the mesh of close, filthy lanes. There was no relief in the business of the waterside, the unloading and hauling, the traffic of wagons and men. Carver looked about often, sometime repeating the name of a street under his breath. Pryor seemed to shy away from contact with the dockyard labourers, splashing in the mud and detritus under their burdens, and sometimes halted and drew into the shelter of the nearest wall.

"We must make haste," said Carver testily.

"Where are we going?" said Pryor. "It wouldn't do, you know, to meet with an accident. Not with what I am carrying."

"We'll be there soon enough," said Carver.

Plodding horses and laden carts with axles grinding went past them. Carver traced more of his circuitous route down the footpaths. Pryor stopped and coughed. Carver glanced behind him, but saw only the human mass confined by brick walls dense with signs and pasted bills.

Closer to the river, Carver could hear ship's bells and the calls of the stevedores, and piping whistles, high as bird calls, eerily persistent along the foreshore. He gathered himself, chivvied Pryor, and went over the boards until he came to a squat pier at the edge of the water. There, they were poised before open space.

The tainted river flowed swift and charged with secrets fit for the sea. The air was cool; rainclouds were massing to the east, but the darkening sky stood clear above. Carver rested at the top of the steps that led down the side of the bricked and slimy bank to the water's edge. He breathed deeply and steadily. Perhaps his abstraction troubled Pryor, who was jigging back and forth, glancing upstream and down.

"This is the boat you mean us to go by?" said Pryor abruptly. He scowled at the low, narrow boat, such as the watermen and river scavengers used, drawn up by the bottom-most step.

"It means we must go alone," said Carver, "and be seen as we do so."

Pryor, thick-chested and bundled in his coat, was breathless and clumsy on the steps. Carver held the craft steady while Pryor stepped in.

With Carver rowing, they slipped out onto the Thames. A breeze rippled the current, fresh and cold. Carver angled downstream, the bridges behind him. He kept an eye on the docks and steeples and river markers. Cutters and other small boats skimmed and bobbed around them. Long whistles, the bellow of ship's horns, and bird cries carried clearly across the open water. Rotherhithe slipped by. At a certain point in the dusk, Carver began to turn the boat, working against the current to hold steady. They were not far from the bank, a succession of crumbling wharves and slipways.

"What's the time?" said Carver, breathing heavily through his teeth.

Pryor fumbled with the heavy fob and chain of his watch. "Near enough seven o'clock." He craned his neck and peered along the expanse of water.

"Almost the hour, then." Carver unhooked the yellow boat-lamp near the stern and stood with great care, to wave the lamp slowly above his head in a wide arc. He studied the shoreline.

"We are of a mind, then," said Pryor emphatically. "When I have that damned book and the fiend at hand, then you shall have the means to go free. But not a moment before, and until then, you are my man, body and soul. Afterwards, all is silence, and we never knew the other."

Carver crouched again, to get his balance in the light craft. Wavelets lapped at the side. "I will keep your secrets. Unless you think to play me for the fool like everyone else."

"Everyone else? What the devil does that mean?" Bundled in the stern of the boat, Pryor looked anxious and petulant, like a weary invalid on a late outing.

"Does your wife know you ran off with a married woman and abandoned your commission in Sydney cove?"

"She doesn't need to know. She's plain, as you can see. And simple about business matters—all women are. I did her a courtesy by marrying her. I was quite the man about town, quite the prospect. Her brother drank and whored himself to an early grave. The company needed a firm hand, a man with an eye for the market. I did that. The family business was a shell when I stepped in. I restored it."

Carver smiled thinly. "And you enriched them, no doubt, by devising that scheme of fleecing convicts the price of a return from the colonies?"

"We pack every ship high for revenue and profit, do we not? What's one body more or less? There are good government contracts in transportation—if you are frugal with the costs. Money to be made with the hulks, too. Why shouldn't we profit by the same cargo going back? That's how I restored the house to its position."

At the tip of a narrow stone peer, some way downriver, a green light appeared, blinked, and then dipped three times.

"There," said Carver, "he has come at the appointed time."

Carver settled to the oars again, and began to row straight and sure towards the pier. The river, in the last overcast, was grey and hard as stone.

CARVER BROUGHT THE boat steadily closer to the pier. The stench of polluted mud thickened. The pier was a black heap of ill-fitted spars and planks, spindly, canted, and half derelict, like a collapsing gallows or a burnt-out house. Behind it retreated a dry dock and a stretch of filthy shore on which lay the dismembered relics of countless vessels, their beams and prows, planks and masts thrown up in great masses of timber, wreathed in coils of rope and rigging, and piled about with stacks of old iron, nails, hoops, and capstans: the boat-breaker's yard—still, dark, and sombre in the tatters of day's ending.

Carver let the oars ride slack a little short of the pier and called up.

A voice came down to them: "Carver, Mr. Pryor. Two of you only?"

"Two of us," shouted Carver. "As you may see."

"And what of you?" called Pryor. "Are you alone?"

"Perfectly alone. There are steps down there. You may tie up and come to me."

Carver guided the rowboat in to the side. As he looped the bow line, Pryor lumbered onto the slimy green steps, cursing, and began to climb. Carver mounted after him.

Pryor stopped at the top of the stairs. Carver was one step behind. Eight or nine feet towards the shore stood the other man, straight and neat, a muted outline in the gathering gloom.

"What is this?" said Pryor softly, as his steps slowed. "This is no common sailor or ruffian." He paused as Carver put one boot on top of the last step. "Do you mean to betray me to the police after all? Who is this fellow here?"

Moynihan inched forward. "I am the man who holds the fate of all your crooked ventures in his hands."

Pryor swayed, as if to spin and bolt to the boat. "Carver, you have played false with me."

"You mean all that noise about a sailor?" said Carver tonelessly. "That was to fox the police and keep them off-guard. Before this business is settled, you will also need a simple account of all this to give to the authorities."

Pryor glanced at the slick stairs to the rowboat. His heavy face was drawn, doubtful. "Convicts and liars." His right-hand moved down his coat pocket and he peered at Moynihan. "Do you have my book, at least?"

"I have it here," said Moynihan, without stirring.

"Do you doubt that you are face to face with your tormentor?" hissed Carver. "Hold steady, and do not play it false, and we may come out of this still. Go on!"

Carver cleared the last step as Pryor lurched forward. The warped boards wobbled underfoot. The prying wind freshened and shifted about them, and all light was almost lost from the sky. The clouds had drawn closer, muddled with rain. All three men were poised above the water on the splitting planks. Ferries and small boats crossed silently on the river, but the breeze blended the faint cries of the waterman, sea-birds, and steam-whistles piping.

"Let us make our damned exchange and be done with it," said Pryor.

Moynihan extended his hand from his side, and in it was a small book, bound in beaten leather. "Here is your record."

"There must be no other copies," said Pryor. "I shall be certain on that point."

"There are no other copies," said Moynihan. "You may take my word for that. And I would gladly be quit of this one."

"Then give it here."

"Presently."

"What else then? I have no more money to give."

"There is one more thing." Moynihan stepped forward and his features were resolved. Carver saw him press his lips together, and a faint, yearning light sparked in his eyes. "The record we have is not complete. There is one other name that should be here, should it not? The name of the adulteress and rebel who came with you when you quit your regiment and your post in the colonies."

"Who spoke to you of her?" said Pryor quietly. "That was a private matter."

Moynihan drew three breaths, quick and shallow. "Old Staines was persuaded she had robbed him and run off with you. Call it a token of your earnest, if we are to deal plainly tonight."

Pryor shrugged. "She left me on the dock at Portsmouth. She has no part in this business."

Behind him, Carver chuckled. "You told me she went back to her own people. Is that not so?"

"For all I know. What does it matter?"

Moynihan spoke flatly and quickly, but Carver marked the faint tremor in his arm, "She fled the prison colony under your gallant protection, and yet you cheerfully let her go the moment you left the ship? Were there no tears, no pleading, no lovers' quarrel?"

"She used me to get away from her sentence and a brute of a husband. That was all there was between us."

"And did she graciously leave her husband's pilfered fortune with you, so you could set yourself up as a gentleman about the town, a retired officer, and buy your way into business?" said Carver.

Pryor flinched, but he did not look back. "I am not here to answer your questions."

"Then answer me!" barked Moynihan, advancing along the pier with rapid steps. The planks shook and bowed under his movement. In his right hand he raised an unpolished pistol, no gentleman's toy but a solid cavalry wheel-lock with the hammer primed.

Pryor shied and tried to back away, but Carver was too close on his heels. Moynihan levelled the pistol at Pryor's chest; they were no more than three feet apart. He was blinking and panting, but his sure surgeon's hands did not waver.

"Answer!" shouted Moynihan, his voice rising over the ruffled waters. "Did you lie when you told this man she went back to her people, or are you lying now? Where is Ruth Tremaine?—on your life."

Pryor made to raise his hands. "This is madness. I do not know, I swear. I thought she went back to her kin. I said as much. I do not know. What does it matter?"

"She did not come back to me," whispered the surgeon. A low sigh, like a sob or a hanged man's last gasp of air, came fluttering from his chest.

"What then?" said Pryor. He lowered his open hand. "She lied, I hazard, to every man she knew."

"She would not lie to me," said Moynihan. He looked to Carver, who was but a single pace distant. "You have seen enough men about to die. You have heard the condemned speak. Is this fellow lying to us now? Will he not confess?"

"He lies to me out of habit," said Carver flatly, "and to you out of fear." The wind danced around them. "Do you mean to murder this man here?"

"I recall that when we first met, one death or another, guilt or innocence, did not matter much to you at all," said Moynihan.

"You have led me into a trap," said Pryor. He tilted his head towards Carver, but did not let his attention leave the pistol. "You know this man. I care not what you thought to do, but you will be as much a murderer as this madman here."

"What is it to me?" said Carver. His voice was a low growl. He shifted on his feet and shook his head. "What does it matter? We are all too eager to deal upon death. Well, I am weary of it. Can any of us unwind the past or bid Lazarus rise?" Carver did not look at the gun, but only the surgeon's face, drawn with grief and yearning. "I have brought you here so that you may have your answer. Set the book down. Then let the truth serve the living, and for pity's sake make an end of this."

Moynihan leaned forward minutely, and the barrel of the pistol settled a foot from Pryor's heart. "You are in mortal peril," he husked. "For the sake of your soul, confess."

Pryor looked down, to the gaps between the boards, where the muddy waves plashed and mingled. "I do confess. I do, in earnest. She died at sea. That's all. She took a shipboard fever in the long crossing. We committed her body to the deep. And yes, I took her stolen money, every last penny, to make my new life. There is my shame. That's why I kept silent. But what was she? A convict, an adulteress, an escapee, in my company. It was better she died at sea, unknown. They would have hanged her ashore, sooner or later."

"Look up!" snarled Moynihan. "What ship was this? What name did she use? Look to me! I will have proof." Moynihan shook the book in his left hand. "I will keep this until I have sure and certain proof. What do you say, Carver? I have seen enough of the dead and dying and the truth in their eyes. And you have stood by the condemned at the gallows, when they confess all. Is this wretch lying still?"

"I say enough," said Carver, steady and grave. "Your love is gone, and you are hunting a ghost. Is that not what you would know? Take comfort in that, and be at peace. She is dead."

Cold tears rolled down the surgeon's cheek, yet he did not blink. His finger moved minutely on the trigger of the pistol. "And this man, who took her under his care, with his promises and lies, who would not think of her family and friends but only of his own gain, should he yet live when four others have died for naught in this cause? Have I laved my hands so deep in blood to let this wretch go and prosper on the scarred backs of others?"

"For God's sake," said Pryor, twisting sharply towards Carver. "I have paid you in full. Will you betray me to this murderer?"

Carver raised his right palm towards Moynihan. Pryor shifted and the loose planks groaned. Carver edged in, almost as close to the slight surgeon as Pryor. Moynihan wavered, and whatever he feared, in that instant of wild doubt the barrel of the pistol wavered and turned a fraction towards Carver. Pryor's arm flew, striking at the stock of the pistol. Moynihan flinched, and in the same motion Pryor lunged, leading with his heavy shoulder. He carried the slighter man back and knocked him down. Perhaps he hoped that the gun would misfire, but instead it clattered from Moynihan's hand. Carver reached for them both as Moynihan toppled and sprawled. Pryor broke into a lumbering run and pelted down the pier. The structure shivered in his wake. Beyond him was the ship-breaker's yard, sunk in morbid shadows.

Carver crouched at Moynihan's side. "Get up! He's gone afoot and knows us both." He hauled the other man up by his coat-front.

Moynihan nodded, but drooped as though dazed. "What a pitiful fool I have been. I am sorry."

Carver raised his head. A whistle, thin and high, came from the direction of the boat yard. "What's that?"

As though helpless, they waited, and the whistle sounded again from farther in the breaker's yard. In moments a shrilling returned from the river.

Carver recalled Pryor shaking hands with Gally, taking his packet of bank-notes, patting his pocket flat, the countless noises and signals of the riverside, all about them as they walked. He shook his rough head. "Pryor and his clerk. They know the docklands better than we two. The whistles are their signal. They have followed us on the water, and he is calling them in. He meant to collect his book and turn us both over to the police. We shall be cellmates if we don't stop him."

Moynihan looked around. "The book. The pistol."

Carver twitched and reached down to pluck the slender, leather-bound book from a gap between the boards. Moynihan rolled past him and gathered up the firearm. Then he scrambled to his feet, and before Carver could speak again he sprinted in the direction Pryor had taken.

Carver glanced at the notebook in his hand. It was convict work, frayed and bent, the stamped leather peeling. How many names it contained, he could not then guess. It was surpassingly light in his hand for a record of such consequence. He scowled, took three sure steps to the edge of the pier, and tossed it into the water. The shivering dark waters took the book, but Carver was already running.

THE ROTTING PIER quaked and creaked as though it would shudder into splinters as Carver thumped over it. He heard the piping whistle again; this time it was answered by the shouts of men on the river. He let loose a stream of convict's curses. Ahead, he saw Moynihan speed from the end of the pier down to the boat-breaker's yard.

A fatal moment to decide: join the pursuit or flee. There was no pause, no hesitating before the drop, only haste and surmise. The image of escape, the shadow of Oliver Kempe, was projected before him. He could take himself from this place. Leave Moynihan and Pryor, the policemen and the judges, to their exhausted revenges. He would be as a hidden man, nameless in the London crowds. But it was the sketch of a hunted life—fearful, suspicious, stealthy—subservient to the terror of the law and its retribution. And a name, and a vision of a distant shore, struck through his thoughts like the flash of lightning over a southern harbour.

Where the pier ended above the waterline, he caught his breath and jumped down after Moynihan.

He reeled into a wasteland of dismembered ships and skeleton hulls, the broken landfall of the Empire. The weak glow of the grey hour dribbled out between the tattered ships' sections, the heaps of lumber, scrap iron, tin, copper, the coils of rope and corroded chains. Sand and mud and fragments of ship's glass were compounded, slippery underfoot. Naked keels, planks, and toppled masts lay in every direction. Carver could see no one. All was chaos and wreckage, a fractured world. He put his hand against an oaken prow, lowered his head, and forced himself still, to listen, as he had often done in the impenetrable darkness of the prison hulk.

Standing so, like a penitent, he waited for sensations to resolve. First he detected the lapping of water, the splash of oars, a steam-whistle. Then, he heard the surgeon's footsteps, light and sure. Cautiously, Carver moved on, fearing to stumble and fall among the loops of rope and piles of splintered wood that littered the ground. Carver shuffled and picked his way down the branching salients, scored like trenches among the gutted shells of vessels and their spoils. Moving again, he lost track of the surgeon. He imagined more sounds: shouts, scuffles. Occasionally, there would be a gap, admitting faint illumination, or a stretch of open ground left by the breaker's men.

Carver guessed that Pryor would attempt to get back to the shore to meet the incoming boat, and that Moynihan would surely follow. He went on, ever towards the sounds and smell of the water, pressing between the hulls. For one moment he had a glimpse of another person ahead of him, a scrap of a shadow slipping between two leaning, half-stripped cutters. Snags and splinters in the wood caught at the edges of his coat; hanging lines brushed his head. It was maddeningly dim down among the wrecks, the twilight flat and tenuous, and the air befouled, like the bilges of the transports.

Then, with no transition, he was in the clear again, up on one of the slipways used to draw the boats up to their destruction. Rain, falling in a thin spittle, blended with the sawing wind. Carver looked along the path towards the water's edge. Two colourless shapes, the bleared forms of men, writhed and twisted halfway down. Abruptly, they broke apart, and the slighter figure tumbled and sprawled on the ground between the rails with one hand held up as if to defend himself. The heavier man swayed and lurched above him. He set his feet and back. In his right hand he raised a long-handled mallet with a worn block for a head: a workman's discarded tool.

Beyond Pryor, some way off yet and set against the river's flow, Carver could see a longboat making for the cluttered shore, six oars rising, and faintly hear the man at the prow shouting commands.

Carver began to run, clumsy on the soft ground. The hammer swung and struck the upraised forearm of the fallen man. Moynihan did not cry out, but his arm was dashed down, loose, like a broken branch. With a grunt, shifting his hands on the haft, Pryor raised his weapon again.

Carver scanned the slipway, stooped and grasped at a discarded wooden pulley trailing a hank of frayed rope. The pulley was as heavy as a man's head. With a bellow and all his strength, Carver hurled the pulley. It struck Pryor on the thigh and he stumbled, one leg buckling. Moynihan, quick as a cat, rolled to the side.

Carver broke his own forward sprint, skidding almost down onto one knee. Pryor pivoted and regarded him, red faced and huffing with rage.

"You damned bully," grated Carver.

Pryor rushed at him, swinging the great mallet. Carver jumped back, extending his arms for balance, quicker than Pryor had judged. But Pryor swung back again, like a farmhand working with a scythe, and Carver, sensing an obstruction at his heel, rebounded into the arc of the blow to try and grasp the handle.

Instead, Pryor's sweep smashed against his side and he reeled, momentarily breathless, falling on a heap of splintered wood and scrap copper.

Pryor drew a half breath and raised the hammer over his shoulder. A convict facing the whip or the bully-club learns not to extend his arms but to keep them close, curl up, and endure, and so Carver wrapped his hands over his head and waited for the blow.

Then came the *click-hiss* and the immense charge of light and noise, as quick and final as the snapping of the hangman's rope.

Pryor dropped the hammer. He buckled and fell. His head struck the sand, and only then did Carver see the gout of blood spurting at nose and mouth.

Carver looked across to see Moynihan, sitting, with the pistol clasped in one hand, smoke curling about the hammer and barrel.

"He meant you ill," said Moynihan in dull seriousness.

Carver gulped at the air. It took a terrible effort to force out the first few words. "So he did. For the sake of all his secrets."

"Oh, the book!" Moynihan's feet scrambled in the sludge. He could not lean on his shattered arm. "I have dropped it!"

Carver glanced to his right. The longboat nudged the shore and the constables had spilled out and were advancing. Near the front, he made out the lanky form of Ellington, swaddled in his coat. Inspector Meade, with water up to his ankles, pointed towards them.

"I cast it into the river," gasped Carver. "For better or worse, those who are listed there are safe from the judges' bench."

Moynihan blinked at him. "Then you have discovered some moiety of pity. What becomes of the hangman, so?"

Moynihan frowned at Pryor's corpse, with a faint interest. "I expect you could still take the money and make your escape."

"Everything I meant to do here is in tatters. I escaped once, better than you know, and it only led me back to this," said Carver.

Moynihan nodded, like a weary child. "What shall we do?"

"You must go with the police. Everything is muddled here." Carver tried to wipe off some of the mud on his hands.

Moynihan clambered stiff and hesitant to his feet. The spent pistol he held as though it were a naturalist's specimen. "I shall speak to them, and set this right if I can. I am so utterly weary. Will you call on me before the end?"

Carver breathed deep and met the pain in his ribs without a grimace. "I shall."

They turned to face the line of policemen, who picked their way up through the wrecker's yard as the swirl of drizzle descended and all became vague.

CHAPTER 22.

The Shadow on the Scaffold

THE ROOM WAS painted a pallid white, cold, with moisture perpetually beading on the walls. It was set deep under the courts to hold prisoners between sessions. The silence was awful and emphatic, so far from the tainted air and commotion of the streets. The prisoner sat in prison weeds, chained to the table with his back to the covered grate that admitted no freshness. Visitors faced the prisoner as they entered, and whenever they pleased, the guards looked in on prisoner and guest through a slot in the door.

Carver, dressed for the street with dry mud on his boots and trouser cuffs, sat across from Moynihan without any outward sign of discomfort. The surgeon's arm was resting in a sling, but he did not fidget with it.

"True to your word," said Moynihan, "you call at the last."

"I'm not particular about much," said Carver, "except my promises. But I don't call as a hangman."

"I am comforted, nevertheless."

"In reference to what you did in the boat wrecker's yard," began Carver. He stopped, and then started again. "Well, Pryor would have broken my thick skull open, for he feared what I guessed or knew of him. But you could have taken that moment to get away yourself. You would have left an escaped convict alone with the man he cheated. And you might have stayed a free man—a little longer at least."

Moynihan tilted his head and laid his good arm on the table, resting his manacled wrists. "I think not. I had to follow Pryor. He was at the end of all my errors, all I had thought or done, or failed in. But he got the better of me down in the dark there. I remember running, thinking where he might hide, being struck from behind. I had no time to raise the pistol. Then we struggled. There was nothing said. He threw me down. I was sorely hurt, and for a moment I could not think of anything. When I recovered and looked up, he was threatening you, and the police were still too far away. His plan from the beginning was to turn us both in once he had reclaimed his secrets, and I know he would have killed you at that moment. He was a wicked man. A betrayer of countless trusts. And you had done me no wrong but trying to stop me. I know there are some strains of compassion in you, and besides, you alone can relate the story of my Ruth. I do not believe that one death more, mine or his, makes an atonement. But I am weary, mightily weary, and would fain rest."

"So you shall," said Carver, "if you don't agitate against it."

Moynihan blinked and tapped the blank table. "I have taken great care in my confession to put all the ill-deeds on myself. I destroyed the book of names, you understand. Your conduct was singular and blameless, and it was by your initiative alone I was captured."

A faint quirk of satisfaction touched Carver's lips. "Sergeant Ellington ain't so sure. But if he admitted that I got the better of him once more when I went free, it would look like a dereliction of duty. Besides, he has his murderer and a confession and a sure path to promotion. You won't return to Sydney for trial, but the Rats' Line is broken up for good. As for the book you mentioned, as far as the Colonial Office sees it, the less said on that matter the better."

"The system is satisfied with you, therefore," said Moynihan, with a wry nod.

"I don't give a damn for the system," said Carver fiercely. "The system is always the shadow on the scaffold. I've had it at my shoulder long enough. We owe the system nothing. Let it serve, or let us dismiss it."

"This puzzles me still: you, also, could have fled the system, when Pryor and I were engaged," returned Moynihan, more calmly. "You had the opportunity, and pounds in your pocket, and a great city to disappear into."

"No. A transported convict? Leaving the scene of a murder? Whatever name I chose, the system would always be at my heels. And I don't expect these new police are going to shrink away either."

Moynihan sighed. "And what now, if you return to the colony with the sergeant and his report?"

Carver looked at the blank brick walls, the dull paint. The great mass of the prison, inviolable, hung above them. "The magistrates will fuss, I'm sure. Fitchett will scold. But I have done my part, and I am owed a conditional pardon. Malloch will have had himself a new hangman, I expect. There's always a need, and a man ready to put his hand up." Carver halted, and for a moment a quizzical look passed over him, and to the prisoner he seemed remote and inward. "And there is one other there on the sandstone shore besides, with bright eyes, who guesses more, and will know more, if I return."

Slowly, Carver gathered himself, but before he pushed back the chair, Moynihan said, almost shyly, "Do you believe him or not, Mr. Carver? Do you think Pryor lied when he said my Ruth died at sea?"

Carver looked down on him and said, "The shot that saved me severed you from the one man who bore the truth. All else is speculation." But then he yielded and added, "If she died a-ship, there will be a record of it. But I suspect that Pryor had no intention of leaving the colony in her company, a rebel and convict. Think of the risk if she was found out at the dock. He used her for what she could get from her husband, just as she meant to use him to secure her a place on board an English ship. If that is the case, then she never left New South Wales. I shall look into it, on my return—but all that means her journey ended before yours began, either way."

"Is that all we have to take from this?" said Moynihan. There were tears on his cheeks.

"You may bid her farewell," said Carver finally. "Mourn, also. But I say this: she was true to her wish to return to you, whatever befell her."

The prisoner hung his head and Carver spoke no more. He knocked briskly on the door to alert the guards. Since the courts were in session, the corridors below were silent and shadowed in the low gaslight. Carver settled his coat about his shoulders, but his steps were slow and measured. The stairs to the streets were before him, admitting a diffident light. His thoughts followed the strange and terrible lines between the great city, the courts, the gallows yard, the hulks, and the sea, and at last flew beyond to the mottled green surge of waves breaking beneath high red cliffs.

Sydney, New South Wales, June 1830

THE GREAT RAINS were over and the cool season had arrived. Inside, the light that came in by the dusty slats was frail and copper-coloured. Antonia Fitchett sat near the open windows, breathing in the breeze from the bay, reading, as she often did, with her head tilted slightly to the side.

The mail from England had arrived three days before, on a swift three-master loaded with free colonists, clutching at their sea-chests and staring about with dazed interest at the rows of white cottages and green gardens above the port.

At the periphery of vision, by the front of the house, Antonia sensed movement. When she glanced up, a woman in the clothes of an upper servant had ducked in at the gate and was walking firmly towards the steps of the house. Antonia rose, and then her frown dissipated. The woman was Meg Harper. Quickly, Antonia slipped out of the front room. Quietly, she unlatched the front door and darted onto the porch before her servants could hear.

"Good evening, Meg," said Antonia.

"Good evening, ma'am."

"Have you business with the magistrate?"

Meg looked around. "The master ain't at home, is he?"

"No. He is at his club with Hoare and Fordham. They are celebrating the final sale of your old master's estate."

"Then, ma'am, begging your pardon, I have business with you."

Puzzled, Antonia stepped lightly down to the ground. Without looking to either side, Meg pushed a thick letter secured with a red seal into her hands. Then, without speaking of the thing, she stood back.

"Are you well, Meg?" said Antonia hesitantly.

"I have a position again. Housekeeper to a family in town."

"I am glad of that—what's this?"

Meg Harper grinned and tapped her thumb to the side of her nose. "A delivery, ma'am, from a faithful friend. Best not to read it where his honour can see, if you catch my drift."

"I understand." Antonia held the letter behind her back. "Try to keep clear of schemes, Meg."

"I will, ma'am. But this regards an old debt, and goes from my hand to yours, accordingly."

"Do you expect news from Mr. Carver?" said Antonia.

"Well ma'am, any debts between us are pretty well settled. I should say he's looking in a different direction henceforth."

The convict made a slight curtsy, and before Antonia could frame any new question, she hastened towards the town.

Returning inside, Antonia set a flame to her lamp and examined the letter. There were many pages, and the handwriting—close, accurate, and swift—was so unlike the assumed character of the man who had written the letter that at first she paused often in her reading, with a faint frown. The script crawled to the edge of each leaf. But then she began to read more attentively, and after a few pages her absorption was complete.

On the last page, she read:

> After the trial for escape, I was transported, for life then, without hope of reprieve, and with convicts who knew me only as Gabriel Carver. And so, when the captain called for a hangman that first day in Hyde Park Barracks, as the assignment clerks scribbled names in their great books, I answered the call, for fear of being recognized and revealed all too soon by my old cell mates, who had since passed onto the system from the transports. In truth, it was not long before Simon Chalke came to the noose, although in the extremity of his fear I doubt he knew me. Among his effects I found the book that he had pilfered from Carver, who had taken it from Stanton as a keepsake: the volume of Shakespeare that was, at times, my only anchor and link to my first life—at least, until I met you.

A brief space afterwards the writer had added a salutation and a name: Oliver Kempe.

When she finished, she laid her hand upon her breast beneath her throat, where her heart was beating wonderfully and painfully. Her hands shook, though there was no one to see her, and by effort only she stilled them.

"Returning," she murmured. "He is returning."

It had grown very late and the night chill freshened at the windows. She gathered up all the sheets carefully, arranged them, folded them, and tied them with a thin ribbon. She placed them in her desk, closed the lid, turned the small brass key to lock it, and slipped the key into a fold of cloth at her waist. She stood up, and leaned back, arcing with her hands on her hips to stretch her long spine.

IN THE MORNING, Antonia sipped her tea on the veranda. Three birds, a strike of green and red, hurled themselves across the road before her. Kathleen was sweeping heavy, curled leaves off the boards.

"I must call on Colonel MacNeish," Antonia said, half to herself. "I expect he will have received some distressing news lately."

"As you will, mum," said Kathleen, puffing as she pushed the broom.

Antonia settled her shawl a little lower, for there was no discernible chill outside. After a moment she said, "Kathleen, have you ever had a man confess himself to you? Confess a very great crime, I mean?"

"I can't say I have. I ain't a priest, and convicts don't care to tell much of themselves."

"And if one did, what would you make of it?"

Her maid stopped and touched her sleeve to her brow. "I would say that it shows a very great faith and trust in the one that receives the confession. For ever after, the confessor would have the power of life and death over the one who confessed."

"Yes," said Antonia, "I expect so. A great danger. And a great liberation, also."

"As you say, ma'am. Shall I call for the carriage?"

"No. Not yet. I shall go into the garden first."

Antonia went down the rough red stone steps, and the green brilliance of the leaves and the boundless southern skies enfolded her.

THE END.

AUTHOR'S NOTE

THE PAST IS SOMETIMES a dusty window. For a general history of Australia's convict-colonial past, I peered first into Robert Hughes' monumental *The Fatal Shore*, some elements of which, such as the story of Charles Anderson, who was chained to the rock of Goat Island for two years, were too brutal and fantastical to include. To visualize early Sydney and its environment, I drew on Grace Karsken's excellent ecological and social history of the city, *The Colony: The History of Early Sydney*.

I quickly learned that the Old Sydney Gaol was long gone, but an online search of the city archives revealed an annotated scan of an archaeological report on the 1970 rescue excavation of the early gaol, written by Patricia Burritt, and dated 1980. This document furnished a handful of critical details. Although there was relatively little to be found on the matter of the prison hulks that were visible to Dickens in his youth, the library of The University of Queensland provided W. Branch John Johnson's *The English Prison Hulks*.

Many facts, of course, were altered or invented in service of the narrative.

I would like to acknowledge the peoples of the Eora Nation, as the first guardians and occupiers of the land that became Sydney and its surrounds. Sometimes history is a story, a song, red pigment on stone.

ABOUT THE AUTHOR

ANDREI BALTAKMENS was born in Christchurch, New Zealand, of Latvian descent. He has a Ph.D. in English literature, focused on Charles Dickens and Victorian urban mysteries. His first novel, *The Battleship Regal,* was published in New Zealand in 1996. His short fiction has appeared in various literary journals, and his first historical mystery, *The Raven's Seal,* was published in 2012. Since 2004, he has lived in the Ithaca, New York; and Brisbane, Australia. In 2017, he completed a doctorate in Creative Writing at The University of Queensland. He now lives in Palo Alto, California, with his wife and son, and works for Stanford University as an instructional designer.

A NOTE ON THE TYPE

The text of this book was set in Dante, a typeface created over six years by the printer and designer Giovanni Mardersteig and the punch-cutter Charles Malin. It was first used in 1955 to publish Boccaccio's *Trattatello in Laude di Dante*, from which it took its name. The slight horizontal stress creates text that flows smoothly across the page and is ideally suited to books and longer texts. The digital version of Dante used in this book was first redrawn by Ron Carpenter and released by Monotype in 1993.

CPSIA information can be obtained
at www.ICGtesting.com
Printed in the USA
LVHW03s0210120718
583510LV00003B/276/P